HUNTER'S GAMES

JAMES P. SUMNER

BOTH barrels PUBLISHING

HUNTER'S GAMES

FOURTH EDITION PUBLISHED IN 2021 BY BOTH BARRELS PUBLISHING LTD.

COPYRIGHT © JAMES P. SUMNER 2015

EDITING AND COVER DESIGN BY: BOTHBARRELSAUTHORSERVICES.COM

ISBNs:
978-1-914191-09-1 (PAPERBACK)

VISIT THE AUTHOR'S WEBSITE: JAMESPSUMNER.COM

Sequels are always hard...

HUNTER'S GAMES
ADRIAN HELL: BOOK 2

1

I step off the Greyhound bus and take a deep breath. It's a refreshing sixty-eight degrees, and the light breeze is cool against my face. I look around the crowded, temporary transit center in downtown San Francisco. It's a little chaotic but bearable. The original Transbay Bus Terminal closed back in 2010, and the new transit center isn't due for completion for another couple of years. In the meantime, this temporary terminal acts as the hub for all bus travel both in and out of the city.

It's been a long ride, and I read up on it to pass the time...

I've been on the Greyhound for just shy of nine hours. I came from Oregon and headed straight down the West Coast on Route 101. I rest my shoulder bag at my feet and stretch. My back cracks as it celebrates no longer being cramped up on a bus. I grab my bag, sling it over my shoulder once more, and fight through the masses of commuters. I take a right onto Beale Street. It feels good to walk again. My legs are stiff from the journey down here, and I relish the chance to get some exercise.

It's a nice, bright September afternoon. I look around as I walk, soaking up the surroundings. San Francisco is a nice enough place. People are friendly, the streets are clean— even the air smells fresh compared to some places I've been.

I'm in town on business. And yes, by *business*, I mean *to kill someone*. For the past twelve years, I've worked as a freelance contract killer. I can safely say, with no ego whatsoever, that I'm one of, if not *the* best assassin operating in the United States. Maybe even the world. My reputation borders on legendary in certain, shall we say, *unsavory* circles. To everyone else, I simply don't exist, which is exactly the way I like it.

A local gangster called Nathan Tam has hired me to take out a government official named Richard Blake. Apparently, Blake recently bought a sizeable amount of cocaine from Tam and proceeded to mouth off about it. Given the company he keeps, Mr. Tam has subsequently attracted some unwanted attention from law enforcement. He wants his client silenced, so he can go back to running his business unhindered.

Someone who buys and uses drugs shouldn't be in a position of responsibility of any kind, so I'm more than happy to do everyone a favor and kill the bastard.

I walk for almost twenty minutes before I come across a nice bar advertising a meal and a drink for seven dollars. A quick glance at the menu on the wall outside tells me they have both steak and beer. Those are pretty much my only criteria when choosing a place to eat, so I walk inside and find a table at the back.

I sit facing the room with my back against the wall. It's

one of many old habits instilled in me. It allows me to see if anyone is approaching whom I might otherwise want to avoid.

Inside is spacious, and there are plenty of tables and chairs—many of which have people occupying them. The décor's simple and clean, with plain colors and small indoor plants strategically placed throughout. There's no theme to the place. It's just somewhere nice to come and eat.

There's a TV mounted on the wall in the corner, showing a news reporter somewhere in the city. It's muted, but the caption running across the bottom of the screen says something about an explosion, and there's crime scene tape behind the reporter. It looks like a restaurant, but whatever happened destroyed most of the exterior beyond recognition.

A waitress walks over and offers me a menu. I smile and tell her there's no need, then order a medium steak, beer, and onion rings.

I take out my phone. While I'm waiting, I'd better check in with Josh. He'll only shout if I don't.

Josh Winters is my handler and superhero office boy. He finds me work and gathers information so that I can carry out the contracts to my usual high standard. The guy's like my brother. I'd be nothing without him, and I have no problem admitting that. We've been through a helluva lot together in our time. I just call him my office boy because it gets on his nerves, which keeps me entertained.

He picks up after the second ring. "Hey, Boss. You made it to 'Frisco safe and sound, then?"

I smile at his overly enthusiastic tone. It's like his trademark, being so damn happy all the time. While I sometimes poke fun at it, there's no denying it provides me with a level of comfort.

"Yeah, got here about a half-hour ago. Just getting something to eat now."

"Let me guess, steak and a beer?"

"You know me so well."

"Yeah, I also know you've probably found a meal deal that includes both, and you've sprung for a serving of onion rings on the side."

I laugh. "Whatever."

"So, are you all set for this job? Are you sure you know what you're doing?"

"You could argue that I never really know what I'm doing..."

"You said it, Boss."

We both laugh again.

He means no harm, but I know he has little faith that I'll remember the finer points of any plan we make. In my defense, plans rarely work. More often than not, I have to improvise anyway. Consequently, I see no point in worrying about the plan. If you focus on it, you risk losing sight of the immediate situation around you, which can get you killed.

"I've got everything covered, Josh. Don't worry."

"Adrian, I *always* worry!"

"Oh, ye of little faith! But... just to make sure *you* know all the details, remind me—what does this Blake guy actually do again?"

Josh sighs, and I can picture him shaking his head at me. "Tricky Dicky's a senior administrator in the Department of Public Works. That's like sanitation and restoration."

"That sounds... really boring. And what do you make of our employer?"

"Tam? From the little interaction I've had with him, he's a businessman who's simply looking after his interests. He's attracted a lot of attention since Blake's been running his mouth. He prefers discretion in his line of work, as I'm sure you can appreciate."

"Blake doesn't sound like the type to blab about his personal habits, though. Sounds more like a working stiff in a dead-end nine-to-five job to me."

"Well, it's always the quiet ones."

"So they tell me..."

"I've made you an appointment to see Blake tomorrow morning at eleven. You're going in as a reporter for a local magazine who's writing an article on the upcoming plans the city has for recycling."

"That sounds phenomenally dull, Josh."

"Sure does. Better take him out quickly before you die of boredom."

"Y'know, you don't have to sound like you're enjoying this so much."

"You have to admit, it's a little funny..."

"It's possibly the dullest contract I've ever taken. Remind me again why I'm doing this?"

"Because Nathan Tam is paying you one hundred and fifty thousand dollars."

"Oh, yeah... that'll do it."

"Oh, and you've remembered the *no guns* rule for this one?"

"Yeah, it's fine. Going into a municipal building with a gun is impossible these days, even for me. But I've got it all worked out. Don't worry."

"I get a bad feeling when you act all confident and proactive..."

I smile. "Thanks, man."

He laughs. "Not entirely sure that was a compliment, but never mind. I'll leave you to eat your steak and drink your beer, Boss."

"Thanks. I'll give you a call tomorrow when it's over."

I hang up just as the waitress returns with my food. I cut into the steak and take a bite—which is succulent and cooked to perfection—and then sink back into my chair as I relax and mentally prepare for the task ahead.

21:56 PDT

After finishing my steak and beer, I left in search of a place to stay for the night. Usually, Josh would arrange something prior to me arriving, but I told him I'd like to have a look around the city, so I'd handle it myself.

As always, my idea of tourism only got me as far as the nearest bar. I found a place that served Bud and was showing a baseball game on TV, so I sat down for an hour or so, relaxed, and had a drink. Or two...

Then I decided to get my ass in gear and find somewhere to stay. I left some money on the table, headed outside, and jumped on the first cable car that passed by. I traveled through another part of the city, up a steep hill, and eventually got off near the Chinatown district.

The first building I saw was another bar...

And here I am. I'm just finishing my sixth beer and still have no clue where I'm sleeping tonight. This place I'm in is nice—the décor's warm and relaxing. Not my usual scene, but it's quiet, and I'm actually enjoying soaking up the culture around here. The waitress comes over to collect my empty bottles. I settle my tab and leave her five bucks as a tip. She smiles gratefully before walking away.

I really should find somewhere to stay. I need to be in top form for the job tomorrow. Having too many beers and not enough sleep isn't the way to prepare. I take out my phone. I'll call Josh and ask him to find me somewhere...

Actually, wait. No—he'll shout at me for getting drunk without him.

No, I'll sort it.

I finish my drink, pick up my bag, and leave the bar. I step outside and take in a deep breath of cool night air. It's dark, but the streetlights are doing their job. I head left. When in doubt, always go left. I hope this way will lead me toward the main street in the district. That's where I'm more likely to find somewhere to stay.

I walk on for another five minutes. I can't help but notice how the buildings seem to be getting smaller and more run-down. Every other store seems to be a Chinese supermarket or a pawn shop...

Hmmm, maybe should've turned right when I left the bar...

I approach a pawn shop and consider going inside to ask directions. There are two guys standing outside, whispering to each other conspicuously. I walk past and look through the window. There's an old Chinese guy behind a counter, reading a newspaper. He's wearing a vest I imagine used to be white.

No... I can't see him being particularly helpful. I'm sure I'll find somewhere soon.

I carry on past, but one of the two guys at the door steps in front of me. He's tall and thin, wearing a jacket three sizes too big for him. I can see part of a tattoo crawling up the side of his neck, which I guess covers some of his shoulder and arm too. His baseball cap is on backward.

He looks me up and down, then flicks his head up. "Yo... help you?"

Assholes are assholes, wherever you may be...

I sigh wearily. "No, I'm good, thanks."

I'm not in the mood for a confrontation. I know, I know—that's not like me at all. But I'm a little tired and a bit drunk, and I just want to find a bed for the night.

His friend steps out to join him and stands just behind my left shoulder. "You sure?"

I glance back at him. He's dressed in similarly over-sized clothes but without a hat. He has a tattoo on the side of his shaved head, which looks like a flame.

I nod. "Pretty sure."

"You look lost, man..."

"Is being lost the same as not knowing where you're going?"

The two guys exchange slightly confused looks.

"Whatever, man," continues the first guy. "What you got in that bag?"

I sigh.

Well, we all know where *this* is going...

Fine, have it your way.

I frown, feigning confusion. "What bag?"

"The one on your shoulder," says the guy at my side.

I look over at him. I take a small sidestep to my right, so the two of them are in front of me. "Whose shoulder?"

They look at each other again and puff their chests out. They frown and glare at me, preparing for violence.

The first guy takes a step toward me. "Yo, are you stupid, old man?"

I frown.

Me? Old?

"Hey! Since when is forty-two *old*, dickbag?"

The second guy taps his friend on the shoulder. "Let's fuck him up, bro. I'm getting tired of this bullshit."

8

I hold my hands up. "All right, fellas. Trust me—you *don't* wanna do this."

"Oh, yeah? And why's that, *old man*?"

I throw my bag on the ground in front of them. As expected, they both momentarily glance at it. That means, for a split-second, they're not looking at me.

Idiots...

I whip my leg forward and kick the guy on my left hard in the gut. As he doubles over, I spin around counterclockwise and slam my elbow into his temple, aiming it perfectly. He drops to the ground.

I come to a stop facing the guy in the cap, who's frozen with shock. I throw a stiff jab, hitting him flush on the nose. It doesn't break, but it hurts him and makes his eyes water. As he clutches his face, I launch the same right kick to *his* gut as well. He sinks to his knees from the impact, wincing in pain and unsure where to put his hands. I step forward and slam my knee into his face, hitting him in his nose again. This time, it breaks. He falls to the side, out cold.

I take a few deep breaths to compose myself, then bend down to retrieve my bag. As I straighten up again, the shop door opens, and the old Chinese guy comes out. He's short, maybe five feet tall, if that. He's bald on top with long gray hair on the sides. He's wearing brown trousers that are way too short; they finish above his ankles.

He looks at the two guys on the ground, then at me. He seems pissed. "What the fuck you doing?"

I shrug. "They tried to rob me..."

"You any idea who they work for?"

I shake my head.

"Oh... you fucking dead man!"

He turns and walks back into his shop, slamming the door behind him.

What just happened?

I glance through the window and see him talking animatedly on the phone to someone.

Huh... *that* was weird.

I set off walking to the end of the street. I look both ways and see the sign for a hotel a little farther along, on the right.

Finally!

2

September 23, 2014 — 10:39 PDT

I'm sitting on the edge of the fountain in the center of Fulton Street, facing the Civic Center Plaza. It's mid-morning, and the rush hour crush is dying down. It's another bright day, complemented by another cool breeze. I've been sitting here about a half-hour, composing myself before my appointment with Blake.

I've never been to San Francisco before, and it's nice being a tourist as well as an assassin. I look around, taking in the sights that the city has to offer. The Public Library is on my left, with the Asian Art Museum opposite. Both are large, picturesque buildings that flank the street on both sides.

Directly ahead of me, across the plaza, is City Hall—which is where I'm heading for my meeting. It's a huge building made of brilliant white brick. It must be a real pain in the ass to keep it as clean as it is. The roof is a gray-silver dome with golden decorations all the way around and up the sides. Because it's such a sunny day, the light's reflecting off the building, making it all the more impressive to look at.

I set off walking, cross over Polk Street, and stroll through the plaza. Trees adorn either side, forming a walkway that leads to the front doors of City Hall. I'm dressed for the part, wearing beige pants, a light blue shirt, brown shoes, and a matching brown leather laptop bag. To finish off the look of a career asshole—sorry, *journalist*—I've opted for an unfastened navy blue jacket.

Yeah, I hate myself right now.

This is the part of the job I openly despise—the acting. Having to dress up and pretend I'm someone I'm not to work my way into a position where I can take out my target. It detracts from the purity of the job. I like things simple and straightforward. I'm not deceptive by nature, and I find this uncomfortable. I'd much prefer to just walk up to people and shoot them in the face.

If I were in charge...

I make my way up the steps and through the middle of the three doors at the front of the building. The lobby is enormous. It's a large, circular space with a distinctive dark marble floor and light marble pillars, which are there seemingly for effect rather than necessity. Around the edges are doorways leading to all the different departments housed within these walls. There's a huge, carpeted staircase leading to the second floor at the far end.

Just inside the main doors, a rope barrier directs me toward a security checkpoint over on the right. There's a guard sitting behind a desk and another standing just in front of a metal detector. It's a gateway scanner, like the kind you see in airports.

I watch the guards process the people in front of me.

They approach the desk and give their name. The first guard checks his list and, assuming they're on it, sends them to the scanner. The second guard waves them through the machine. Presumably, he'll check them if the scanner beeps. Once through, a third guard issues them with a security badge, which is to be displayed at all times while on the premises.

There's no way inside the building without going past these guards and through that scanner.

I'm next in line. I'm ticking off in my head all the things I need to do, making sure I have everything I need in my bag and that my story and credentials are fresh in my mind for when I'm inevitably asked to present them.

It's like I'm an actor learning a script...

Have I mentioned how much I hate this?

The first guard gestures me forward. I step toward him and smile. "Good morning. Brian Johnson from *Life and Times* magazine. I've got an appointment with Richard Blake at eleven."

I'm doing my best to sound upbeat. I actually asked Josh's advice on how to sound happy. Is that bad?

The guard scans down his list. After a moment, he nods as he finds my name. "Mr. Johnson... Thank you. Step over to the metal detector, please."

He gestures with his hand and I walk toward it.

The second security guard is standing on the other side of the scanner, smiling at me. He's a tall, slightly overweight man with a thick mustache. His hair is going gray at the sides, and his body language tells me he's probably been doing this job a long time. He moves like someone who accepted their own monotony years ago.

"Step through the scanner, please, sir," he says, waving me toward him.

I place my bag on the table at the side and step confidently through. It's not like I have anything to hide, right?

The machine beeps.

Uh-oh...

I'm just kidding. I expected that to happen.

The guard smiles apologetically. "Just step to the side, please, sir."

I do, and he takes out one of those electronic wands from his back pocket. He gives me a once-over with it. It beeps as he moves it over my jacket. He looks at me and smiles again, in that *this happens all the time* kind of way.

"Can you empty your pockets, please?" he says.

I nod. "Oh, of course. My apologies."

I empty the contents out on the desk. My phone, wallet, and some loose change from my pants. I reach inside my jacket and pull out a small, black metallic case.

The guard looks at me, then at the case. "Can you open that up too, please, sir?"

That's got him worried. He suddenly sounds more formal, professional.

I shrug. "No problem."

I unfasten it, lift the lid, and turn it toward him, displaying the contents. The inside has a foam lining with spaces cut into it, protecting a hypodermic needle and two small vials of yellowish fluid.

The guard looks at me again, and I see the growing concern on his face.

I shake my head like something's just occurred to me and laugh, trying to sound embarrassed. "Oh my God. I'm sorry! I have diabetes. This is my insulin. I have to take it everywhere with me."

The guard smiles, visibly relieved. "That's fine, sir. I apologize for the formalities. You can never be too careful."

"Oh, I know. Especially nowadays. It's reassuring that people like you do these types of checks."

He stands to his full height and sucks in his gut, puffing out his chest and brimming with pride at the fine service he's providing. "Just doing my job, sir. Go and see my colleague to get your pass."

"I will. Thank you."

I pack away my things and walk over to the smaller desk on the other side. The third security guard hands me a visitor's pass attached to a lanyard, which I place around my neck.

"Could you tell me the way to Mr. Blake's office, please?" I ask.

He nods and points to the stairs at the end. "It's just up and to the right. Follow the signs for Public Works. You'll find his office at the end of the corridor."

I smile. "Many thanks."

Following the directions he's given me, I head over to the staircase, looking around me as I walk. It's an impressive building on the inside too. The artwork hanging on the walls looks expensive and makes the place look like an art gallery.

I climb the steps and head along the corridor, following the signs for the Public Works department. At the far end is a waiting room. It's a small, open-plan area with corridors branching off on either side. A few chairs are positioned in an L-shape against the right wall. In front of them is a low table with magazines scattered across the surface.

Ahead of me, a young woman is sitting behind a desk, just to the left of a large wooden door. She looks up and smiles as she hears me approach. Her designer glasses highlight her friendly brown eyes, and her dark blonde hair is tied back in a ponytail. She's wearing a navy blue suit and white blouse.

"Can I help you?" she asks.

I nod. "I certainly hope so. I'm here to see Richard Blake."

She glances down at her desk, presumably checking a schedule, and then looks back up at me. "Mr. Johnson?"

I smile. "That's me."

She gestures to the door. "Please, go right in. He's expecting you."

"Thanks."

I walk past the desk and knock once as a courtesy, then enter Richard Blake's office and close the door behind me.

I quickly take in the spacious office. A large window dominates the far wall, offering a beautiful panoramic view of the city. Roads and buildings spill out below us in every direction, all the way to the horizon.

There's a desk directly ahead of me, with two plain black leather chairs in front of it. On the surface is a flat screen monitor, keyboard, and mouse positioned on the left at an angle. To the right is a telephone and a stack of four trays, each one overflowing with paper.

Against the right wall are two filing cabinets, standing roughly five feet high, each with four large drawers. The wall opposite is clear, apart from the artwork hanging in the middle. It's a black and white photograph of the Golden Gate Bridge.

There's a slightly worn, brown leather sofa to the left of the door. There's a small coffee table just in front it with a fruit basket in the middle.

Richard Blake is sitting behind his desk in a nice walnut leather chair. He stands to greet me as I enter. He's wearing an expensive-looking charcoal gray suit. He has a thin frame and deep-set eyes. He's clean-shaven, which exposes a slightly weathered but otherwise blemish-free complexion.

He's definitely giving off a vibe, but I can't quite put my finger on it...

He flashes me a wannabe politician's smile and extends his hand as he walks around his desk toward me. "I'm Richard Blake. You must be Brian."

His voice sounds older than he looks, even though he's probably the same age as me. But the look suits him, as do the streaks of gray in his thick, dark brown hair.

I shake his hand and smile back, playing my part beautifully. "That's right. Brian Johnson. Nice to meet you. I appreciate you sparing some time for me today."

He waves his hand dismissively. "It's my pleasure. We're working on some exciting new projects to clean up this city. Any opportunity to talk about them and get people involved is beneficial to us. We've had some really positive reactions to our *Bin and Win* recycling initiative—which was my idea, by the way."

Oh my God... I can feel myself glazing over already. This guy's duller than a knitting convention! I've just figured out what his vibe is. He's a fully-fledged nerd. Y'know, that guy who had his lunch money stolen every day in high school?

Jesus... Josh was right. This guy's going to bore the shit out of me. I need to get this job over with quickly, or I'll end up killing *myself* first.

He gestures to one of the chairs facing his desk, and I accept the invitation to sit down. I rest my bag on the floor next to me and reach inside. I take out a notepad, a pen, and my diabetes kit and place them on his desk in front of me. He sits back down in his chair, and I see him staring at my things. He frowns and looks at me. He smiles like he's silently asking for an explanation.

Time to play the part again...

I shake my head. "Ah, sorry! I'm diabetic, and I forgot to take my shot on the way here. I just need to get my insulin before we begin. Is that all right?"

Blake nods, still flashing me his increasingly annoying smile. "Of course. We're in no hurry. Take your time."

Now obviously, I'm not *actually* diabetic. The two vials contain a lethal dose of highly concentrated Indian Cobra venom, which is a rare and deadly poison. One bite from the snake will inject around two hundred and fifty milligrams of venom, which will induce full-body paralysis and cardiac arrest in under two hours if left untreated. The fluid inside each vial contains around three *thousand* milligrams, so the effects will occur in seconds, not hours.

I stand and move over to the window as I load the hypo-dermic needle with venom. I smile apologetically and act like I can't see properly, using the light from the window to see what I'm doing. When the needle's full, I start to un-tuck my shirt, as if I'm about to inject myself in the stomach. As expected, Blake respectfully turns away.

Straight away, I rush behind him and place my hand over his mouth. I hold his head firmly against the back of his chair. In one swift, accurate motion, I jam the needle in the side of his neck. I slowly press the plunger down, injecting the venom into his bloodstream. I watch as the liquid gradually disappears inside him. I remove the needle, quickly discarding it on the floor, and clasp both hands over his nose and mouth, keeping him silent while the venom works its vicious magic.

He struggles feebly as the poison attacks his muscles and respiratory system, making it harder for him to breathe. It takes just over thirty seconds for him to stop struggling and another twenty to stop breathing altogether. I hold on for an extra ten, just to be certain.

I let go of Blake's head and guide him forward, resting him gently on his desk so as not to make too much noise. I retrieve the needle and put it back in my bag. Quickly, I pack everything else away and give the room a once-over to make sure there's no trace of me ever having been here. I didn't touch anything, so there are no fingerprints to worry about.

I cover my hand with my sleeve, pick up the receiver of his phone, and rest it on his desk next to him. I fasten my bag, sling it over my shoulder, and walk out of Blake's office.

The receptionist looks at me, puzzled, as I step out and close the door behind me. I gesture to the room with my thumb. "Oh, he had to take an important call. He said he'd be a while, so I figured I'd leave him to it."

She glances at her own desk phone and sees the light flashing that shows his line is busy. "Oh, okay. I'm sorry your meeting's been cut short, Mr. Johnson. Would you like to re-schedule?"

I shake my head. "No, it's fine. I'll have my office call another time."

She hesitates a moment. "Maybe... *I* could help? I work closely with Mr. Blake. You could interview me, if you'd like? I break for lunch at twelve. Maybe we could get a coffee?"

She smiles at me and takes her glasses off.

I'm no expert, but I'm pretty sure she's flirting with me.

I mean, did she just ask me for a drink?

Oh, man... I'm *terrible* at this. I don't want to hurt her feelings.

"That's, ah, really kind of you to offer, Miss..."

"Jenny. Call me Jenny."

I smile, feeling uncomfortable. "That's kind of you to

offer, Jenny, but... the thing is... my... editor only commissioned me to interview Mr. Blake. I'm not sure they'll be too happy if I come back having interviewed somebody else..."

She looks a little dejected and I feel bad. Should I try to make her feel better?

I keep smiling. "I'm sure you'd be really helpful. I just can't use you for this particular piece, that's all."

She nods and stands, looking away momentarily to untie her hair. She whips around to face me again, and her hair flows down to her shoulders like in a shampoo commercial.

Are you kidding me?

"Well, it doesn't have to be a business meeting. Maybe we could just grab a coffee?"

I'm struggling for words and feeling more awkward by the second.

I take a small step back and chuckle nervously. "I've got... ah... deadlines to hit. I'm sorry. Maybe some other time?"

Jenny smiles reluctantly through a deep breath, accepting her advances haven't worked. She composes herself as she puts her glasses back on and returns to her seat. "I'll let Mr. Blake know you'll be in touch. Have a nice day, Mr. Johnson."

Very professional. I think I pissed her off.

I nod courteously. "You too."

I've never been more desperate to leave somewhere. I'm just glad Josh wasn't here to witness that. The only time I lose my cool is when I'm talking to women. I feel like I'm cheating by just speaking to someone who seems to like me. I know that might sound crazy, but it's just me. I'm not ready. I'll always love my wife and daughter. I've not forgiven myself for what happened to them, so I can't allow myself to carry on without them. Not yet.

I hastily walk back down the corridor the way I came in —past the expensive works of art, down the carpeted grand staircase, and across the entrance hall. I walk over to the desk with the third security guard behind it and hand over my lanyard. I nod a polite goodbye to the other two guards, who return the gesture, then walk through the front doors, back out into the sunshine. It's bright, and I have to squint while my eyes adjust. I stroll down the steps and set off back across the plaza.

Well, that's a job well done. No resistance at all from the target, which is always nice. Ignoring the embarrassing run-in with his not-unattractive secretary, it all went smooth and according to plan.

There's a first time for everything, I guess.

I take out my phone and call Josh.

He answers, and I'm deafened by the music he has blasting in the background. "Hey, it's me. Will you turn that shit down? Christ!"

It goes quiet and he laughs. "Sorry, Boss. I was just... Y'know what? It doesn't matter. You all right?"

"Yeah, all good here. The target's been taken care of."

"Excellent! In record time too. Was he *that* boring?"

I laugh. "You have no idea."

"I'll let our employer know. So, no issues at all?"

I think back to the secretary. Should I tell him? Would he ever let me live it down if I did?

Yeah, you're right.

I smile to myself. "No, everything went smoothly."

I'm halfway across the plaza, approaching the crossing at Polk Street, when I hear shouting behind me. I turn around and see FBI agents appearing from out of nowhere, swarming toward me.

What the...

They converge on the walkway of the plaza, falling into a trained formation and completely surrounding me. There are nine agents in total, all armed with either a Remington 870 shotgun or a Heckler and Koch MP5 submachine gun. One of them steps into the middle, facing me, and holds his badge out in front of him.

"Freeze! FBI!"

3

"Don't move!"

What the fuck is going on?

I'm completely stunned and probably look like an idiot. I'm standing still, staring at an FBI SWAT team with my mouth open and my eyes wide, holding a phone to my ear.

"Adrian? Adrian? What's going on?"

Oh, yeah, Josh is on the line...

I shake my head, re-focusing. "I'm not sure, but I think I'm about to get arrested by the FBI. I might have to call you back."

I hang up as the agent at the front with the badge steps forward. "Adrian? I'm Special Agent Green. I've been instructed to detain you and bring you in for questioning."

I regain my composure. My brain kicks into gear, processing every possible reason that could've led to this moment, as well as every likely outcome.

I stare at Agent Green, trying to ignore all the others

who have their guns trained on me. "You not gonna read me my rights?"

He shrugs. "You're not under arrest. We just want to talk to you."

I look around and gesture to all the agents he's brought with him. "Then why the show of strength? You could've just asked if you wanted a conversation."

"Fair enough. Adrian, can you please come with me, so we can ask you some questions?"

He walks toward me, putting his hand on my arm like he's trying to lead me away. I don't move. I look down at his hand, then back up at him. "I might. But then again, I might not. You said yourself I'm not under arrest, so you can't make me."

He smiles and tries again to lead me away, but I hold my ground. When that doesn't work, he looks at me with something akin to an apology in his eyes. Like he really doesn't want to have to do it, but he's going to anyway. "Adrian, don't make this any harder than it already is."

"I'm not. On the contrary—I'll make this as easy as I can for you. Move your hand, or I'll give you a reason to arrest me."

I see the circle of agents twitch. Agent Green is getting more nervous by the second. His eyes move like he's checking to see if anyone's watching him struggle. He's losing control of the situation and losing face in front of his SWAT team. I don't think he was expecting any resistance, under the circumstances. They clearly know who I am. Otherwise, they wouldn't have come so well prepared. Plus, who would argue with an armed SWAT team sent to detain them?

"Listen, I can arrest you any time I want, all right? I'm trying to be nice about this."

I know they've got nothing on me. I'm too good. I raise an eyebrow. "Just out of interest, on what grounds would you place me under arrest, exactly?"

"Pre-meditated murder, for one."

"Bullshit. You can't prove something I've not done."

The agent laughs. "Just do yourself a favor and come along quietly, or else."

He turns and starts walking away, presumably thinking I'll follow him.

Oh, dear.

Those two words are like a red rag to a bull.

Or else.

I wish people would stop pushing me. Nothing good ever comes from it. I feel the adrenaline building up inside me. My heart rate's slowly increasing, along with my anger. I look around me once more. There's no way they're going to shoot an unarmed man in public. Even if they *are* trying to arrest me, the most they'll risk is a non-lethal takedown, and I can live with that.

I feel my jaw muscles clench. "Or else... what?"

Agent Green stops and looks back at me. His eyes narrow. He takes a step back, then spins around to face me, stopping a few feet away. He raises his hand. I have no idea why. Maybe he intends to shake a disapproving finger at me. Or maybe he's going to grab me again. But I've no intention of waiting to find out. I'm past caring.

I grab his wrist and twist it counterclockwise, away from me. I catch him off-guard and he almost overbalances. He instinctively moves his body in an effort to ease some of the pressure, which I anticipated. As he does, I thrust my hand into his throat, hitting him with the curve between my thumb and trigger finger. He goes crashing to the ground, coughing profusely.

I drop my bag and step back into a loose fighting stance. I turn slowly and stare into the eyes of each agent in the circle. I feel enraged... trapped... and my instinct is to react the only way I know how: violently.

It's not the smartest thing I've ever done. I know they came here with nothing they could use to justify an arrest. That said, something is definitely amiss here. I mean, how did they find me in the first place? And why would the FBI want to talk to me anyway? It has to be some kind of misunderstanding.

But now all that's irrelevant. Now they *have* something to arrest me for: assaulting an FBI agent. I can imagine what Josh would say to me if he were here. In his sarcastic, British voice, he'd say, *"Nice one, Adrian, you muppet!"* I don't fully understand the reference, but I know that *muppet* means *idiot*... and he'd be absolutely right.

They swarm toward me, forcing me to the ground, holding me in position as they place handcuffs on me. I don't offer any more resistance. I've proved my point. You can't get away with threatening me.

Two of them drag me to my feet. The others follow in a wide arc, guns trained on me from all angles. Agent Green has managed to get back up and is dusting himself down, massaging his throat. He catches up with us and takes the lead, escorting me toward a fleet of cars parked a short distance away. "That was a grave mistake, Adrian! Now you *are* under arrest."

He reads me my rights as I'm ushered into the back of one of the cars. The door's slammed shut behind me, and everyone disappears to their own vehicles.

We drive off a moment later. I look out the window at all the onlookers lining the sidewalk, pointing and staring.

That went south really fast...

What the hell just happened?

14:31 PDT

I'm sitting on the world's most uncomfortable chair, with my hands flat on the table in front of me. I look around the small, generic room and note every detail. Not that there are many.

The walls are plain, gray brick and probably haven't had a fresh coat of paint since the seventies. At the top of the wall on my right is an analog clock. The door's just to the right in front of me. It's made of old, thick wood with frosted glass in the top half. I can see the outlines of things outside but nothing clearer.

A two-way mirror takes up the wall to my left, stretching from waist-height to ceiling and running the full width of the room.

My wrists are cuffed and chained to the table in front of me through a small metal hook. The table is bolted to the floor, though the chair I'm sitting in isn't.

In the corner, just above the mirror, is a security camera, which can easily see the entire room. I imagine there's sound recording on it as well.

I glance at the clock. I arrived at the FBI field office a couple hours ago, and Agent Green hustled me straight into this room. He secured me to the table and left without saying a word. I've been here ever since, and no one's been in to check on me yet.

Standard operating procedure when you need information from someone is to leave them on their own for a while. People tend to get nervous and paranoid, which leads to them feeling guilty. So, when you finally ask them a question, they've worked themselves up into such a state, they'll tell you everything.

But this isn't my first visit to an interrogation room, either as a prisoner or the one asking the questions. I relax back into my chair and close my eyes. In these situations, patience is the best way forward. There's nothing I can do right now to improve matters, so I'll wait and let things play out. I'm here for a reason, even if I don't know what that reason is.

That's getting to me. I know they can't possibly have any real evidence against me for a crime. I'm one of the best contract killers in the world. When I carry out my hits, I'm like a ghost. To the criminal underworld, I'm a legend. But in the eyes of any law enforcement agencies, I'm just a myth —a story told to new recruits to scare them. They have nothing on me. I'm sure of it. Which begs the question... how did they know where to find me?

I look at the two-way mirror. I wonder who's behind there, watching me. There's always someone behind those mirrors. I study my reflection. I need a shave. My ice-blue eyes stare back at me, looking as tired as I feel.

It's my own fault for having a few beers last night...

Despite the lack of sleep and the mild hangover, I'm in great shape, both physically and mentally. The last year has been both productive and profitable. Overall, I'm feeling better than I have in a long time.

I briefly look at the scar underneath my left eye, which runs down my cheek. My mind flashes back to that cabin in the Nevada desert twelve months ago. Ironically, I was restrained to a chair *then* as well...

Nothing good ever comes from me being tied up.

I sigh and begin drumming my fingers on the desk to break the silence. I hate not knowing what's going on.

After another few minutes, the door opens and two men walk in. The first guy is likely the younger of the two. He's a black guy, probably late twenties. He has short dark hair and is clean-shaven, wearing a suit and tie with the jacket open. He walks over to the table, places his cup of coffee and a document folder carefully on the surface, and sits down opposite me. He's fresh-faced and serious. I'm guessing he's new to the job and keen to impress.

His colleague remains standing near the door as he closes it behind him. He's a little older and looks slightly more... cynical than the first guy. Like me, he needs a shave, bordering on the scruffy side of fashionable with his beard. He doesn't have a suit jacket on, and he's rolled his sleeves up. He leans against the wall with his arms folded, staring at me.

A doomed-to-fail attempt at intimidation.

I find it amusing when people underestimate me, assuming I'm like everyone else.

I look at the young and enthusiastic man in front of me. He seems to be trying not to look terrified as he reads the file he brought in with him. After a few moments, he closes it and looks at his watch, then at me.

"Interview started at fourteen thirty-nine hours. Special Agents Wallis and Johnson present. For the record, Adrian... *Hell*, can you confirm that you've been informed of your legal rights and that you understood them?"

I nod once but say nothing.

Silence is the best strategy when you're under arrest. Pick any one of the million metaphors that exist to prove it. If you say nothing, it puts you in control. The authorities can't do anything if you don't talk, and more often than not, they'll crack before you do. Let them form their own opinions. Speak only when necessary.

I know what you're thinking. I'm going to find this really hard. And you're right. I'm resisting the urge to have some fun with Bert and Ernie over here. But I have to play this smart. I still don't know why I'm here, which means as things stand, they know more than I do.

"For the benefit of the audio recording, Adrian Hell nodded." He glances over his shoulder at his colleague, who nods back at him. He turns to me again. "So, let's begin. Adrian, my name is Special Agent Tom Wallis. I'd like to start by establishing why you're in San Francisco."

I look at him, then at his colleague, whom I assume is Special Agent Johnson. I clench my jaw as I run through everything in my head. I obviously have a cover story in place. It would be downright amateurish of me not to have everything planned and every angle covered before I carry out a hit. But I need to be sure of every detail before I speak, for my own peace of mind. Something's not right. Must be something here I've missed because they arrested me the moment I stepped outside City Hall...

But I'm still confident they don't have any real evidence against me. I've spent too many years learning how to be too good to leave any. But that doesn't explain how they knew where to find me or what they want.

"Staying silent isn't as beneficial as you might think, Adrian," Wallis says after a few moments. "Tell us why you're in San Francisco."

I stay quiet a beat longer. "I'm here on business."

"What kind of business?"

"My own."

Johnson pushes himself away from the wall and walks over to the table. He leans over next to his colleague and rests his hands on the surface. "What were you doing at City Hall?"

"Sight-seeing."

Wallis smiles humorlessly. "There are better things to see around here than City Hall."

I shrug. "Just want to see everything this town has to offer, that's all. Why do you care, anyway?"

"We care about the safety of the people who live here," says Johnson.

I note the edge in his tone, and I don't care for it. "How noble of you. You want a medal or something?"

"Are you not curious how we know who you are?"

I smirk. "You *don't* know who I am."

"We know *exactly* who you are," says Wallis. He taps his index finger on the file he brought in with him. "Let me show you."

I shrug again. They don't know a goddamn thing, but I'll let them have their fun.

He opens the file. "Adrian Hell—born Adrian Hughes, February 14, 1972 in Omaha, Nebraska. Joined the Army in 1990 and was involved in Desert Shield. Your military record is a little hazy from '93 to '02, but you're rumored to have worked in some capacity with the CIA. No details on record of any operations you may or may not have carried out during that time...

"In 2002, after officially being given an honorable discharge from active military service, you moved to Pennsylvania to marry your partner of five years, Janine, with your three-year-old daughter, Maria, in tow."

Huh. I'm surprised they have so much on me. They're clearly well prepared. But they've made the mistake of showing me their hand straight away.

I smile. "Why stop there? You were on such a roll. Please, continue."

Agent Wallis says nothing. I look at him, then at Agent Johnson. They exchange frustrated glances but remain silent.

"What?"

More silence.

"You can't continue, can you? That's all you have. You've got nothing on me since 2002, and everything you *do* have is on the military's databases anyway, and therefore easily accessible if you know who to ask. Am I right?"

Wallis looks down at the table in defeat, closing the file as he realizes his bluff has backfired. Johnson paces away from the table, sighing heavily.

"C'mon, guys. You have nothing to justify holding me here, which brings us back to square one. What do you want with me?"

There's a tense silence in the room.

Johnson looks at me. "We want to know why you're in the city."

"And I've already told you, so if there's nothing else..."

He approaches the table again and leans forward, so his face is mere inches from mine. His expression changes from attempted intimidation to genuine anger. "Well, this morning, a man died in City Hall of a suspected heart attack. Roughly around the time you were in the building."

I look at him innocently. "A tragic coincidence..."

"Our Forensics team is running blood tests. I wonder what they'll find..."

I shrug. "How should I know? Maybe he needed to cut out fatty foods."

"Look, asshole, we might not have anything in a file, but we know who you are and what you do, all right? Everybody does. The FBI, the CIA, NSA, Homeland Security—*everybody*. I don't care if we can't prove it. We all know it. You're a goddamn psychopath and you should get the chair!"

Wallis quickly stands and pushes Johnson away. I wink at him, which infuriates him further. You know me—I'm not one to pass up an opportunity to piss someone off for my own amusement.

But what he said concerns me. I doubt *everyone* knows who I am and what I do, but given I'm sitting in an FBI field office, there's possibly *some* truth to it. I think back to my dealings with the secretary of defense last year in Nevada. I wonder if word has gotten around.

I dismiss it for now.

After a moment or two of whispering, seemingly happy he's defused the situation, Wallis returns to his seat across from me. He clasps his hands in front of him and leans forward, suddenly coming across as a lot more experienced and comfortable than he probably is. I'm impressed.

He looks briefly at the two-way mirror and sighs, like he's reluctant to say what he's about to. "Adrian, like it or not, my colleague is right—you *are* on several agencies' watch lists after your involvement in the Nevada incident last year."

Shit. I knew it.

I sigh.

C'mon, Adrian—poker face.

"It's kind of an unspoken agreement that we all know what you do, but we keep it to ourselves because we know we can't prove it. You want the truth? You're so good at what you do, it scares us. But that's not why you're here. You're here because the FBI needs your help."

I wasn't expecting so much honesty. I'm confused. What could they want *my* help with?

Before I can say anything, there's a knock at the door. Another agent enters, followed by a man with shoulder-length blond hair, wearing a suit and carrying a tattered briefcase.

The agent looks at Wallis. "Sorry to interrupt, but this gentleman says he's Adrian's lawyer, and he's demanded access to his client before any further questioning takes place."

Johnson rolls his eyes. "Jesus Christ..."

He turns and walks out the room, followed by the other agent.

Wallis stands and turns to my lawyer. "I'm Special Agent Wallis. Adrian has been formally arrested for assaulting an FBI agent."

My lawyer looks at me with raised eyebrows. I shrug.

"But that's *not* why we originally wanted to bring him in. I was just about to explain that we need his help. Consequently, I don't think legal counsel is necessary at this time."

My lawyer nods. "That's a valid opinion, and we can absolutely discuss that in more detail... once I've spoken with my client in confidence."

"I can assure you there is no need to—"

He holds his hand up. "Did you or did you not place my client under arrest?"

"Well, yes."

"And I assume you followed procedure and read my client his rights?"

"We did."

"In doing so, you advised my client of his right to legal representation, and on his behalf, I am exercising that right immediately. Please clear the room and turn off any recording equipment, so I can talk with Mr. Hell confidentially."

Wallis sighs, realizing there's no point in arguing. He leaves the room and closes the door behind him. A moment later, the little red light on the security camera goes out, signaling it's no longer recording.

My lawyer sits down opposite me and places his briefcase on the table. I regard him for a moment. He looks younger than me, but I know he's a few years older. I've not seen him in a few months, and under the circumstances, I'm glad he's shown up.

I smile at him. "Hey, Josh."

4

"Don't *hey, Josh* me! Why in God's name did you assault an FBI agent? Have you completely lost your mind?"

"It's good to see you too, man. How did you get here so fast?"

He waves his hand dismissively. "I was... in the area. Stop changing the subject. Walk me through what happened, Adrian."

I sigh. "I came out of City Hall on the phone to you when they swarmed at me from out of nowhere. They knew exactly who I was and where I'd be."

"So, again, what possessed you to beat up an FBI agent?"

I look down at the table. I feel like a guilty child being given the *we're not angry, just disappointed* speech. "I hit the agent trying to bring me in for questioning because he told me to come along quietly... or else."

He frowns. "He used those exact words?"

"Yup."

36

Josh is quiet for a moment, then shrugs. "Fair enough. All things considered, the guy's lucky you didn't kill him."

We both fall silent, then burst out laughing.

"It's good to see you, Boss."

I nod. "Likewise. How *did* you know to come here, anyway?"

"You know I don't like giving away trade secrets, Boss. Don't ask me that."

"Josh..."

I stare at him until he can't hold my gaze any longer. He looks away, lost in some inner turmoil, like a magician asked to reveal how he does a trick.

"Just because I'm handcuffed doesn't mean I won't kick your ass..."

He sighs. "All right, fine. I'm never more than a couple of hours away from you when you're on a job. I have a Winnebago, which I've kitted out as my own little mobile command center. Ever since Philly, I've tried to stay close when you're working. Y'know... just in case you need any backup or anything."

I stare at the wall behind him, my mind flashing back to Philadelphia eight years ago. Finding my wife and daughter murdered in our family home. The result of a drug kingpin called Wilson Trent taking revenge on me for unknowingly killing his son.

I re-focus my gaze on Josh and smile. This guy is the closest thing I have to family. He's always had my back, and he's the only person other than myself whom I trust with my life. But right now, I can only think about one thing.

"You have a Winnebago?"

I fail to suppress a laugh.

He rolls his eyes. "Ah, screw you! I like it, and it beats having to stay in all the crappy motels *you* sleep in."

We laugh together again for a brief moment, then fall silent.

"So, what's the score here? Why does the FBI want you?"

I shake my head. "I honestly have no idea. They have my background up until I moved to Philly. And along with every other acronym, they know my real name and what I do for a living. I think the secretary of defense may have started talking after last year."

"Oh, how thoughtful of him... prick!"

"Exactly. But apparently, the FBI wants my help with something."

"Okay, well let's just see what they have to say. The way I see it, if we can do them a favor, it buys us a free pass this time, and we can get out of here and lie low for a couple of weeks."

This is why we work so well together. I'm the impulsive, violent, loud-mouthed, borderline-sociopathic member of the team. Josh is the calm, patient, sensible one. Together, we're unstoppable.

I nod. "Sounds like a plan."

Josh stands and walks over to the door. He opens it, sticks his head out, and says something I can't quite hear. A moment later, Special Agents Wallis and Johnson re-enter the room.

Josh closes the door again and moves to stand behind me. This time, Agent Johnson sits down opposite, placing a file on the table in front of him. Agent Wallis is at his side. I look up and notice the red light is back on the security camera.

"Are you going to formally charge my client?" asks Josh, back in character as the no-nonsense British lawyer.

Agent Johnson glances behind him, then looks at me. "Despite the circumstances surrounding his arrest, we don't intend to press charges following Mr. Hell's assault of an FBI agent at this time."

"Good, then you can take the restraints off him."

Wallis steps forward and produces a key from his pocket. He unlocks the handcuffs, allowing me to pull my hands free. I massage each wrist in turn, getting the blood flowing back to them.

I nod to him. "Thanks. So, you were about to ask me for help?"

"Reluctantly... yes, we were," replies Johnson.

"So, go ahead."

"Are you aware of the recent terrorist attacks that have taken place in this city in the last seventy-two hours?"

I shake my head.

Johnson opens the file and spins it round for me to read through. "Yesterday morning, a bomb went off in a restaurant in Chinatown. There were over fifty casualties."

"Oh, wait—I think I saw this on the news. There was a TV in the place where I ate yesterday. It looked pretty bad..."

I skim through the folder. It contains photographs, both black and white and color, taken at the scene. It looks like total carnage—much worse than the TV had implied. Bodies and body parts litter the remains of the annihilated restaurant and the street outside. There's a report attached, which seems to detail witness statements and forensic information, but I don't bother reading it.

"Jesus..."

I close the folder and pass it over my shoulder to Josh, who takes it and starts flicking through.

"Two days ago," continues Wallis, "there was a seemingly random sniper attack outside the Transamerica Pyramid. Two people were shot dead from roughly seven hundred yards away."

"*Seemingly* random?" asks Josh.

"I'll get to that. Both victims were shot through their right eye. Whoever pulled the trigger was exceptionally talented."

I wouldn't say they were *exceptional*. Seven hundred yards is a good distance, sure, but it's not earth-shattering. Any half-decent sniper with six months of military training could hit a target at that distance. Admittedly, getting them in the right eye is a little more impressive, but it's still no cause for concern.

I gesture to the folder. "So, you think there's a link between the two attacks?"

Before either of them has chance to answer, the door opens and a woman walks in, carrying another folder. She's average height, maybe five-six, and she's wearing a gray suit and black heels. "I'll take it from here."

Her voice is a perfect blend of icy authority and warm comfort.

Agents Wallis and Johnson excuse themselves and leave the room. She sits down opposite and regards me silently for a moment. Her jacket's open, and I see her gun resting in its holster, strapped to her shoulder over her white blouse.

She's staring at me, unfazed. Her steel-gray eyes look out of place on her otherwise welcoming and friendly face. "I'm Senior Special Agent Grace Chambers. I'm well aware of who you are and what you do for a living." She glances up at Josh. "Both of you."

I raise an eyebrow at her. She's well informed. Apparently, more so than her colleagues, if she knows who Josh really is.

"You're here because we need your help with an ongoing investigation. I believe the other agents gave you the details of what we have so far?"

I nod. "I've seen the photos and heard the details. I still don't know what any of it has to do with me. How could I possibly help?"

"These attacks weren't random. They were meticulously planned with one purpose in mind."

I frown. "Which was?"

"To send a message to you, Adrian *Hell*."

I stay silent. My mind instantly starts racing in every direction. Josh is pacing behind me. I look up over at him and see the look of concern on his face. My face betrays nothing, but this has left me speechless and confused. I'm wracking my brain, trying to think of anyone who could hold this much of a grudge against me and have the means to execute a plan of this magnitude. They must—

What am I thinking? The list of people who hate me is likely to be extensive.

I re-focus my attention on Agent Chambers. "What makes you think they're trying to send a message to me?"

"Each crime scene has a clue that leads to you. We haven't had time to piece everything together since we received the phone call. We were too busy trying to find you."

Josh steps toward the table. "Whoa, whoa... what phone call?"

"We received an anonymous call yesterday morning, which is how we knew where to find you, Adrian."

I look at Josh and shrug. "Can we hear it?"

"I don't see why not."

She looks at the mirrored wall and makes a circular motion in the air with her index finger. A crackling sound fills the room over a speaker system.

"This is a message for Senior Special Agent Grace Chambers of the FBI. The attacks on this city over the last two days were my doing. I wanted to get your attention. I trust I've succeeded. We both want the same thing, Agent Chambers. We both want Adrian Hell. I know the FBI, along with every other government agency in this country, knows who he is. I want him to suffer, and I want him to die by my hand. These attacks are for him. I've left a message for him at each scene— a little game for us to play. We shall see if he's smart enough to figure out who I am. If you want the attacks to stop, you will detain him for me. I'll know when you have. Then you will stay out of my way. If you want to catch him, he'll be coming out of your City Hall tomorrow morning, about eleven a.m. I'll be in touch."

The line clicks dead. I look at Chambers. She's staring at me, watching me with a professional curiosity. Her eyes are asking me a million questions all at once.

I don't know what to think. The caller used a device to mask the sound of their voice, so their words were digitally distorted. My first impression is they sound like a complete psychopath. Maybe even a serial killer. And what do they want with me? It could be any one of hundreds of people who would gladly see me dead, so running through my job history won't do me any good.

I stand up and pace around the room for a moment, trying to focus my mind. There has to be something... some detail I'm missing that will help me.

I look at Josh, who's standing near the mirror. "Any ideas?"

He shakes his head. "It could be anyone. Pretty much the entire world hates you."

"Only the people who know me..." I look at Agent

Chambers. "You said there were clues at the crime scenes that led to me?"

She nods. "You heard the same recording we did. We're working on the evidence we have. That's why we wanted you here. Aside from keeping you out of the line of fire, we were hoping you'd help us find who this person is, so we can stop them."

Josh sits down in the chair I've been keeping warm for the past couple of hours and looks at Chambers. "Show me the evidence."

She opens the folder she brought in, flicks to the back, and spins it around to face him. Josh places the other folder down on the table and starts scanning through the new one, casting a professional eye over the reports and photographs.

It's amazing watching him work. Normally, I just call him and ask him something, and then he'll call me back a few minutes later with the answer. I have no idea how he manages to do even half the shit I ask of him. The guy's a genius. But actually *seeing* him work on something is incredible. He looks at each page, each photo, nodding to himself periodically when he finds something I imagine everyone else has missed.

Out the corner of my eye, I catch Chambers looking at me looking at Josh. I don't think she finds me attractive, thank God—you saw what I was like with the secretary this morning. I just think she's trying to figure out the dynamic between us.

"I travel a lot with work," I say to her, unprompted. "Josh typically handles the logistics and administrative side of my day-to-day life."

He doesn't look up from the folder. "Whatever. If I could wipe your ass down the phone, you'd make me do *that* as well."

I smile at Chambers. She shakes her head in disbelief. "It's hard to believe *you* are what the rumor mill says you are. If there were a shred of evidence in existence to prosecute you, every agency in the United States would be fighting to arrest you. And here I am, sat with the pair of you, and you're both coming across as nothing more than a clueless comedy double act."

She's half-laughing as she speaks, so I'm not sure how much of that is derogatory and how much is a polite observation. But it makes Josh stop reading the report.

He looks up at her. "Clueless? You think we're *clueless*?"

I smile to myself. I think he's genuinely offended, and his British accent always makes him sound that little bit more confrontational than he probably means to be.

He gestures to the report. "Tell me, how many people have you got working on this?"

She thinks for a moment. "We have a task force consisting of four of our best agents. They're currently analyzing the data."

He stands, holding the file. "Well, let me save you the trouble. The shootings are the most obvious message. Both victims, like Adrian, are white men in their early forties. The first victim is Alan Holding. The second is Aaron Henderson. The obvious link to Adrian? Both he and the victims have the initials A.H. But I'm sure you've already figured that out?"

Chambers frowns but remains silent. I'm not sure whether she's dubious of Josh's analysis, or quietly pissed off he's figured that out in less than three minutes. It's hilarious! I lean against the back wall and cross my arms, enjoying the show.

He throws the folder down in front of her. "But that's not all. The less obvious link is in their financial statements.

They both donate a modest sum every month to a charity called Guardian Angels. Or at least, they *did*. The link to Adrian is that angels are found in Heaven. As in, Heaven's Valley."

Even I'm speechless at that level of deductive reasoning!

He's on a roll now...

"The bomb at the restaurant earlier today is a bit trickier. Working with Adrian is the only way you'd pick up on the link. You reported a poker chip from The Dunes casino found at the scene. That's the message." He turns to me. "Adrian, The Dunes casino was in Las Vegas up until '93, when it was demolished to make way for another larger, more impressive, establishment."

I have no idea what he's talking about.

He smiles sympathetically at the blank look on my face. "It was knocked down so that they could build The Bellagio..."

I stand up straight and stroke my chin. How does *that* relate to me personally? I think about the other clues. They were cryptic and obscure, but once you understood them, the meaning was obvious. So, I need to think of the most obvious reference to something relating to me...

Bellagio... Bellagio...

Then it hits me. "Well, that sounds an awful lot like *Pellaggio*, doesn't it?"

"Bingo." He turns back to Agent Chambers, who's still watching us with fascination. "Whoever this is, the beef they have with Adrian has something to do with what happened in Heaven's Valley, Nevada twelve months ago."

Saying it out loud makes it hit home a lot harder. There's only one person I can think of with the ability to carry out this level of vendetta against me, and who knows the full extent of what happened in Heaven's Valley. Only one person unaccounted for in the aftermath. One of only two names on my personal hit list.

Clara Fox.

"You boys ever thought of a job as FBI agents?" asks Agent Chambers. She almost sounds impressed. "If what you say is right, then we can start putting together a profile of our terrorist and hopefully track them down before they take any more innocent lives."

I shake my head. "It might not be as easy as that. If it's who I think it is, they're a stone-cold killer. Highly trained in the art of espionage, deception, and being invisible. You won't get to them unless they want you to."

"And what have you done to him to make him this mad, dare I ask?"

"Not him. *Her*."

"You think this is a *woman*?"

Josh looks at me with something akin to fear in his eyes. "Adrian, if this *is* Clara, you need to tread carefully. Think about where we are, all right?"

I nod. "Agent Chambers, am I under arrest?"

She shakes her head. "At this moment, no, you're not."

"Then I need to leave right now."

"I'm afraid that's out of the question. You're still in our custody for questioning, and we have twenty-four hours before we legally have to charge you with something and place you under arrest. You can't just leave. You heard the phone call. They're coming for you, Adrian. I can't just let you back out on the streets alone. I'd be putting you at risk. Not to mention any collateral damage that could potentially harm the people of this city. Whoever's behind this has already shown they have no regard for the consequences of their actions."

I smile. "Why, Grace, I never knew you cared so much..."

"I will not put any more people at risk until we know more about who we're dealing with and what their plans are."

There's a knock at the door and Agent Johnson enters. He looks flustered and out of breath. "Ma'am... they're on the phone right now... asking for you."

She frowns. "Who is?"

He looks at me momentarily. "The terrorist, ma'am."

Chambers looks at me.

I smile. "What are we waiting for? Let's go and say hi."

5

_____

Chambers walks out of the room in a hurry, leaving Johnson in the doorway.

He looks at each of us in turn. "Follow me."

He disappears, so Josh and I head out the door and along the corridor after him. Halfway down, it branches out into an open-plan area full of desks, phones, and FBI agents busying themselves with their work. We carry on as the corridor doglegs to the left. We come out into another office space, slightly smaller than the one we just passed. There are a few desks with chairs either side. On each one are laptops and more telephones. The furniture looks like an IKEA clearance sale. It's all standard with a beechwood finish. The carpet is navy blue, and the fluorescent lights on the tiled ceiling overhead are buzzing away happily. The FBI agents in here stop and stare at us as we walk in.

Have you ever seen those old western movies, where the hero walks into a bar and the music stops and everyone turns to look at them? The hustle and bustle, the chatter, and the piano all goes quiet to the point where you can hear a mouse fart. And they all take a simultaneous breath in...

It's like that.

Josh looks at me and smiles. I simply shake my head and continue across the floor, toward a conference room in the far corner that I see Chambers entering.

Inside, there's a large table in the middle with several chairs along both sides. Agent Wallis is standing over by a large TV screen on the back wall with a phone to his ear and his hand over the mouthpiece. In the center of the table is a black speakerphone system used for teleconferences. Chambers is standing on the opposite side of the table, facing the door, leaning over it and resting on both hands.

She looks at me as I walk in. Johnson stays at the door, turning to face the other agents and giving them instructions. I guess they'll be recording and tracing the call.

She points to the chairs, then puts her finger to her lips. Josh and I sit down and observe. She looks over at Agent Wallis, who gives her the thumbs-up, then stares at the device. "This is Senior Special Agent Chambers. Who am I speaking to?"

There's moments of tense silence.

The line crackles. "Have you done as I asked?"

It's the same low, distorted voice I heard a few minutes ago.

"If you mean, have we managed to apprehend Adrian Hell, then yes, we have. I guess I should thank you for the tip-off."

"Put him on the phone."

"I can't do that until you give me something. I want to work *with* you to resolve this, not against you. Can you at least tell me your name?"

There's silence again. Everyone in the room exchanges worried glances.

"Call me... The Shark. Now put him on the phone. I know he's listening."

Agent Chambers looks at me and shrugs. She gestures to the device, giving me the go-ahead to talk. I look at Josh for any last words of wisdom before I open my mouth and cause mayhem. He holds his hands up in resignation.

Okay. I officially have total freedom to talk to a terrorist who's already attacked the city twice, all in the name of playing a game with me. I have to handle this delicately.

"Hey, dickbag, it's Adrian. What kind of a name is *the Shark*? You sound like a really shit comic book character. The kind of expendable doodle that doesn't make it past the first issue because they're killed off in spectacular fashion by our well-drawn hero. Which, in this instance, would be me."

Have you not been paying attention? I don't do delicate!

There's more silence on the line. I take that as a sign to continue antagonizing them.

"Oh, have I offended you? I'm sorry, *Jaws*. I didn't realize you were such a sensitive soul."

On the other side of the table, Agent Chambers rests her head in her hands. In the corner, Agent Wallis is trying to hold back a smile.

"I'd heard you had a mouth on you." The distortion masks the tone of the voice, but I can still tell when someone's pissed at me. "You should really learn some manners, Adrian."

"Tell you what. You stop randomly killing people, and I'll address you as... Mr. Shark. How's that?"

"My killings aren't random, Adrian. I'm sure you and your friend have figured that out by now."

"Yeah, we got your messages. Not very subtle. The shootings were particularly amateurish if I'm honest. Nevertheless, we're here. So, what do you want?"

"I want you, Adrian. I want your head on a spike for the world to see."

"Mom, is that you?"

Josh laughs out loud involuntarily, then clasps his hand over his mouth to suppress any further outburst.

"You think this is a game, Adrian?"

"Oh, sorry—was I supposed to be taking you seriously? I figured you're just a nut-job with a grudge who's been dying to find an excuse to squeeze off a few rounds and get their fifteen minutes of fame, and I've seen no evidence to the contrary."

"You took everything from me, you sonofabitch! I will have my vengeance."

"So, tell me who you are, and I'll come and apologize to you, all nice and civilized."

"You'll find out soon enough, Adrian. In the meantime, I have another message for you. And I want to give you this one in person."

"Great. We're at the FBI field office. Just come on over and we can talk about it."

"I think not. You have one hour to come and get the message, or there will be penalties. You want to treat this like a game? Fine. Let's play a game, Adrian."

"Where do you want me, douceface?"

"In the parking lot of the California Academy of Sciences is a school bus. On that bus are forty-three schoolchildren and three teachers. Underneath the bus is a brick of C4. Do the math, Adrian. Be there in sixty minutes, or there'll be a large hole filled with small body parts."

The line clicks dead. There's a split-second where

everyone in the room holds their breath and looks at each other, the panic clear on their faces.

I feel somewhat numb after how that ended. "Huh..."

Time resumes its normal speed. Chambers strides hurriedly out the room, barking orders at everyone outside. Organized chaos erupts all around, the likes of which I've never seen.

The room quickly empties, and everyone dashes to their respective desks, shouting to each other as they go. Chambers walks into the center of the open-plan office as she takes her firearm out of its holster to check the magazine is full. It's the standard FBI issue Glock 22 pistol, which holds seventeen .40-caliber Smith and Wesson rounds. Everyone quickly huddles around Chambers's desk as she outlines the plan. Josh and I stay at the back, just outside the conference room, out of the way. I figure it's best to let them get on with it.

I turn to Josh. "I don't suppose—"

"—I went to your hotel and retrieved your bag and guns? Yes, they're in my Winnebago."

I smile. "You're so pretty."

"Ah, shucks. You sure know how to make a gal blush!"

We chuckle to ourselves, making sure we—

"Hey! If you two have finished blowing each other, maybe you could join us and try to look like you give a shit about what's going on here?"

That was Agent Johnson, trying to exert some authority over the two people most likely to rebel against such things. We look at each other and huddle together.

Josh frowns. "Is he talking to us?"

I shrug. "I dunno. He can't be. He doesn't look that stupid."

"I think he was, y'know..."

"You reckon?"

"Yeah…"

"Well, it's probably not the time to retaliate, is it?"

"Nah, I wouldn't…"

"Okay. We should go over there…"

Josh gestures for me to go on ahead. We approach the group of agents, who have fallen silent following Johnson's outburst. I can't tell whether they're simply embarrassed on his behalf, or if they're genuinely interested to see how I'll react, given my reputation. Which everyone is aware of, apparently…

I ignore Johnson, making a point of turning my back to him as I look directly at Agent Chambers. "What are your plans?"

She seems reluctant to answer, knowing that telling me probably violates too many rules to list.

"Hey, regardless of what you say, I'm free to go whenever I want, all right? I'm here because I want to help. This guy's after *me*, and I'm going to sort my own shit out. But believe it or not, I don't want anyone to get caught in the crossfire who doesn't deserve to. So, if there's anything I can do to help you guys out, tell me."

She raises an eyebrow. "Well, regardless of what *you* think, Adrian, you're in an FBI field office. Which means the FBI is in charge, not you. I know you'll help out because I'm telling you to. And if you think you're walking in there and doing everything the way you want, you can forget it. Around here, we focus on saving lives, not settling scores."

I like her. She's *by the book,* for sure, but she has a little twinkle in her eyes when she speaks that makes me think she'll come through when it counts, rulebook or no rulebook.

Still, this is ultimately my fight. Consequently, I consider myself responsible for those kids. And unlike all these desk jockeys stood around watching me, I'm not restricted by procedures and regulations, which means I can do what's necessary, not what's appropriate.

I nod. "Fine. How far away is this place from where we are?"

"In traffic, about twenty minutes. It's near Golden Gate Park. Our Hostage Rescue Team won't make it in time, so we're liaising with the San Francisco PD and mobilizing our SWAT team as we speak." She checks her watch. "They'll be on site in fifteen minutes."

I look at one of the clocks on the wall. "We've got a little over three-quarters of an hour until his deadline. We'd better get moving, eh?"

"You two aren't going anywhere on your own."

"You'll only slow us down, and I'm better equipped to handle this than you are."

"How do you figure that?" asks Johnson, stepping to Chambers's side.

"Look, I think we're all done flirting around the subject of who I am and what I do. Under the circumstances, I suspect you'll overlook all the things you know you can't prove and let me help you any way I can. If this Shark asshole is nearby, they'll shoot at me pretty much on sight. Which means their focus won't be on you guys, so you'll be in a better position to save those kids. Whereas if you try to confront them directly, you'll have to stand there beating yourselves off, waiting for all kinds of authority to give you the green light to even think about pulling a trigger. I have the luxury of doing what I want if I need to. You guys don't." I turn to Josh. "Come on, we're leaving."

We both head for the main corridor, but Chambers runs over and blocks our path. She stands in front of us, arms folded. She sighs begrudgingly. "If you screw up, it's my ass that gets fried, so watch your step, okay?"

I grin. "I will do what I can to make sure your ass remains intact."

She almost succeeds in holding back the smile, but it slips out a little. She looks over at the huddle of agents. "Wallis. Johnson. You're with the Two Stooges here." She looks back at us both. "Play nice, boys. We'll be right behind you."

We walk out the office and back along the corridor toward the elevator. We ride it down to the first floor and walk across the entrance hall, eventually making our way outside to the small plaza in front of the building. It's late afternoon, and the sun is shining brightly, reflecting off the windows of the surrounding buildings.

Josh checks his watch. "We've got about forty minutes. We'd best get a move on."

Special Agents Wallis and Johnson appear behind us.

"You're riding with us," says Johnson. Wallis moves past us, taking his car keys out of his pocket.

I shake my head. "No chance. We'll go in Josh's car and meet you there."

"Agent Chambers said—"

"Agent Chambers isn't here. Why don't you boys live a little? I won't tell—promise."

"Come on!" shouts Wallis from over by his car, which is parked close to the entrance. "We're wasting time."

Johnson sighs with resignation. "Fine. But don't be skipping town or anything."

He turns and walks over toward Wallis' car.

Josh looks at me. "What a dick."

I smile. "Aren't they all? So, where's your ride?"

I scan the street, seeing nothing but government-issue

sedans and the occasional civilian vehicle parked against the sidewalk.

Where's his—

Hang on.

No...

That can't be it, surely...

My eyes rest on a dull, dirty, cream-colored Winnebago with a huge aerial sticking up from the roof and a windshield that's so filthy, I'd be surprised if you could see through it.

I look at Josh, who's smiling like a proud father. "Really?"

He shrugs. "What?"

"The money we make, and you have *that* piece of shit?"

"Don't knock it till you've tried it."

"I wouldn't want to knock it at all. It might fall apart."

We walk over and get in. Josh starts it up—on the third attempt—and we set off toward Golden Gate Park.

I look over at him as he navigates the steady flow of traffic. "Do you know where we're going?"

"Yup."

"Is my stuff in the back?"

"Yup."

Inside, the vehicle is open-plan, meaning you can get out of your seat in the front and walk into the back area. There's a fitted worktop running down one side with a ridiculous amount of tech on it. There's a barstool just in front of it. Opposite that, separated in the middle by the side door, is another worktop, also brimming with equipment, printouts, maps, and God knows what else. Against the back window is a battered sofa with my bag on it.

Bingo.

I walk over, eagerly open it, and retrieve my babies. Two custom Beretta 92A1 pistols. Each one is metallic silver with an ebony plate fitted either side of the butt. On it, embossed in silver, is an upside-down pentagram. Helpful in keeping the Adrian Hell persona alive and well. I take out my back holster and fit it around my waist, then slide the guns into place. I make my way back to the front cab and sit beside Josh.

I check the clock on the dashboard. We've got just under twenty-five minutes left before the Shark's deadline expires.

"You got a plan for when we get there?" asks Josh.

I shake my head. "Not really. Figured I'll try to stop the kids from getting blown up. That's about as far as I got."

He shrugs and smiles. "A good a place as any to start."

I look out the window as Josh threads through the traffic as fast as he can. Wallis and Johnson are just ahead of us. The same SWAT team who apprehended me earlier will be on site by the time we get there. I imagine Agent Chambers is en route behind us as well.

I sit back and close my eyes, trying to push everything else aside in my mind, so I can focus on whatever shit-storm I'm about to walk into.

6

Josh is a good driver and seems to know exactly where he's going, despite presumably having never been to San Francisco before. He's reliable and frighteningly resourceful, which is why he's been by my side in some capacity for over half my life.

We turned right on Fell Street after leaving the field office and followed it until we merged onto JFK Drive. We've been lucky so far that we've not hit any major traffic. We follow the road around and turn onto Kazar Drive. I look out the window and watch the skyline of the city flash past me. Under any other circumstances, I'd probably enjoy seeing more of the place, but right now there's no time for sight-seeing.

I look over at Josh. "It's good to see you, man."

And it really is. I've seen him twice in the last twelve months. I speak to him probably fifteen times a day, but when I'm out and about on your own, the solitude does get me down sometimes. I've always enjoyed moving around from place to place, remaining anonymous and seeing the world. But every once in a while, it's nice to have some company.

He smiles as he focuses on navigating the slow but steadily moving traffic. "You too, Boss. Shame it's under these circumstances, though. Can you please just have a normal contract for once?"

"Hey, you're the one who finds me these jobs, remember?"

"Don't start blaming the logistics. Things only ever seem to turn to shit when you arrive in town. I'm just saying..."

"It's not my fault bad people tend not to wanna roll over and die willingly with no fuss!"

We both laugh.

That's another reason we work so well together. We understand, regardless of how enormous the task at hand is, it's always best to approach it instinctively. Don't think about it—do it. It's too easy to over-think things, which inevitably leads to indecisiveness and hesitation. And those things can cost you your life. To an outsider, it might look like I don't care, or that I'm not taking things seriously. In reality, I'm simply keeping detached so I can rely on my instincts.

Believe me, I'm taking the current predicament seriously.

"I don't think this is Clara," says Josh. "The voice is too masculine, even through the distortion. And from what we know of her, this isn't her style. She wouldn't have the patience or subtly to pull something like this off."

I sigh regretfully. "No, I know. I think that was wishful thinking on my part. But it's definitely someone who knows the truth about what happened in Heaven's Valley."

"I think most people know what happened, though. You

almost created a second Grand Canyon in the middle of the desert..."

"Very true. But if you're right about the Pellaggio reference, this has gotta be someone who knows I was also responsible for wiping out his organization, which was a separate thing entirely. Even the news reports at the time said it was likely a gang-related hit carried about by a large group of people."

He thinks for a moment. "GlobaTech?"

I shrug. "They certainly have the resources. But what's their angle? We're on pretty good terms with them last time I checked."

"Maybe they're pissed that you blew that military compound into a billion pieces?"

"I think they would have conveyed their displeasure before now. This sounds too... I dunno. Too personal."

We fall silent again. I'm not sure what to expect when we get to this academy, and I must admit I'm feeling a little out of my depth. I try to picture how it will go down. I imagine the bus will be parked inconspicuously. Will the Shark be there? My instinct says he won't be, but he'll be watching from a safe distance. From speaking with him earlier, he seems to have a good idea where the FBI are at with the investigation, which immediately says to me that he can either see them himself, or he has an inside man. Neither possibility bears thinking about.

Assuming he won't be on site, how is he keeping the kids on the bus? They must know they're in danger, surely? I figure it won't be much fun for him if he can't see people afraid.

I have no idea how to stop this asshole, either. I still haven't worked out why he's doing all this just to get to me.

I hate not knowing everything...

"Trying to figure it all out?" asks Josh, breaking both my train of thought and the silence.

"Just trying to prepare for what we're walking into here, yeah."

"I don't think anything can help with that. This is painfully new territory for the both of us."

I look ahead and see Wallis and Johnson a few cars in front of us. I wonder how far behind us Agent Chambers is...

Grace Chambers.

I like her. She definitely doesn't take any crap from anyone and is undeniably in charge, but she has a kindness about her at the same time.

We turn right on Martin Luther King, Jr. Drive. I check the clock again. We've got just under ten minutes before the deadline, but we're almost there now. After another quarter-mile, we turn right on Music Concourse Drive. We follow the road as it turns to the right, bringing us to the main entrance of the California Academy of Sciences, one of the largest natural history museums in the world. The building looms into view as we approach. It looks impressive.

I sigh heavily. Why am I even here? Things like this are the FBI's show, for God's sake. What use am I going to be? I've just admitted to a room full of agents that I'm the assassin they all think I am... what's to stop them arresting me the moment all this is over?

Assuming I don't get blown up or shot first.

Shit.

"We're here," says Josh.

He pulls over and stops opposite the main entrance. The scene is total chaos. Despite my efforts on the way here, I now realize nothing could've prepared me for what I'm about to walk into.

The local SWAT team must've been here for at least fifteen minutes, given how organized they are. There's a yellow school bus parked at an impromptu angle in the middle of the road, on the crossing right outside the main entrance to the academy. The area around the bus is cordoned off in roughly a hundred-yard radius. All around, police, SWAT guys, reporters, and onlookers are standing and staring at it with a mixture of shock, uncertainty, and regret. A chopper's hovering overhead. I can't see any markings, but it's more likely to be the police than the media.

We climb out of the Winnebago and walk toward the scene. I catch a glimpse inside the bus as we pass. It's full of schoolchildren, just like the Shark told us. They look terrified. I can see them crying and screaming, although I can't hear them from where I'm standing.

So, they *are* fully aware of the danger...

Agents Wallis and Johnson have parked across the road and are talking to someone who looks in charge of the scene. Johnson looks over and sees us approaching. He taps Wallis on his arm, and they walk over to us.

I hold my hands out to the side and look at each of them in turn. "Well, I'm here. Not sure what I'm meant to do, though."

"Neither are we," says Johnson. "I've spoken to the SWAT team leader, and they've seen nothing out of the ordinary."

"Apart from the bus full of terrified school kids?" observes Josh.

"He means there's been no sign of any suspects and no communications," says Wallis, professionally. He checks his watch. "We've got seven minutes until the Shark's deadline is up. I think we need to wait for him to contact us. He'll be watching, I'm sure."

I completely agree. I turn a slow circle and scan the crowds of people and the surrounding area. I can't see anyone who looks like they could be him, but I didn't expect to. If it were me, I'd be looking on, for sure—but from a long way away.

The cordon stretches all the way to the main entrance, so the building and the immediate area are clear. Just over the road from where we're standing, the SWAT team are milling around, seemingly unsure of what to do but doing their best to look like they're in charge anyway. They won't be sure what move to make, as no one knows what the endgame is, only that I need to be here.

Well, I'm here. Come on, you sonofabitch. Show yourself.

I'm sure the SWAT team would've done a full assessment of the situation when they arrived, but for my own peace of mind, I lie down on my stomach and look over at the bus. It's been parked with the back angled toward the academy's entrance. I scan underneath it as best I can from where I am. I can just about make out a red flashing light.

So, he wasn't bluffing about the bomb, either.

Shit.

I stand and find Johnson looking at me funny. "What the fuck are you doing?"

I frown and look at him like I'm staring at an idiot. "I was seeing if I could see the bomb he told us about."

"And what, are you some kind of expert on car bombs?"

I momentarily flash back to Heaven's Valley, standing outside the hospital as Clara's car blew up, sending me hurtling backward.

I smile faintly. "I've had some experience with them, yeah. You have a problem with me trying to help?"

We square up to each other, our faces only inches apart.

I could kill this prick with my bare hands, but I restrain myself, if only for the fact we have bigger problems to deal with. But I'm not backing down.

"I don't know who the fuck you think you are, but—"

"I'm the man you think *you* are. Now take a minute to remember we're meant to be on the same side, then take three steps back before you find yourself waking up with a crowd of people looking down at you."

"I thought I told you boys to play nice?" says a voice behind us.

I turn to see Senior Special Agent Chambers walking toward us. Even though she's harassed and in a hurry, she still has this casual demeanor about her, which seems to stop me from getting stressed when she's nearby.

Johnson steps away and stands up straight. "Ma'am, we were just discussing how best to approach the situation." He glances at me. "Aren't we?"

He emphasized his words in that way people do when they're trying to drop hints to get someone to say what they want them to.

Rookie error.

I look at Agent Chambers and smile. "Actually, Grace, I was just checking to see if there's a genuine bomb threat here, and Agent Johnson decided to take his life into his hands and start mouthing off at me. When you arrived, I was simply explaining how quickly and painfully the conversation could end for him."

Petty? Yes, I'm afraid it probably was. But the guy's an asshole, and I'm not doing him any favors. Besides, my comments make her smile a little bit, which is what I was aiming for. She has a great smile...

She rolls her eyes. "We've got three minutes until the

64

Shark's deadline. We've heard nothing from him yet. Adrian, have you any idea what this has to do with you?"

I shake my head. "Not a clue. Given that his previous clues seem to reference me or my history in some way, I've been looking for something along the same lines here, but I've got nothing. Josh?"

Josh shrugs, which isn't like him at all. "I have no idea what this guy's angle is. We have no clue who he is, nor what he's got against Adrian—aside from the fact he's clearly met him once, which is enough for anyone to want to kill him, frankly. But we're pretty sure it's not who we first thought it might be, so I've got nothing."

He gestures to the scene around us.

I know him well enough to know it would've hurt him to admit he didn't have an answer.

Agent Chambers' phone starts ringing. She takes it out of her pocket and looks at the caller ID on the screen. Looking confused, she answers. "Chambers."

I can't hear the voice on the other end of the line, but given how wide her eyes are, I'm guessing it's our guy.

"Okay," she says after a moment. She holds the phone out to me. "It's him. He wants to talk to you."

I take the phone from her and put it to my ear but say nothing. I listen. I'm convinced he's nearby. Even though he's distorting his voice, there could still be some background noise that might offer a clue as to where he is. But I get nothing.

"What?"

"I'm glad you could make it, Adrian," says the Shark. "Are you ready for my next message?"

"Just get on with it, you arrogant bastard."

"Now, now, Adrian. There's no need for name-calling. Put me on speaker, so all your friends can hear."

I do, and we gather around the phone in a tight circle, listening intently.

"Here's my message, Adrian. I can do things even *you* can only dream of. You once did what many thought was impossible. And in doing so, you took everything from me. Now there are no clues this time. No hidden meanings. Just a demonstration of what *real* power can do."

He hangs up, leaving us all looking at the phone and listening to a dead tone.

"What the hell does *that* mean?" asks Johnson, sounding confused.

I don't get the chance to answer because the whole world suddenly goes to shit...

7

_____

We all instinctively hit the ground as the deafening roar of an explosion sounds out nearby. I can just make out the screams of people around us over the ringing in my ears. I wait maybe ten seconds before standing and looking at the school bus, expecting to find a flaming wreck and the bodies of forty-three dead kids. But I'm relieved to see it still intact. Agent Chambers appears next to me. We exchange a confused glance.

I'm obviously happy the kids are still alive, but what the hell blew up?

Disoriented from the blast, I quickly scan the area to see if—

Ah, shit!

The SWAT van's completely destroyed, along with the entire team who were either inside it or standing close by.

Jesus Christ...

I hear what sounds like two gunshots, but they're faint

amid all this noise and chaos. I look around, trying to see where they came from, but it's futile. There's too much smoke and too many people running around and screaming. My gaze rests momentarily on some scattered body parts on the road—probably what remained of the SWAT team...

Agent Johnson runs over to a small crowd of people nearby, waving at them wildly and imploring them to get back. Agent Wallis takes his time standing and looks a little concussed. He would've been closer to the blast than the rest of us, so he probably caught more of it.

I know what that feels like...

"What the hell's happening?" shouts Chambers. "Where is this guy?"

I shrug. "I have no idea!"

A second explosion sounds out, farther away than the first. We all half-duck again before realizing it isn't nearby.

But it must be...

I look up, trying to see the tops of the buildings in the mid-distance in the vain hope of seeing a small figure looking down at us. Instead, I see the chopper that's been hovering above spinning out of control, in flames and plummeting quickly toward us.

Straight for the bus.

My eyes go wide. "Oh, shit!"

Without thinking, before anyone else can react, I race over to the school bus and yank the doors open, no longer caring about the initial bomb threat. The way I see it, if he were going to detonate the bomb under the bus, he would've done it already.

I climb on board and look at the sea of shocked and scared children. I have no idea what to do. For a valuable second, I freeze completely as I gaze down the bus, seeing nothing but small faces with mouths hanging open in unimaginable horror.

Then my brain resumes normal service.

"Everyone, I need you to listen carefully and do exactly as I say. I want you all to make your way to the front of the bus as quickly as you can and jump off, okay? Single file, right now. Once you're off, you have to run as fast as you can and get as far away from the bus as possible."

I clap my hands together to speed them along.

"Come on... *Now!*"

They don't need telling twice. A stampede of small feet run to the front of the bus and jump down to the parking lot. I look for the teachers in the crowd and make eye contact with one of them, a woman, probably mid-forties. "Hit the ground running and get them as far away from here as you can! You've got less than ten seconds!"

I stand, watching as the last of the kids escape the bus. The last one, a little girl, jumps off and starts running but loses her balance and falls forward on her face. She's probably about seven years old. She has pigtails in her hair...

I look at her lying on the floor, crying and screaming, and think of my own daughter, Maria. She was roughly the same age when she was taken from me. Everything stops, and I feel my heart breaking all over again.

I'll be damned if I'm going to lose another little girl...

I jump off and rush to her, scoop her up in my arms, and run as fast as I can. A couple of seconds later, I hear the flaming chopper hit the bus. The impact is deafening. The explosion knocks me off my feet. I managed to get maybe thirty feet away, but the blast hits me like a freight train and throws me forward. Instinctively, I throw the little girl out in front of me; I'll crush her if I land on top of her. It'll hurt when she lands, but it's better than the alternative, and I'm sure she'll forgive me.

I hit the ground hard, landing face-down. My head smacks against the concrete. As my skull bounces up again, I catch sight of the little girl landing some feet in front of me, seemingly safe from the blast.

Everything goes quiet. People's screams are reduced to a small echo, drowned out by the loud, constant ringing in my ears. My body feels hot and my eyes are stinging. Disoriented, I roll over on my back and look down my body.

Holy shit, I'm on fire!

I quickly roll over and over, mindlessly slapping at the flames to put them out. People I don't recognize are surrounding me. They cover me in a blanket, then help me to my feet.

My eyes are sore and my vision's blurring...

I wipe my hand across my face. It feels wet. I look down to see my hand covered in blood.

The world around me keeps fading to black and back again in slow motion. I look around and see blurry outlines of people running toward a body on the ground a few feet away, then toward me...

I'm lying on the ground again. I open my eyes. I must've blacked out. I struggle to push myself up on all fours. Johnson and Chambers appear next to me and help. They lift my arms around their necks and help me walk away. They're saying something, but I can't make out what.

I stumble and they guide me to the ground. I'm on a grass verge, away from the carnage and chaos behind me. I wipe my eyes again and look over to the entrance of the academy. I see the burning wreck that was once a SWAT van. Across the front of the building, whoever isn't dead or injured is running and screaming, trying to get away but ultimately falling over each other. Nearby is what's left of the school bus, with the remains of a chopper sticking out of it, on fire.

Sweet Jesus... this is insane!

I look up and see Chambers talking hurriedly into her phone. Johnson's kneeling beside me with his hand on my shoulder. I can't see where Wallis has gone. He's probably helping anyone who's injured.

Johnson is saying something to me and nodding, but I have no idea what. His voice sounds hollow, drowned out by a loud ringing. Looking at his face, I think he seems positive...

My head starts to spin. I lie back, preparing for the world to turn black once again. In my mind, all I can see is an image of the Shark looking on, laughing. I can't believe he would endanger the lives of so many innocent people— innocent *children*—just to get to me.

This has to stop. It's just too much. I've always said my anger is kept behind a closed door. Every now and then, someone will try to push that door open, and they never like what awaits them on the other side. This guy just kicked my door off its goddamn hinges! He has no idea what's coming for him—what I'm prepared to do to put a stop to this. The scary thing is, as I close my eyes and feel the world slipping away from me once more, neither do I.

??:??

"He's awake. Go and tell Agent Chambers."

That voice sounded miles away. I frown and then open my eyes, blinking a few times to clear the fog. I look over and see Agent Wallis standing next to me. He isn't smiling, but he seems glad I'm not dead, which is something.

I look around. I'm in a hospital room, lying in bed, hooked up to a heart monitor. The door is open. I look briefly out the window; it's dark outside.

I turn back to Agent Wallis. "Where am I?"

He smiles weakly. "You're in San Francisco General Hospital. You've been here just over four hours."

My head's killing me. I try to turn on my side, but all the wires stuck to my chest restrict my movement. I look at the machine, which is beeping steadily. That's good— I'm definitely not dead. First bit of good news I've had all day.

Memories of the chaos outside the academy come rushing to the forefront of my mind. "Christ... Wallis, what the hell happened back there? Is everyone all right?"

"The kids are safe, thanks to you. I don't know if you're a hero or just plain stupid. You were on that bus before any of us even registered the chopper had exploded. That was some good work, Adrian... Thank you."

"I'm glad they're all right. What about the SWAT guys?"

Wallis purses his lips together and shakes his head, solemnly. "All dead. I've no idea how the sonofabitch managed to rig a bomb to a fucking SWAT truck..."

"Shit. Listen, I'm sorry, man. I mean it."

"None of us saw it coming. We were too focused on the school bus..."

His voice trails off. I look at him. He's maybe six months into being a fully trained agent, but nothing at Quantico can prepare you for a day like he's just had. He's probably still in shock.

"Hey, no one's to blame here, okay? The bus was clearly just a distraction, so we wouldn't think about the possibility of anything else happening. Nobody saw that coming. How are we all doing?"

He starts to answer, but Agent Chambers walks in, followed by Agent Johnson, and he stops himself. They both look like they've been dragged ass-backward through a trash heap, but they're in one piece at least.

Chambers looks at him. "Can you give us a minute?"

He nods and heads out the door. Johnson follows him, then stops and turns back to look at me. "Listen... everything else aside—that was a real gutsy move back there, Adrian."

He walks out without waiting for a reply and closes the door behind him.

I look at Agent Chambers. Grace. She stands next to me, where Wallis just was. She smiles a weary smile.

I return the gesture. "You all right?"

She nods. "I've had better days, but I'll live."

"I'm just glad we all survived. You might not believe me, but I do genuinely feel for those SWAT guys. I know this is my fault."

She puts her hand on mine and squeezes gently. "This isn't your fault. This is the Shark's fault. And whether I like it or not, we were lucky you were there."

"Ah, team effort." I laugh a little, but it makes me cough. "Hey, where's Josh? I don't remember seeing him in the chaos back there."

Chambers says nothing but looks down and squeezes my hand again.

I frown. "What is it?"

She sighs. "Your friend was shot. He's in the ICU now and listed as critical. I'm sorry, Adrian."

I instantly feel sick to my stomach. Like I'm on a rollercoaster and I've just been flipped upside-down at a hundred miles per hour. The room starts spinning almost as fast as my mind is. How the hell could Josh have been shot?

I replay the scene in my head as best I can. Parts of it are still blurry to me, thanks to what I can only assume is a significant concussion.

The first blast was over to our left. That was the SWAT van. The second blast was high above, which was the chopper. That crashed down on the school bus, causing a third blast—which was the one that just about got me. So, how did Josh get shot?

I close my eyes and rub my temples, trying to make sense of everything.

The gunshots...

There were two gunshots. They were barely audible, but there was no mistaking them. I remember hearing them in the few moments between the first two explosions. I dismissed them as random at the time, but I was wrong. Their timing was too specific. Two bullets.

The Shark intended to take Josh out.

I don't have the energy to get angry. I'll save that for later. I'll save that for when my hands are around the Shark's throat.

I look at Chambers. "I need to see him."

"You need to rest..."

"I wasn't asking."

I sit up and pull all the leads off me. The constant beep of a flat line sounds loud on the machine next to me. I swing my legs over the side of the bed just as the door bursts open and three nurses run in, shouting.

"Sir, you must stay in bed!" barks one of them.

I wave them away and stand up slowly, gradually adding weight to my legs to make sure I can actually get out of bed under my own strength.

Another nurse places her hand on my shoulder. "Sir, please, you need to rest."

I look at her. She seems like a nice person. Short brown hair and brown eyes. Probably late forties. A career nurse, for sure.

"Where is he?"

The nurse looks confused and glances at Agent Chambers for verification. I see the look on her face as she realizes who I mean. "Your friend is in a critical condition."

"I know. What happened to him?"

"He was shot in the center of his chest and at the top of his left thigh. We've done our best to remove the bullets, but the damage was extensive. The loss of blood was significant, and one of his lungs has collapsed. Luckily, the bullets missed any major arteries, so we were able to stop the bleeding, but he's still suffered a massive trauma. We're keeping him in a medically-induced coma until he stabilizes."

I nod, taking in the information while at the same time barely hearing a word. That's Josh she's talking about. My friend. My partner. My brother. And he's lying in a hospital bed because of me.

"I still need to see him." I stand and stagger over to the door. "Where is he?"

The nurse sighs, giving up the argument. "He's down the hall to your left. Go through the double doors. It's the first room on the right. Let me get you a wheelchair."

I wave my hand dismissively, then set off to find him. I realize I'm wearing a hospital gown and underwear and nothing else. But I don't care. I have to see Josh. Even if he's in a coma, he'll hear me.

I need to tell him I've just figured out who the Shark really is.

8

I'm standing at Josh's bedside, looking down at him lying motionless, connected to a heart rate monitor with an oxygen mask over his nose and mouth. His machine's beeping a lot slower than mine was.

The bedsheet is down by his waist. His chest has a bandage across his left pectoral, with a red circle in the center of it over the bullet wound. On his left hand, a clip on his index finger also links to the monitor at the far side of the bed.

I stare at him, feeling an emptiness inside I haven't felt since losing my family all those years ago. It feels like a black hole in my stomach, gradually sucking in and crushing every remaining ounce of humanity I have.

Josh is all I have left. My life doesn't exactly allow for many friends. My family has already been taken from me. All I know is him, the open road, and me. Josh keeps me grounded... keeps me sane. He rescued me from a dark place and helped me channel my anger into something positive. Granted, to call killing people for a living positive is arguably still pretty dark, but it's a job with a big market and lots of money to be made. Over the years, I've probably accumulated close to thirty million dollars. When the time comes to walk away from this life and retire, we'll be set. But right now I'd trade every cent to get him back.

I take a deep breath and let it out slowly. "I'm sorry, Josh. This is my fault. For every hit I carry out, I make two enemies. I should've done a better job of keeping you away from this. I'm supposed to be the one in the line of fire, not you. You're the one who sits behind the desk and tells me what to do. Why did you even come here, you dumb sono-fabitch? We both have phones. Why didn't you stay away from all this, like you normally do? Now you're lying here attached to some fucking machine, and it's all because of me!"

There are no signs of life from him at all, other than the slow, constant beeping of his heartbeat on the machine next to him.

But I know he can hear me.

"I've figured out who the Shark is. You'd be so proud of me. I know who he is and why he's pissed at me. And I promise you, I'm gonna find him. I'm gonna torture him, and I'm gonna watch him die screaming in pain."

Still nothing. But he can hear me—I'm sure of it. He's far too talented to let something as simple as a coma stop him from utilizing all his senses. He can hear me, and if he could reply, he'd tell me to watch my back. He'd tell me to remember the FBI are in charge, and if I'm not careful, I'll expose myself and risk spending the rest of my life in prison. Or spend the last three minutes of my life strapped to a chair. He'd say it in his bouncy, happy, optimistic tone that makes me sick and makes me feel at peace, all at the same time.

And I'd look him in the eye, man-to-man, brother-to-brother. Without saying a word, he'd know I was going to ignore him and tear this world apart to have my vengeance anyway. And he'd help me without question.

I take another deep breath, which hurts more than it should, and place my hand on his shoulder. "Thank you. For everything. And when this is over, and you've woken up and gotten over all your little cuts and bruises and shit, we're gonna go out and buy you a brand-new Winnebago. It'll have all the trimmings—no expense spared."

I wait for the inevitable retort, but it never comes. He just continues to lie there, eyes closed, breathing slowly.

I pat his shoulder and turn to leave the room. Agent Chambers is standing in the doorway, leaning against the frame.

Busted.

I smile to myself and look at her. "You been there long?"

"Long enough." She turns back into the hallway and waits for me to follow. "You all right?"

I stagger out of the room, and we walk slowly down the corridor side by side.

I nod. "Yeah, I'll be fine."

"You need to rest up and let us handle this."

"Well, seeing as you've done such an amazing job so far…"

She looks at me with an expression that's half resentment and half sympathy.

I close my eyes for a moment. "I'm sorry. That was uncalled for."

"Damn right it was, asshole."

"I deserve that."

We fall silent. The sound of her heels echo down the corridor as we approach the nurse's station by the elevators on our floor.

She takes an extra step and turns, stopping in front of me. She puts her hands on her hips and cocks her head slightly, asking a million unspoken questions. I look her up and down. Even with bruises and cuts on her face, neck, and hands, she looks amazing. Her fitted trouser suit clings to the body I figure she spends every spare hour working on in the gym.

I shake my head and look away, slightly embarrassed. I haven't looked at a woman like that in years. Must be the concussion.

I shrug. "What?"

"You gonna tell me what the hell's going on, then? You were quick enough to tell your friend, and he can't do anything to help you. I can."

"Actually, no, you can't. From what I've seen, you're a damn good agent, Grace. But thanks to that oath you took when you joined the FBI, if I told you anything about this, you'd be obligated to arrest me immediately."

She raises an eyebrow. "I can imagine..."

"I'm not under arrest, and we both know I'm not going to be any time soon. It's probably best to leave it at that. You have my word I'm going to fix this. I'll help you with your investigation as much as I can, but please just step back and let me finish this. He won't stop until he's got me, so I'm going to give him what he wants."

"You're going to turn yourself over to him?"

"I'm going to use myself as bait, yeah. If I can see him with my own eyes, I can stop him."

"And how are you going to do that?"

I smile. "Don't ask me questions you don't wanna know the answer to."

She smiles back, but there's no humor there. "Then don't do things that make me want to arrest you."

Grace Chambers. I like her. One of the good guys.

I gesture to my gown. "Let me slip into something less revealing, then we'll talk, okay?"

She gestures to the front desk. "I'll wait for you here. I assume you'll be doing the stupid thing of checking yourself out of here?"

"The thought had crossed my mind, yeah."

She shakes her head. "Figures."

She walks away, takes out her cell, and dials a number.

I walk back to my room and sit down on the edge of the bed, resting my elbows on my knees and my head in my hands.

I might be a full-time killer and part-time idiot, but I'm not stupid. I need help, and with Josh out of the picture, the list of people willing and able to give me a hand is narrowed down to one.

The FBI.

If I don't ask for their help, I'll be flying blind with no clue how to stop the Shark from carrying out more attacks. But if I *do* ask for their help, I'm going to implicate myself in more crimes than I care to count, which would quickly lead to my incarceration and *still* wouldn't stop the Shark.

I sigh. Either way, I'm screwed.

21:43 PDT

. . .

I finish getting dressed and pull my jacket on as I walk out the room. I head down the corridor and see Chambers sitting patiently on the end of a row of chairs opposite the front desk, among the patients. In addition to the three nurses working behind the counter, there are six patients scattered around the waiting area.

I imagine she's grateful to rest a few minutes. It's been a hectic day.

When she sees me, she stands. We both walk over to the desk.

"So, you're definitely checking yourself out?" she asks me as I approach. "Despite the advice of everyone who works here?"

I smile humorlessly. "I'm no use to anyone lying in bed in here." I turn to the nurse and take a clipboard from her with some forms attached. "I need to be..."

I trail off as I look across the waiting area, toward the elevators at the far end. The doors have dinged open, and four men have just stepped out and are now walking toward us. Three of them are wearing black suits with blood-red shirts and black ties. They're all oriental, with jet-black hair in different styles, walking with purpose behind the fourth man. He's short and wearing a dirty white vest and brown pants that aren't long enough, finishing just above his ankle. He's bald on top, with his long, scraggly gray hair starting at the sides and falling down to his shoulders.

It's the old guy from the pawnshop last night... and these guys with him look—

They open their jackets, revealing guns in shoulder holsters, which they immediately draw.

Yeah, they look like trouble!

I turn to Chambers. "Grace, get down!"

I grab her shoulders and push her to the floor. She

doesn't get a chance to respond before gunfire sounds out around the waiting area. People scream and start running. An alarm starts ringing. I crouch in front of the desk, instinctively reaching behind me for my Berettas.

Nothing.

Shit, where are they?

I look over at Chambers, who looks confused but is quickly coming to her senses. She reaches for her gun and her badge, preparing to stand.

I grab her wrist and hold her down. She looks at me and I shake my head. "Grace, that badge isn't going to do shit besides get you killed. Give me your gun."

She shakes her head at me as bullets continue to splinter the desk around us. "No chance, Adrian! If you fire my weapon, it's a federal crime."

"Only if I take it from you first. If you hand it to me willingly, it's fine."

"No, it's really not!"

"This isn't the time to start arguing with me over minor details."

"That's not a minor detail!"

I sigh and peek over the desk. The three men are fanning out across the waiting area, taking turns to reload. The old guy is standing with a wicked smile on his face, pointing in my direction.

I have to get them away from here. There are too many innocent people, and there's already been too much death on my account. I won't accept any more.

I look back at Chambers. "Fine. If you're not going to give it to me, will you at least start shooting these bastards?"

She readies herself, straightening her right arm and tightening her grip on her weapon, clasping it in both hands.

She looks at me quickly. "Are they friends of yours?"

I shrug. "I'm not sure. I only met the old guy once."

"Well, you know how to make a lasting impression, I'll give you that."

She stands and fires, hitting one of the three guys in suits in the chest, dropping him instantly. She ducks back down next to me.

I grab her hand. "Come on!"

We stand and set off running back toward my room, away from the waiting area. I glance over my shoulder and see the remaining two guys in suits coming after us, followed by the old guy.

Good—at least they're not concerned about the innocent civilians in there...

As we near the room, Grace pushes me away. She turns to face them, levels her gun, and stands her ground. "I'm a federal agent! Drop your weapons and put your hands in the air, right now!"

They don't even break step. They just keep coming, firing intermittently at us. Luckily, they're terrible shots, but that's not the point.

Without thinking, I step in front of Chambers and hold my hands out to the sides, hoping that they don't shoot me before explaining themselves.

The corridor behind us is a dead end. We're standing level with the door to my room, which is slightly ajar. I shuffle to my right and fall in line with Chambers, who's still aiming her gun at the three guys. They stop a few feet in front of us. We're at a standoff.

The old guy steps to the front and points his finger at me. "I told you... you fucking dead man!"

"What have I ever done to you?"

"You put two of my guys in hospital! You disrespect the Red Dragon!"

Chambers looks at me. She seems concerned.

"You did *what?*" she whispers.

I wave my hand dismissively. "It's nothing. Two assholes tried to rob me last night, and I put them down. That's all."

"You broke my guy's nose!" the old man shouts. "You disrespect the Red Dragon. You die!"

I sigh and look at him. "Will you quit going on about that? What the fuck's the *Red Dragon* anyway?"

Chambers lets out a heavy breath next to me. "It's the gang that runs Chinatown."

I turn to look at her. "Oh..."

"They're extremely violent, and the local PD have an understanding with them. If they keep their own house in order and stop any disputes spilling onto the streets, they leave them be."

"I see."

"And it would appear you've just started a war with them single-handedly."

I smile. "Whoops..."

Chambers doesn't look happy.

"Look, I didn't even do anything. *They* started it, completely unprovoked."

"That doesn't matter to them, Adrian. It's about respect."

The old man steps closer to us. He looks at me and smiles. "FBI bitch is right." He turns to her. "Now drop your weapon. If you lucky, you might only get shot."

The piece of shit.

"Hey, General Chow—watch how you're speaking to her, all right?"

The two guys with guns behind him look restless, like

they really want to start shooting at someone. I need to take them out.

The old guy keeps smiling, still looking back at Chambers. "Put... your gun... down..."

It's pissing me off that he's ignoring me.

He's within arm's length of me, and his men are maybe three feet behind him. He's short and looks like he doesn't weigh much. I'm far from a hundred percent, but I reckon I've got enough in me to take these guys out before it's too late. Bottom line, if they're Triad, they're likely to take the both of us hostage. They'll torture me and do God knows what to Chambers... neither of which I care to think about.

I look at her. "Do as he says. Trust me."

She scowls at me. "Adrian, I'm a federal agent!"

I shake my head. "It doesn't matter. Just do as he says. It'll be fine."

She sighs and gives me a frustrated look before crouching and placing her gun on the floor. Just as I'd expected, all three of them watch her do it. With legs like hers, they'd have to be blind not to.

Her gun touches the floor.

I step forward and quickly grab the old man by his throat with both hands. I launch him with all my strength into the guy on the left behind him. I was right—he is pretty light. He crashes into his man, sending them both sprawling to the floor.

I quickly close in on the remaining guy. I grab his wrist and point it to the floor, controlling his weapon. I swing my hand around and connect with the side of his head. I'm nowhere near full strength. He takes the blow and replies with one of his own, slicing his hand across my face, causing me to lose balance. I let go of him and see out the corner of my eye that he's raising his gun toward me. I bring my forearm across, knocking his aim off to the side. I jab him hard in the face. He takes a step back, slightly dazed. I move in and, without breaking stride, slam my foot into his kneecap, pushing through and breaking his leg. He goes down screaming, dropping his gun.

"Adrian!"

I look around to see Chambers fighting off the old man. She takes a decent punch and gives him the same back...

She can handle herself. I'll give her that.

The remaining gunman is getting back to his feet. I walk over to him and slam his head into the wall as he stands. It leaves a dent in the thin drywall. He collapses to the floor. I retrieve his gun, turn, and aim it at the old guy.

"Hey!" He turns and freezes. Chambers steps to the side, picks her gun up, and aims it at him. "Okay, listen up."

He ignores me, more concerned with Chambers. I don't know whether that's because she's an attractive woman or because she's an FBI agent with a gun on him.

I frown, a little frustrated. "Hey, don't look at her. Look at me."

He turns to me, glancing at the gun in my hand.

I nod. "There we go. Now pay attention. I meant no disrespect to your organization, all right? I was simply defending myself against those two pricks who came at me. I have no idea who you are, and you *really* don't want to know who *I* am. Let's just chalk this up to experience and move on."

The old guy looks at Chambers, then at me. He shakes his head. "You... fucking... dead man!"

His words were slow and deliberate. And a little condescending, I think.

I sigh. "Fine, let's try this a different way." I gesture to his men. "You see these two ass-clowns, all broken and beaten on the floor? Well, go and run back to your boss and tell them *this* is what happens when people come after me. Consider it your only warning."

He looks at me blankly, like he can't comprehend why anyone would think it's okay to talk to him like that.

I raise my eyebrows, wondering why he's hesitating. "Go on... off you fuck."

I step aside and motion him past me. Reluctantly, he walks off. I watch him go through the waiting room and over to the elevators. He presses the button and steps inside without looking back.

I turn to Chambers. "You okay?"

She holsters her gun. "You're an idiot."

She walks past me to greet the security guards who are approaching. She produces her badge and starts explaining what's just happened.

And here's me thinking I handled that rather well...

So, I have a Triad gang who run Chinatown called the Red Dragon gunning for me now. Well, they can get in line. My priority is the Shark. And if I'm going to get the FBI on my side, I need to be honest with them.

I look at Chambers, taking control of the situation with ease.

I sigh.

I need a beer.

9

It didn't take long for Chambers to explain what happened. Content to leave it in the hands of hospital security and local PD, we made our way downstairs and out of the hospital.

We're standing outside the main entrance. The temperature's dropped and there's a chilly breeze. She's spoken to Wallis and Johnson, and they're on their way here to pick us up. I've promised her the truth and made her promise *me* I could have a beer while I give it to her.

A few minutes pass in awkward silence before the car pulls up in front of us. We climb in the back. Johnson, who's driving, sets off again. We travel in silence for about five minutes before coming to a stop outside a bar. We get out, and I stand looking at the place. It looks old and run-down, with a faded green theme to it. The three agents walk in like they're going home, so I'm guessing they come here a lot.

I follow them inside and stand in the doorway, gazing

88

across the bar. The interior keeps with the green from outside and has an old-fashioned Irish feel to it. There are blue neon signs dotted around the walls. The place is more long than wide, with the bar talking up most of one side.

It's reasonably busy but not packed. It's mostly couples or small groups. There aren't many empty tables left. A few singles are propping up the bar on worn stools. Some of the patrons glance over with a look of vague recognition at my companions. I eye each of them for a moment.

All cops.

They've brought me to a goddamn cop bar...

Well, this makes me feel much more comfortable about spilling my guts to these people.

The barman's slightly overweight and losing his hair on top. I'm guessing he's been here half his life—probably owns the place and knows all the local cops and G-men.

We order our drinks and sit in a booth at the back of the room. Wallis is next to me, against the wall. Johnson's opposite him with Chambers adjacent, facing me.

I'm nursing my ice-cold beer. My mind is racing, trying to figure out what I can and can't say. I need to give them enough that they'll agree to work with me but not so much that they'll place me under arrest on the spot.

What would Josh do?

I smile to myself. I think he'd be pleased that he's had such a positive impact on me. Not that I'll ever admit that to him.

Chambers looks at each of us in turn. "So, where are we?"

There's silence for a minute. I look at Wallis and Johnson, who look like they're trying to decide what information's worth sharing.

"We're still getting details from the forensic teams

working the scene," says Wallis finally. "We know the bomb under the school bus was a decoy."

"Clearly, he wanted something authentic to get us there," adds Johnson.

Wallis nods. "Exactly. They've found traces of C4 on the SWAT truck. It was remotely detonated, probably using a cellular signal. God knows how he got close enough to plant it. Nothing yet from the chopper. It was a local media station covering the scene."

Chambers lets out a taut, frustrated sigh. "He had the whole thing planned meticulously... He knew which vehicles to rig and clearly had line of sight because he knew exactly when to detonate."

I lean forward in my seat. "What about the bullets?"

It goes quiet again. The agents all exchange glances.

"Nothing's come back yet from the ballistic tests on the bullets they removed from your friend," says Johnson regretfully. "Once we know what the bullets are, we can work backwards and find the rifle, then hopefully where it came from and who bought it."

I take a sip of my beer. "Well, there's no way he was within eight hundred yards of the academy, which rules out anything smaller than a .300-caliber bullet. That, in turn, narrows down the list of possible rifles. He'd also have needed to be close enough to get a decent view of what was going on, so I'd put him within twelve hundred yards, which narrows things down even further. I heard the gunshots, and there was enough of a delay between them that they had to have come from a bolt-action rifle, which means he was probably using a Remington XM2010. It fires .300-caliber Winchester Magnum rounds. The weapon basically replaced the old M24, and it's the weapon of choice for the

U.S. Army. It wouldn't be too hard to get your hands on one if you knew where to look."

Everyone exchanges wide-eyed glances with each other before looking back at me.

I shrug. "What? I know things..."

"You clearly know quite a bit," remarks Chambers, still sounding unimpressed. "You've admitted you know who's behind all this, so spill. Help us, Adrian."

I sigh.

What am I meant to say?

I sit in silence for a few moments, weighing up the best approach. Judging what their reaction would be to every level of detail I choose to divulge.

I'm going to have to go for full disclosure. I reckon I've done enough to help them already that they'll at least postpone any pursuit of an arrest. If I don't tell them everything, I can't see any way of them giving me the freedom or the help I need to go after the Shark. They have to know it all.

I sigh.

Here we go...

"This whole thing stems from Heaven's Valley, twelve months ago."

Chambers tilts her head slightly. "You figured *that* from when you and Josh worked out the clues from the first two attacks."

I take a deep breath. "Tell me what you know about what happened in Nevada."

She shrugs. "It was a military operation, so all us lowly government employees officially know is what was on the news at the time: an extremist group called Dark Rain were operating out of an old military base in the desert. The compound was ultimately blown up, taking their operation with it."

"Okay. What about unofficially?"

"Unofficially, your name was all over whatever happened there. No one really knows why you were there, but everyone suspects what your involvement entailed. Hence why you're on everyone's watch list."

"I'm telling you what I know because I genuinely want this whole thing to end, and I don't want any more innocent people getting hurt. Think of me what you will, but I'm not a bad guy and I'm not a monster."

"You wanna know what I think? I think you have a good heart but have made some seriously bad career choices."

I smile wearily. "Like the old saying goes: the road to hell is paved with good intentions. But you have to understand, by telling you what I know and why it's happening, I'll be giving you details of situations that may cause you to re-think my involvement in all this, and I don't want that. I have to help, and I have to be the one to stop him."

Silence falls for a few moments.

Wallis pushes his glass out in front of him and turns to me. "Look, I might be way out of line here, but if it weren't for you, we'd have forty-three dead kids on top of everything else. The fact we know this guy is doing all this specifically to get at you means you're as much in the line of fire as we are. And you've suffered casualties like the rest of us. All due respect..." He glances briefly at Chambers before looking back at me. "I don't care what you may or may not have done in the past. I only care about what you've done *here*, and as far as I'm concerned, you've proven yourself an asset." He turns to Johnson and Chambers in turn. "Am I right?"

They both shrug and nod, though I notice Johnson seems more reluctant to agree than Chambers does.

I nod. "Okay. Well, I appreciate that, Wallis. Thanks. I'll

be sure to remind you of this moment when all this is over and you try to arrest me."

He smiles but says nothing, which makes me think that prediction might not be too far wrong.

I let out another heavy, begrudging sigh. "Okay. The Shark's real name is Danny Pellaggio, and he's doing this because twelve months ago, I killed his entire family."

Silence.

Wow... you could hear a pin drop at our table right now, and I'm very aware I'm sitting with three FBI agents in a bar full of cops. I've just admitted to killing someone. Well, lots of people, actually. This isn't the smartest thing I've ever done, but I've got no choice.

I place my hands on the table, face up, wrists together. "I promise I'll come along quietly if you want to stop this here and now."

Wallis and Johnson look at Chambers for guidance on how they should react.

She looks away for a moment and sighs. Probably wrestling with her conscience. "Start from the beginning. Leave nothing out."

"You'll forgive me if I'm quiet and slightly vague, given you've brought me to a bar full of police. So, Heaven's Valley didn't start out being about Dark Rain. I went there because a mob boss named Roberto Pellaggio had hired me to..." I pause, choosing my words carefully. "...ask a former business associate why he backed out of a property deal. It turns out, this former associate was going to sell him some land under the table. However, he didn't realize that some people he worked with at GlobaTech Industries also had plans to sell the land to Dark Rain."

Johnson frowns. "Aren't GlobaTech one of the biggest defense contractors in the country?"

I nod. "They certainly are. Luckily, I now count them as friends. Anyway, I removed the associate from the picture, but I couldn't hand the deeds for the land over to Pellaggio. He was pissed at me, and we had a... disagreement, but it was left with me advising him to leave me alone."

"Which I'm assuming he didn't do?" asks Wallis.

"I'll get to that part. Anyway, it turns out GlobaTech wasn't aware of this deal with Dark Rain. They soon had an internal reshuffle, and the deal was dead in the water. However, I opted not to give the deeds to Pellaggio because the land was actually above a Uranium mine... which obviously opened up a whole new can of worms."

Chambers shakes her head. "Wait a minute. Uranium? In the United States?"

"Yup. Long story short, the land and the mine are now property of the U.S. government, following a brief conversation with the secretary of defense."

I think I just committed treason by saying that, but never mind.

"Jesus Christ!" says Johnson, a little too loudly.

"Oh, it gets better. Both Dark Rain and Pellaggio's mafia outfit then started taking it in turns to try to kill me. I got blown up by a car bomb, which I thought Pellaggio's men had planted. It turns out he'd not even started trying to take me out—it was Dark Rain. But given how pissed off I was, I went to his house and... *explained* my unhappiness in short, loud, lethal movements to Pellaggio and the small army he had as protection."

Wallis holds up a hand. "Wait, I remember that... The Mansion Massacre, right? They said that was a professional mob killing. That was *you*?"

I nod.

Johnson shakes his head. "Bullshit. One man couldn't do that. There must've been twenty guys in there that night."

"Twenty-one, actually. What can I tell you? As a wise man once said: you wouldn't like me when I'm angry…"

"So, what does this have to do with the Shark?" asks Chambers.

"I saw a news report on TV about it a few hours afterward, and it said there was one survivor—Danny Pellaggio, Roberto's youngest son. He'd been shot in the leg and chest and was listed as critical. I thought about going back to finish things but decided against it."

Wallis stares at the table. "Everything the Shark does is a message to you…"

"That's right. The Shark is Danny Pellaggio. He shot Josh exactly the same way I shot him a year ago to send another message to me about who he is."

Chambers leans forward. "This is valuable information, Adrian. I appreciate you being honest with us."

"I just want this to end. Like I said, just because you don't approve of my chosen career, it doesn't mean I'm a bad guy. I don't want people suffering any more than you do. Especially when it's because somebody is playing a game with me."

"What would you suggest our next move should be?"

"First of all, I want someone watching Josh. Around the clock. Just because Shark Boy survived, it doesn't mean he intends for Josh to do the same."

"I'll do what I can for you."

"Thanks."

I stand and stretch.

Johnson looks up at me. "Where are you going?"

I point at the jukebox at the far end of the bar. "I need some music."

I walk casually past three tables full of the SFPD's finest, reach into my pocket for some change, and then feed some quarters into the machine. I scroll through the song list to find something to suit the mood.

It doesn't take me long. This is a good jukebox.

I walk back over to the table and sit down just as the haunting sounds of the guitar at the beginning of *Hell's Bells* by AC/DC is kicking in.

Chambers raises an eyebrow. "You good?"

I smile. "I am now."

She looks at all of us in turn. "Right, the way I see it, we need to work on everything we can as quickly as possible. We don't know where to find Danny Pellaggio or what his endgame is. So, until we hear from him—which I assume will be soon—Wallis, I want you to work on tracing the gun used. I think Adrian's logic is sound, and I'm confident the ballistics will confirm his theory. So, start checking everything we can to find where he got the weapon from. Distributors, the military, whatever you can."

He nods. "Will do."

"Johnson, I want you to work with forensics and put together a real picture of how today happened. Look at how he was able to orchestrate such an elaborate attack—the materials used, trajectory of the bullets to pinpoint a location... anything. It might give us some clue about what he's got planned next."

He nods in acknowledgement.

She turns to me. "And you... you don't work for me, and you're likely to disregard any type of order I think about giving you—"

I smile and wink at her. "You know me so well."

"But I don't want you doing anything stupid in the

meantime, so you're with me. You don't go anywhere without me or my say-so. Is that clear?"

"Crystal."

"Then drink up, gentlemen. We've got work to do."

She stands and walks through the bar and out the front doors without looking back. I watch her leave. She looks fantastic.

Johnson gets to his feet, stretches a little, and then waits. Wallis goes to stand, but I remain in my chair.

He looks at me. "You coming?"

I shake my head. "Not until this song's finished."

They look at each other and shrug before sitting back down in their seats.

10

The last twelve hours have passed by surprisingly fast. After leaving the bar last night, we all headed to the FBI field office. From there, people took turns sleeping and running around getting stressed. It didn't take long for me to feel out of place and useless, so I resigned myself to trying to get some sleep and sorting everything out in my head.

Chambers insisted I stay by her side as much as possible, but for the most part, I stayed in the conference room while she moved around the office. She must be running on fumes by now, but she hasn't skipped a beat.

Johnson and Wallis worked hard through the night and turned up some good information. I'm sitting opposite Chambers now, reviewing what they've managed to find out so far.

Johnson was working with the crime scene investigators and the forensic reports to piece together details. One of their tech guys has generated a 3D computer model of the scene using reports and video surveillance footage of the surrounding area at the time.

The computer model is on the big screen at the far end of the room, and Chambers is working the keyboard and mouse, navigating it. I'm the first to admit that high-end technology is beyond my mental capabilities. The whole thing looks like something out of Tron. And I don't mean that recent disaster of a movie either. I mean the classic from 1982, which starred Jeff Bridges.

They looked at Josh's gunshot wounds and calculated the angle of entry. From there, they determined an approximate trajectory along which the bullets would've traveled. Factoring in my estimations about distance, the bullet, and the weapon used, they've managed to pinpoint roughly where Pellaggio was standing as the nightmare unfolded.

If Josh were here, he'd be having a geekgasm all over the place...

Chambers points to an area on the topographical layout that's northeast of the academy. "See here? He must have been on the roof of one of these buildings on Balboa Street to have both line of sight and to make the shot."

I look at the screen and imagine myself in Pellaggio's shoes, carrying out the hit. It's easily nine hundred yards away, if not farther. Considering the wind and glare from the sun's position, not to mention trajectory, the fact he hit Josh exactly where he wanted to—twice—is worryingly impressive.

I breathe out slowly. "It's a helluva shot..."

Chambers goes to say something but hesitates. I give her a minute to change her mind, but she doesn't. "What is it?"

She sighs, as if in defeat. "Could you have made that shot?"

She sounds almost timid—nothing like the woman I've

come to know and respect over the last thirty-six hours. Since leaving the hospital, I wouldn't say she's been frosty with me, but she's certainly kept conversation to a minimum. Looking at her now, after she's had time to calm down, I can see she has a lot of questions.

I think about it for a moment. I might as well be honest. "Yes. Quite easily."

She pushes the keyboard away from her, clasping her hands in front of her on the desk. "I don't get you. You're the strangest person I think I've ever met."

I chuckle. "Not the worst thing a woman's ever said to me..."

"Everyone *kind of* knew who you are and what you do, but you openly admitted it to us surrounded by police. You're obviously a lot more intelligent than you act, and you have a curiously adorable arrogance about you. Yet you seem so concerned with doing the right thing all the time, it's like you forget you commit murder on a regular basis."

I stroke the stubble on my chin and face for a moment, thinking about what she just said. "I wanna say it's because I'm mysterious, or because I'm trying to keep this enigma about myself to attract women, or something equally smart and cool. But that would be bullshit, and I won't ever bullshit you, Grace. I don't try to fit into a particular category. I don't live to anyone else's standards. I have my own opinion on what's morally right and wrong, and I'm paid well to kill people who have done bad things. That's all."

She smiles, though it looks like she's trying not to. "I don't get how you can make what you do sound almost noble."

"Years of practice..."

"I'm trying so hard to fight every natural urge I have right now to arrest you. You know that, right?"

"I do. Don't think it's not appreciated."

She regards me a moment longer, then retrieves the keyboard and continues navigating her way around the computer model.

We study the screen in silence for a few minutes. There's a knock on the door. We both look up to see Agent Wallis standing there, holding a file and looking pleased with himself.

Chambers gestures him inside. "Wallis, what've you got?"

He takes a seat at the head of the table. "I've got the ballistics back from the bullets we removed from Josh."

I sit up in my chair. My jaw muscles tense when he mentions Josh by name. "And?"

"And... you were right. The bullets were indeed fired from a Remington XM2010 sniper rifle."

"Any idea where he got the hardware from?" asks Chambers.

"I did some digging around through old and existing cases, and I've managed to narrow down the search for who might have sold it to Pellaggio to two individuals. Both are known arms dealers operating within the city. One of them is small time, so I've ruled him out because we've got no evidence to suggest he has the ability to supply this kind of weaponry. Which leaves us with this guy..."

He turns the page in his file and spins it around to face Chambers. She takes a quick glance and immediately has an *I knew it* look on her face. She turns the file, so it faces me.

In front of me is an eight-by-ten black and white mugshot. It's of a man who looks about my age, with long, spiked hair and piercing, evil eyes. He's clean-shaven, with a network of scars running across his face.

Chambers points to the image. "Joseph Turner. Known locally as Jo-Jo. He's the only real player in black market weaponry in the city, having murdered or partnered up with anyone who could be classed as a competitor."

"We've never been able to make anything against him stick," adds Wallis, "but the guy's a real piece of work. It has to be him who sold the rifle to Pellaggio."

I take another look at Joseph Turner. As far as I'm concerned, he put the gun in Pellaggio's hands, so he may as well have pulled the trigger himself...

My jaw muscles tense again, and a wave of anger washes over me. I push the file away and look up at Chambers. "Where do I find him?"

"Easy, Tiger. You can't just walk in the front door and confront someone like him. We need to play this smart. We need to build evidence and get a warrant and some major backup before we go after him."

"And how long's that gonna take? This piece of shit is our only lead to finding Pellaggio. The longer you take to get permission to go after the guy, the less chance we have of stopping Pellaggio before it's too late."

"Welcome to our world. This is what happens in real life, Adrian. You don't get to just walk up to someone and shoot them because it's easier."

"I would've interrogated him first..."

"There's something else you need to know about him," says Wallis, tentatively interrupting.

We both look at him expectantly.

"He's the biggest arms dealer in the city and has ties to local criminal organizations... including the Triads." He lets the words hang there for a moment. "Adrian, what happened at the hospital... that's just the tip of the iceberg if the Red Dragon has you in their crosshairs. And if they get word that you're going after Turner, they'll protect their business relationship with him any way they can. It could lead to a street war. They'll put a price on your head. You'll have nowhere to run."

I nod. "I wouldn't be running, but I see your point. Enough people have been hurt because of someone's vendetta against me. I won't allow it to happen again."

"So, let us do this by the book," says Chambers. "It's the only way to go about this without causing chaos."

I sit quietly, thinking, looking at every angle and every option. Pellaggio's the priority here. There's no question about that. But to get to him, I have to get to this Joseph Turner—and I can't do *that* without further pissing off a Triad gang who already want me dead for no valid reason.

Unless...

I stand and leave the room, forgetting for a moment I'm in an FBI building. The answer just came to me, and my instincts have taken over.

"Adrian, I'm ordering you not to leave this building!" yells Agent Chambers behind me. I hear her and Wallis running after me. They step in front of me as I reach the main corridor of the building. "Adrian, will you stop, please?"

I sigh, feeling bad for pushing them away. I have no choice if I want to end this. "Grace, all due respect, but I don't work for you. Plus, given I'm still not under arrest, there's nothing you can say to me that I have to listen to."

She sighs. "I know, but *please*, let's just wait and do this properly. Turner is the best lead we have right now, but you're going about this all wrong."

"Am I? I intend to go over there and knock on his front door. I'll say I'm in town on a job and in the market for some hardware. I'm going to negotiate a face-to-face meeting with him and explain what guns I need, then offer him a small percentage as a goodwill gesture for supplying me with them. I'll be inside his operation. I'll know how many men he has and how protected he is. I'll be able to gather intel and give you something to justify getting a warrant. If I'm lucky, and I ask real nice and polite, he might give me something to go on with Pellaggio."

Chambers and Wallis exchange a surprised and embarrassed look. He shrugs, and she looks bewildered for a moment. Then they both look back at me.

Her eyes soften and she glances down. "That's... actually a good plan. I'm sorry."

I smile. Ordinarily, I'd launch into a tirade of sarcasm and I-told-you-so's, but there's no need. Not with Grace. I wink at her. "You said yourself: I'm not as dumb as I look."

She smiles. "I guess you're not. But it *is* stupid thinking you can do all this alone and with no preparation."

I take a deep breath. An image of Josh flashes into my mind, lying in a coma, vulnerable...

"Look, we're not trying to replace your friend, all right?" says Wallis, as if reading my mind. "But we can help each other here. There's no doubt you're the best person for this type of undercover operation. But this is our show. Let us help you prepare for this, and we'll watch your back the whole time."

"I don't need your help."

"I know," says Chambers. "But that doesn't mean it'll do any harm if you accept it anyway."

She's right. They both are. I know it, and they know I know it. It's more of a pride thing, which sounds silly, given the circumstances. But I feel like I'm betraying Josh if I let someone else do his job. But they make sense—going into something like this could get nasty. While that doesn't bother me, and I'm sure I can handle it, it's simply easier if they were outside ready to back me up.

I sigh. "Fine. Do what you need to do to make this happen, and I'll do it your way."

Chambers fails to hide the surprise in her voice. "Really?"

"Well, when I say, 'I'll do it your way,' I mean I'll stick to your plan as long as I think it'll work. If it all goes to shit, as these things tend to, then I'll revert to doing things my way."

Wallis looks nervous.

She nods. "That's fair enough. It's your life on the line in there. Given how little we have to go on and how much worse things could get, do what you need to, all right? Just..." She pauses, as if trying to find the right words. "Just try not to create more trouble than we already have."

I smile and nod. "Deal."

They turn to walk back to the conference room, but I stop them. "Oh, Grace, there's one more thing I need for my plan to work."

"What's that?"

"I need to know how I can get a message to the Red Dragon."

She exchanges a nervous glance with Wallis. "Do I want to know why?"

I smile. "Probably not. But you have my word it's a great plan that will *definitely* work... maybe."

10:26 PDT

After a few minutes of failing to reason with me, we headed back to the conference room. Agent Johnson joined us, and

Chambers has spent the last fifteen minutes filling him in on what's happened and what I intend to do.

He shakes his head and looks at me, bewildered. "You're insane. Are you in a rush to die?"

I smile and shake my head. "I'm just looking at the big picture. I've got the Shark terrorizing the city to get to me, and the Triads have marked me for death because of a misunderstanding in the street. As luck would have it, both problems have someone in common—Joseph Turner. He's supplied weapons to both of them recently, so I need to get to him to track down the Shark. My job here is going to be made difficult by this Red Dragon outfit, so I need to figure out a way to get them off my back. I'm not going to let them come at me. I need to make a pre-emptive effort to take them out."

"And you think *this* is the way to do that?"

"I think it's got a chance of working, yeah."

He shakes his head and falls silent.

"Are you sure about this?" asks Chambers. "We can't protect you from the Red Dragon if this goes south."

"I'm not asking you to. And it'll work. Trust me."

There's a knock on the glass door. Another agent enters and hands a piece of paper to Chambers. He leaves again without a word, and she passes the paper to me.

I frown. "What's this?"

She gestures to it. "*That* is the phone number of Jak Soo Yung—the head of the Red Dragon. We've hit up every contact, undercover agent, and asset we have to get you that."

I'm genuinely surprised. Not just at the fact they seem willing to go along with my admittedly stupid plan, but that they were able to get results so quickly.

"Wow, thank you."

"From what we know of their organization—which admittedly isn't much—your old friend from the hospital is what they call their Vanguard. He's in charge of the day-to-day running of the less reputable business ventures, and he reports directly to Jak Soo Yung."

"We've got a file on them," adds Wallis, "but we haven't really got a formal investigation underway. The Organized Crime Unit might have, but they operate nationwide. This is a localized problem, and there's an uneasy peace on the streets that we don't get involved with. We let the SFPD manage that."

Chambers leans forward in her seat. "Like we've already said, if this plan of yours doesn't work, you run the risk of starting a war that will spill onto the streets."

I nod. "Understood. Can you get me a copy of the file you have on the Red Dragon? On a USB flash drive or something?"

"I really shouldn't, but I guess under the circumstances, we could look at—"

"Good. How far away is Turner's place?"

"He owns an apartment building about fifteen minutes from here," says Johnson. "He lives on the top floor and runs his business from there."

"Okay."

I reach across the table and move the black teleconferencing system closer to me. I dial the number and wait. The three agents look nervous.

The call connects on the sixth ring, but no one speaks.

"Hello? Who's this?"

"Who you ring?" asks an abrupt voice.

"I'm looking for Jak Soo Yung."

"And you are?"

"I'm the guy who took out three of his men in the

hospital last night and sent some old guy back to him with a message to leave me alone."

More silence, but I can hear some movement on the line, like the cell phone's being handed to someone else. The crackling and commotion stop and someone else speaks.

"Who this?"

"I'm looking for Jak Soo Yung."

"You found him... who this?"

His voice sounds young, but he speaks slowly and deliberately, like a man who answers to no one.

"You get my message from last night?"

"Oh... so *you* dead man? Hello, dead man."

"Yeah, whatever. Listen, I've changed my mind. I don't want any trouble, all right? I've just got one last thing I need to do, then I'll leave town and you'll never see me again. Can we chalk this one up to experience and call it quits while I finish my business?"

There's a lengthy pause. "Price on your head... one million U.S. dollar."

Chambers gasps, and the others look like they feel for me being in this position.

I frown. "Is that it? I'm almost insulted. How about I do you a favor and we call it quits?"

"No quits."

"Fair enough. How about I do you a favor anyway? To show you I'm not a bad guy."

He pauses. "Go on."

"I'm in town on business. Got some debts to settle with a man by the name of Joseph Turner. I believe you've had dealings with him?"

More silence on the line.

"He's responsible for hurting someone close to me, and I'm aiming to take him down. I've already confronted him, and I've discovered he's actually undercover FBI... quick to spill the beans about what business he does with you."

"Bullshit."

"How do you think I got this number?"

No reply.

"I'm going to kill him. Originally, I wanted to let you know as a courtesy because of the business relationship between the two of you. But when I found out he's ratting on you and everyone else he deals with to the feds, I thought I'd give you a head's up. Figured maybe we can work something out."

"You dead man. If what you say true, then Turner dead man too. No agreement."

"I'm going to be at Turner's apartment in forty-five minutes. I'll gather up all the information he's got on you, ready to hand over to the feds, then I'll give you a call back. We'll see if we can reach an agreement then, yeah?"

"Who you think you are?"

I hear the anger in his voice, but he's doing a good job of keeping calm.

"I'm Adrian Hell. Look me up, asshole."

I hang up and look at Chambers. "Okay, so who's driving?"

11

The four of us are parked across the street from Turner's apartment building. Wallis is behind the wheel, with Chambers riding shotgun. I'm behind her and Johnson is next to me in the back.

The building is on the corner of the block and looks like what I'd expected. It's ten stories of old, weathered, rust-colored brick. We've got a clear view of the south and east sides.

The south side is basking in the morning sun, all the way to the roof. The sunlight's reflecting off the glass in some windows and highlighting the wooden curtains in the others. The entrance is on the east side, covered in shade. Outside, there's a line of aluminum garbage cans, most of which are brimming over with trash. Just inside the doorway, I see one guy stood leaning against the wall.

Must be the doorman...

I lean forward to get a view of the top of the building

through the car window. I need to talk my way up to the tenth floor and engage Turner long enough that he might reveal something of use about his previous customers.

"You sure about this?" asks Chambers.

I shrug. "As sure as I can be."

"And you think Jak Soo Yung will take the bait and show up?"

"Definitely. He'll be skeptical about everything I said, but he'd have checked my name out after I hung up. He'll believe me after that."

"But what are you hoping to accomplish?" asks Wallis.

"With some luck and good timing on my part, I'll be talking to Turner when the Red Dragon Triad arrives. They'll come in force. With a gentle push in the right direction from me, my plan is to get Turner and Yung to kill each other."

"Jesus, we're gonna lose our fucking badges for this," mutters Johnson. He leans forward to look at Chambers. "And you're all right with this?"

She shakes her head as she stares out the window. "No, but time isn't on our side. At least this way, we're not allowing Adrian to kill anyone himself. If an arms dealer and a Triad gang want to shoot it out between themselves, where no innocent civilians can get hurt, I'm not going to complain." She turns in her seat to face me. "Wear this."

She produces an earpiece and a battery unit with a small microphone attached to it. I take it from her and toss it onto Johnson's lap next to me. "No fucking way am I wearing a wire! Are you trying to get me killed?"

"That's the deal, Adrian. If you're going in there, you're going in wired. If Turner *does* give you anything, I want it on tape, ready to present as evidence to the district attorney."

I massage my temples in frustration. "I'm guessing you've never tried to buy black market weapons before?"

Next to me, Johnson smirks. "Have you?"

I glance at him. "I exercise my right to remain silent." I look back at Chambers. "First thing they'll do is pat me down to check for weapons. Next, they'll wand me to check for any electronic equipment. If this guy's the big player you make him out to be, then show him some more respect. If I put this on, I'll have a bullet in my head before I can take three paces inside that building, plain and simple."

She sighs and turns around, unhappy.

"Wallis, what's the name of the other weapons dealer you dismissed for this?"

He doesn't turn around to answer me. "His name's Mickey Cartwright. He's small time. Has a few counts of possession to his name. He's suspected of supplying small arms to local dealers. Nothing major. Why?"

"Because I'm going to use him as an excuse for being here."

"How will we know if you need backup?" asks Chambers.

"Twelve years I've been doing this, and I've done all right without any so far. But if you mean, how will you know if it's going well or not... just assume if you don't hear gunfire or see bodies falling from the sky, then I'm doing all right."

There's an uneasy silence in the car.

"Oh, by the way, where are my guns?"

"They're in the lock-up back at the office," replies Wallis.

"I want them back. Right, now drive past and circle around the block. Pull over across the street, around the corner by the south side of the building."

He does. I unfasten my belt and get out of the car. I quickly look around and walk down the street and turn left.

I walk casually along until I draw level with the entrance. I stand outside, trying to look like I'm trying to be inconspicuous but failing.

The act works.

It only takes a minute or so for the door to open and the guy to appear. He's an average-looking man—young, maybe late twenties, with long, styled jet-black hair.

"You lost?"

His voice is high-pitched and sounds... slimy.

I shake my head. "I dunno. I'm looking for Jo-Jo. I heard this was his place. You know him?"

"Never heard of him. Who the fuck's askin'?"

"If you've never heard of him, why does it matter who I am?"

He breathes in, trying to bring himself to his full height and width to look more intimidating. Then he brushes his open jacket aside to reveal a holstered gun. "You tryin' to be smart with me, asshole?"

The urge to flatten the guy right now is overwhelming, but I stop myself. I've got a mission here. It's way too early to write it off.

I put my hands up, open palms facing him, to signify passiveness. "Hey, buddy, I'm not looking for any trouble, all right? Mickey C. sent me here. Said to ask for Jo-Jo. Said he'd be able to hook me up."

He visibly relaxes a little. "Mickey sent you, did he? What you lookin' for, man?"

"I'm after some hardware. A couple of serious pieces. I've got plenty of cash. I heard Jo-Jo is the man to see."

"All right, wait here."

He presses a buzzer. When the door opens, he disappears inside.

I breathe out and relax. So far, so good. I glance around

idly, like I've got all the time in the world. I'm sure there'll be at least one surveillance camera on me, so I have to act the part.

With him having to buzz himself in, I figure that means there's maybe one guy on the other side of the door. More likely, there'll be two. Probably armed as well.

I look up, all the way to the sky. If I do manage to get up there to speak with Turner, and it does go wrong, that's a whole lot of building to try getting out of...

I sigh, steeling myself and clearing my mind. I know the rules. Don't think about it; just do it.

The door clicks. The doorman pushes it open and holds it for me. "Come on."

I step past him and through the door into a small lobby. At the end, side by side, are two elevators—both out of order.

Figures.

On one wall is a large cabinet of lockers, presumably used as mailboxes. Opposite, immediately as I walk in, is a table with a chair at each end—both occupied by poorly dressed, grossly overweight men. Farther along is a flight of stairs.

The walls are a sickly pale yellow and are cracked almost everywhere. The fluorescent lights flicker overhead, buzzing faintly in the background. The floor's covered in linoleum, probably laid down in the seventies and never replaced. It's peeling around the edges, with large air bubbles all over it. It's dirty and discolored.

There's a faint stench of excrement as well, which stings my nostrils.

I grimace as I look around. "Nice place..."

The two overweight guys at the table stand. They're slightly shorter than me but easily a hundred and fifty pounds heavier. And it isn't muscle. They could be twins. Both have those bucket hats on that people wear for fishing, with sunglasses and badly designed facial hair. In their pudgy hands are large pistols. I don't want to stare, but I'm sure they're Desert Eagles, fifty-caliber.

Christ, those things are like fucking cannons...

The doorman comes up behind me. I hear the unmistakable sound of a gun being drawn and the safety being clicked off. I turn slowly to face him. The Desert Eagle twins both have their guns trained on me. The doorman's aiming his right between my eyes.

"Now let's try again. Who the fuck are you?"

11:05 PDT

I need to stay calm and relax. My instinct is to fight. I could have all three of them on the floor, in pieces, in a heartbeat. But I need to look like I'm playing it cool. I can't think about this like I normally would. I'm not Adrian Hell right now. I'm just a guy trying to buy a gun, and this is probably normal. This is an intel-gathering operation. I need them to think I'm something less than what I am.

They need to believe they're in control.

I raise my arms slightly and try my best to look afraid. "Whoa! Guys, come on—there's no need for any hostility. I just wanna do some business..."

"What business might that be?" asks the doorman.

"I already told you. Mickey Cartwright sent me here because he couldn't get me what I was after. He said that Jo-Jo would be able to help me out."

"You a cop?" asks one of the large twins.

"Am I a..." I wince in feigned offense. "Fuck you, all right? Fuck... you! I don't need this shit. No, I'm not a fucking cop! I got a job to do in this city, and I need some hardware to help me do it. I got plenty of cash to spend, and I want the best. Word is, this is the place to get it. If you boys are doing so well that you don't need my business, I'll take it elsewhere."

Silence falls. I fight to keep my breathing normal and subdue the rush of adrenaline my body's trying to release. At least I've got nothing to worry about. Obviously, I'm not a cop...

My mind flashes to Agent Chambers, handing me the earpiece and microphone.

She would've gotten me killed.

The doorman turns to the large twin who spoke. "Search him."

He tucks his gun into the back of his jeans and waddles over to me. "Arms out to the sides, asshole."

Jesus, the guy's out of breath after three steps!

I do as he asks. "My pleasure."

He pats me down and finds nothing. He turns to the doorman. "He's clean."

The doorman nods, then looks at the other twin. "Okay, give him the wand."

I frown, playing my part. "Give me *what*? Hey, I don't need these guns *that* much. Nobody's sticking anything inside me!"

The doorman rolls his eyes. "Relax, you idiot. We're just gonna scan you to make sure you're not wearing a wire."

"Oh..." I chuckle nervously. "Well in that case, *wand* me to your heart's content."

So far, it's going as I expected. I hate myself for having to act the part, but I'm getting closer to Pellaggio by doing it. That's all that matters.

The other large twin puts his gun away and pulls out a small black stick, which I know is the wand. It detects the radio frequencies emitted by any electronic device it moves over and beeps when it finds one.

This is where it gets tricky. Albeit reluctantly, Chambers *did* give me a copy of the FBI file on the Red Dragon, stored on a USB drive. It's only small, and it's currently in the heel of my boot, which I hollowed out, so it slides back to reveal a hidden compartment. It's useful for smuggling things such as USB drives. I must admit, I've never had much call to use it, but Josh was insistent.

Thankfully, people rarely think to check as low down as the shoes. Typically, they're only looking for weapons. As a result, they only search your arms, legs, and body.

He quickly waves it around my body, revealing nothing.

Phew...

The guy shrugs. "We're good."

The doorman nods and puts his gun away. "What's your name?"

I've already thought of my cover story.

"James."

"Okay, *James*—follow me."

He sets off up the stairs, beckoning me to follow. I walk after him, briefly looking back over my shoulder at the large twins. I smile at them. "You boys not coming?"

One of them gives me the middle finger. They both sit back on their chairs, which creak loudly under the weight.

"Huh, figured as much."

We walk up two flights of stairs in silence. The décor on each floor mirrors that of the lobby. I suspect any residents aren't overly concerned about the state of the wallpaper in the hallways...

We come up on the fourth-floor landing. Five men are loitering around outside the nearest door to the stairwell. They look like low-level heroin addicts—skinny, their faces thin and drawn, and their eyes set deep in their sockets. They stop talking and all turn to look at me, giving me a disapproving once-over, but say nothing. They nod an unspoken greeting to the doorman before turning back to their own conversation.

Onward we climb, floor after floor, until we finally reach the landing on the tenth.

The top floor looks different. It's cleaner, for a start. There's been more effort made with the décor—a nice carpet replaces the forty-year-old linoleum. White paint instead of the cracked, dirty, pale yellow found on the floors below us. There's even a large plant by the wall next to the elevators.

Joseph Turner must want to make it abundantly clear to anyone who comes here that he's in charge, and they're in his house.

We turn right and walk along the hallway. There are fewer apartments on this floor, which I suspect means they're bigger inside. We walk past two doors, one on either side. Both are open. On the left, I see a room full of muscle —at least four guys, built like bodybuilders and armed with shotguns. There's a woman in there too, counting money at a table. No one looks up as we walk past.

That's not a good sign. There are a lot of people here, which means Turner has lots of protection. It's a large-scale operation, no doubt about it.

I glance through the doorway on the right. From what I can see, it's a living room of some kind, with a couple of worn sofas in the middle. There are three more guys in there, sitting with a cloud of smoke floating above them. I recognize the smell—a strong, high-quality marijuana. Sitting among the guys are a couple of young women— neither looks any older than twenty-one. Both are skinny and under-nourished. Addicts, I'm guessing. Both are completely naked.

Jesus. Their fathers must be so proud...

We come to the end of the corridor. The last door on the left has a guy standing on either side of it, armed with a shotgun. They nod a curt greeting to the doorman as we approach. He steps forward and bangs once on the door with his fist. There's a sound from within, like multiple locks unfastening and bolts sliding back. It opens slowly, about two inches. I can just about see one eye and half a nose in the gap.

"Got a customer here to see Jo-Jo."

The door slams shut again. A moment later, it opens fully. The doorman steps to one side and gestures me through with his gun. "Go on."

I step past him and walk inside the apartment. The guy who opened the door is leaning against the wall to my left. He shuts it behind me and pushes my shoulder to signal I should go in.

The apartment is a large, open-plan expanse, with four doors leading into other rooms. I glance around the room and quickly spot Joseph Turner. He's sitting in a large armchair but gets to his feet as I walk in. He has six guys in here with him, all packing Desert Eagles.

I know that because they all have them drawn...

He must have gotten a bulk discount on the damn things.

There are also three women, similar to the ones I saw

down the hall but with more clothes on. Only just, though.

The main living area has a kitchenette in the far corner. It's small and basic but good enough quality. Next to that is a large flat-screen TV mounted on the wall. It's easily sixty inches. It looks like a goddamn movie theater.

There's an over-sized, L-shaped sofa in the middle of the room, occupied by the three women and two of the guys. In front of me is a large floor-to-ceiling window and a dining table with six chairs around it. Three of the guys are sitting at the table, which I note has a laptop open on it. The remaining guy is standing over by the TV, near Turner.

Everyone turns to look at me as I enter.

Turner steps forward. He's wearing a yellow T-shirt, brown shorts, and sandals. He also has on a beaded wooden necklace and black sunglasses resting on top of his head. He has a couple of days' worth of rough stubble on his face. He looks like a surfer missing his board. Not quite what I'd expect from one of the premier arms dealers on the West Coast.

Turner looks me up and down warily. "Who are you, and what can I do for you?"

His voice is deep and gravelly, like he's smoked forty a day for the last twenty years.

I clear my throat. "My name's James."

"James?"

"Hetfield."

He looks at me funny. "Your name is James Hetfield?"

I nod, trying to look like I don't see what the big deal is.

He laughs loudly and points at me, looking around until his hired goons start laughing too.

"Do you know that's a pretty famous name around these parts?"

I shrug and shake my head. "No kiddin'?"

I know damn well who James Hetfield is. I'm not an idiot.

Turner has a strange smile that would be unnerving to the average person and an aura about him that exudes confidence and charisma. He also has a look in his eye that screams of evil. I know I have to tread carefully.

I step farther into the room. "Listen, I was told you could help me out. I'm looking for some hardware, and your name is top of the list of suppliers around these parts. Am I in the right place?"

Turner paces casually over to the kitchen counter. "That depends. What do you want?"

"I need a handgun. Something light but sturdy. I was thinking maybe a Glock?"

He nods. "Okay. Easy enough to supply."

"I also need a sniper rifle for a .300-caliber round. I'm looking at a thousand yards, easy. Was thinking maybe a Remington?"

"A Remington?" He strokes his stubble with his hand, like he's deep in thought. "Interesting choice. Mind if I ask what you want it for?"

Bingo.

"My backup guy is gonna be covering me from a good distance. I need to make sure he has a reliable weapon, given he's guarding my life."

Turner nods. "A wise choice. You seem to know your stuff, Mr. Hetfield. You're in luck too. I had someone just the other day come in and order the same rifle, so I got my hands on a crate of them."

"Really? Well, that *is* a stroke of luck."

I know I've got to play it right, but I leap on the opportunity to try to get something more out of him.

I frown. "Hang on a minute. What did this other guy

look like?"

Turner cocks his head to the side. His eyes narrow as they flick to one of his bodyguards, then back to me. "Why?"

"I'm just thinking. I've spent weeks researching this job in extensive detail, and that rifle is perfect for it. If someone else is in town asking after the same gun, maybe they've got designs on the same job. I'm in a... competitive business, shall we say. I wouldn't mind checking the guy out if it's all the same to you."

His face softens and his expression mellows again. "Hey, I can understand that. You gotta protect your investments, am I right?"

"Absolutely."

"But while I feel your pain, Jimmy, I'm afraid I'm gonna have to decline in helping you out with your request. I run a reputable business, and the privacy of my clients is paramount. The confidentiality I guarantee with the service I provide is why I'm as successful as I am."

He gestures to the room, as if it's a prime example of his accomplishments.

I best not push my luck too much.

I nod. "I understand. So, how do you want to work this? I can get the money to you by the end of today. You got a bank account I can arrange a transfer to?"

He laughs again. "Jimmy, I sell weapons for a living. I deal in cash. I don't exactly declare things to the IRS, know what I'm saying?"

"Oh, of course—sorry! I can have the cash with you in a few hours. How much are we looking at?"

Turner walks over to me. The bodyguard standing next to him takes a few steps forward but hangs back. I glance around subtly at the rest of the room. The three women on the sofa aren't a threat, so I can rule them out. The three guys at the table, the two on the sofa, and the one backing up Turner are the main concern. Plus, there's the guy behind me, by the door...

Certainly not the best situation I've ever been in. However, it's not the worst, either.

Turner's standing a couple of feet in front of me. I regard him with as neutral a gaze as I can, trying to stay in character.

"Well... for the Glock, I'll do you a good price because I like your name." He laughs again. I hate people who continuously amuse themselves like that. "You can have it for five hundred."

I nod with a slightly surprised look on my face. "That's a fair price. I appreciate that, Jo-Jo. Thank you."

He shrugs humbly. "I'm a businessman. I know how to conduct good business, y'know. Now, the Remington... that'll cost ya. Twenty grand."

I know that a good price for a sniper rifle of that caliber is between ten and fifteen thousand dollars. What he's trying to charge me is extortionate.

I frown. "That's a bit steep, isn't it?"

I feel all the bodyguards around me tense. Turner flexes his shoulders. "Hey, you came to me, remember? You don't like the price list? Fuck off."

I sense the guy behind me take a step closer.

Shit.

I'm sure the whole thing's just gone horribly wrong...

I put my hands up defensively. "I'm sorry, man. I meant nothing by it. Can't blame a guy for trying to negotiate a little, right? Twenty grand is fine."

He shakes his head. "No... y'know what? The price just went up. You want the Remington? It'll cost you thirty grand. Consider it inflation... for the insult."

I sigh. My spider sense is tingling. This conversation is only going to end one way, and I'll be damned if I'm going to cower and grovel. I don't care if I *am* pretending.

Besides, I need to stall and hope the next part of my plan works. But before that, I need to get over to that laptop, which isn't going to happen with seven guys and Turner in the way...

Time for plan B, I think. When in doubt, wind them up so that they make a mistake, then take advantage.

Antagonize and capitalize.

I look Turner dead in the eye. My persona slowly shifts back to normal. I feel my body relax, my breathing slow, and my mind kick in and begin to work on an exit strategy.

The faint sound of gunfire way below us distracts me.

Didn't even get the chance to say anything...

Turner hears it too and the mood changes. He looks over at the three men by the table. "You three, go and find out what the fuck's going on."

They stand and pile out the door. The guy standing by it remains in the room, as do the two on the sofa, who now stand and stare at me.

Turner draws his gun—which is also a Desert Eagle—and aims it at my head. "Who the fuck are you?"

I hold my hands out to the sides. "I told you who I am. Who the fuck are *you*? Is this some kind of setup? Are you a fucking cop?"

He scoffs and seems to take genuine offence. "No, I'm fucking not. Are you?"

"No! I just want to buy a goddamn gun. Is that too much to ask?"

The door bursts open behind me. I turn and see one of the three guys rushing back in, out of breath. "Boss, we got a big fucking problem!"

12

Turner doesn't move. He keeps his gun trained on me and looks at his man. "What the fuck's going on?"

"Triad is storming the place, spreading out across every floor! They're shooting everyone they see!"

"Fuck!" He looks back at me. "Well, haven't you picked the worst fucking time to buy a gun?"

I frown. "What's going on here, Jo-Jo? If there's trouble, I'd like my guns right now!"

"You just wait here and don't fucking move." He looks at the guys left in the room. "You three—you're with me. I want to know what these ignorant Triad fucks are thinking, attacking me in my house!"

He storms out of the room, followed by the men. I'm left standing on my own, with only three high, half-naked women and a doorman who appears unarmed for company.

Perfect.

I look at the laptop, then at the man behind me by the

door. "Hey, I might just take off. I think maybe this is a bad time..."

The guy produces a gun from his back and aims it at me.

Oh, look. A Desert Eagle. Shocker.

"The boss told you to stay put, so you're not going anywhere."

I step toward him, trying to tempt him closer. He walks toward me and stops a couple feet away, placing the barrel of his gun against my forehead.

"I said, don't... fucking... move."

I quickly look him up and down. He's average height and build, no obvious physical limitations. Confident with the gun but probably not used to thinking for himself, given his job is guarding a door.

I lean my upper body back and quickly swipe my hand across, knocking his gun away from me. Unprepared for the attack, he stands frozen and wide-eyed, making my job a whole lot easier. I go to grab his throat but jab my hand into his larynx instead of gripping it. He drops the gun and holds his throat with both hands as he coughs violently. I kick him hard in the balls. He sinks to his knees, moving one hand to cradle the injured area, still coughing. I swing my elbow across, catching him on the side of his head with the thick bone at the top of my forearm. He crashes to the floor, unconscious.

I move over to the table, take off my shoe, and take out the USB drive from the heel. I plug it into Turner's laptop and open up the file directory. I need to copy the Red Dragon's FBI file onto his computer, so it looks like he's had it the whole time, feeding the lie I told Jak Soo Yung about Turner being an informant.

I copy the information across, then begin searching through his files. I need to find some records of his transactions. He must keep them, so he can track his finances. I click through folder after folder but come up with nothing.

Dammit.

What would Josh do?

Who am I kidding? I have no idea what Josh would do. He's way smarter than I am.

Okay, think.

Would Turner keep those kinds of files on this physical laptop?

Probably not. It's not secure.

So, where else would he keep them?

You can store things remotely or wirelessly or whatever, right?

I click on the *My Computer* icon on his desktop.

There's an external server listed here...

I click that.

A file directory opens with folders named by date...

This might be it!

I start clicking into folders going back a week. Turner said Pellaggio came by the other day...

I open a folder dated four days ago.

There's one document in there, so I click on that.

It looks like a shopping list. I quickly scan through it.

Yes!

There's the Remington. This must be it.

There's an address on here too. They must've delivered it.

Wait a minute... is this entire list what Pellaggio ordered? It must be—

Holy shit! There's a *lot* of hardware on here.

I hear movement out in the hall. I quickly copy the file onto the USB drive. It only takes a few seconds. I unplug the drive, put it back in my heel, then close the various windows on the laptop.

I put my shoe back on, walk over to the unconscious doorman, take his gun, and check the magazine's full.

Not sure how I'm going to get out of here.

Turner appears in the doorway, looking pissed off. He's not holding a gun anymore. He only has one of his men with him. They stare at the guy on the floor, then back at me, holding the gun. I smile at him. Before anyone can say anything, the doorway fills as five men pile in behind Turner.

They're Chinese. Three of them are wearing the same black suits and blood-red shirts as the guys in the hospital yesterday. One of them is the old guy, still wearing the same dirty white vest and short brown pants.

Does he ever change his clothes?

The last guy walks in slowly, casually but purposeful. He's wearing a light gray suit and looks younger, maybe closer to my age. He's bald, with smooth, unblemished skin. He's wearing a black shirt with the collar open.

Jak Soo Yung, I'm guessing.

They walk in and fan out, seemingly ignoring me completely. Turner and his man stand in the middle of the room between the sofa and the kitchenette. The three guys in blood-red shirts form a loose line in front of them, standing with their backs to me. The old guy narrows his eyes and frowns, glaring at me angrily as he walks past everyone to sit in the armchair by the TV. The last guy stops in front of me. He's holding a gun. It's a Browning Hi-Power, and it's solid gold.

Nice!

"Adrian Hell?"

His voice is low and deliberate. I lower my gun a little. "Yeah, who's asking?"

"We are Red Dragon."

"So, you're Jak Soo Yung?"

He nods.

I look over at Turner, who looks furious and frightened at the same time. He's glaring at me. "Sonofabitch! *You're* Adrian Hell!"

I smile and shrug. "My reputation clearly precedes me. I'm sorry, Jo-Jo. All this is kinda my fault. You see, I told Mr. Yung here your secret. Y'know... that you're really an undercover fed. That's why he's so pissed off."

Turner's mouth opens and his eyes widen. "What? No, I'm not!" He looks at Soo Yung, fear flickering into his eyes. "Jak, I'm not a cop—you know me! We've done business together for years."

Soo Yung looks at me as he adjusts his grip on his Browning. He raises an eyebrow.

I hold my hands up innocently. "Hey, this is nothing to do with me. Maybe check out his computer or something if you don't believe me."

Soo Yung looks to the old man and nods. The old man stands and pushes past Turner, his men, and me. He sits down at the table, turns the laptop to face him, and taps away on the keyboard.

He quickly finds the FBI file on Red Dragon. He shouts in Chinese—presumably cursing. Soo Yung strides over and looks at the screen himself.

"What? What are you looking at?" asks Turner, panicking. He looks at me. "What the fuck have you done?"

"I think they've just found the FBI file you've been keeping on them on your computer."

"That's ridiculous! I don't have a—"

The old man stands, pushes past me, and walks over to him. He grabs Turner by the back of the neck and ushers him across the room to the table. He forces him into one of the chairs and moves the laptop in front of him, jabbing angrily at the screen.

"You undercover?"

Turner's eyes go wide as he reads the file.

I smile to myself.

Gotcha.

Turner looks at me. "You sonofabitch! You did this!"

I shrug and look at Soo Yung. "I don't know what he's talking about. But I'm not happy he's giving your details to the FBI. It probably means he's giving them information about me too."

I level my Desert Eagle at him.

Everyone else raises their guns too, resulting in a loud, metallic noise as multiple weapons simultaneously cock and take aim. Soo Yung levels his Browning at me. I look over my shoulder and see one of the three men in suits aiming at Turner's muscle. The other two have one gun on me, one on Turner.

I smile. "Well, this is exciting, isn't it?"

Soo Yung gestures at me with his gun. "You dead man!"

"Oh, are we still not okay? That's... disappointing." I move my gun and aim at Soo Yung. "Here's what I propose. I'm going to walk out of here, and you have my word you'll never see me again. You can feel free to dispose of Mr. Turner here and destroy the FBI file, so you guys are in the clear. Everybody wins. Sound good?"

He snarls at me. "No. You dead man. Nobody disrespects the Red Dragon!"

I see Turner getting twitchy out of the corner of my eye. I think he's getting ready to make a move, but what move can he make? He's got one man with him, unarmed. He's sitting down, unarmed. There are three Triad men with guns on the pair of them, and I'm in a standoff with their leader. He'll be dead before he takes a step.

I see his arm moving slightly. His hand's under the table.

That sneaky bastard's got a gun under there, hasn't he?

I turn and look at him, raising an eyebrow. He smiles back at me and confirms my suspicions.

Soo Yung is maybe four feet away from me. Arm's length at a stretch. It's the three guys behind me I'm worried about.

I glance at Turner again. Yeah... he's definitely ready to do something.

I've got to play this right.

I lunge forward and drive my shoulder into Soo Yung's thighs. I aim blindly as I do and fire two rounds at the men behind me. The blast of the Desert Eagle is deafening in the quiet apartment. I don't see if I hit anyone.

As we hit the floor, Soo Yung grunts under my weight. A thunderous blast erupts behind me. I roll onto my back and see Turner standing with a sawn-off double-barreled shotgun in his hand. Smoke is whispering out the ends, and the old man is on the floor. His head has pretty much disappeared; only the mandible and the right half of his face remains. There's a large pool of thick crimson all around him.

I aim at Turner as he fires at the three men in the center of the room. His blast takes out two of them at the same moment I fire. I hit him in the shoulder and nearly sever his arm. He flies backward to the floor. I scramble to my feet as Soo Yung does.

Side by side with little room to maneuver, I drop my gun and grab his head with both hands, clasping them together and pulling him down toward me. I drive my knee up to meet him and feel his jaw dislocate from the impact. I let go and he slumps to the floor, dropping his weapon.

I crouch to retrieve it as a bullet flies over my head. I spin around to see the remaining Triad member taking aim at me. I raise Soo Yung's Browning and fire three rounds, which all hit the guy in the chest.

I stand for a moment, holding the gun ready while I let the scene settle. The echoes of the gunfire fade away, and I hear groaning off to my right. I look over. Turner is slumped against the wall, sitting upright on the floor, holding his shoulder.

I walk over to him. "Well, that was fun, wasn't it!"

He's lost a lot of blood and is fighting to stay conscious. "What the... fuck, man? Why did... you... do this?"

I crouch next to him, gesturing with the gun as I talk. "Well, initially, this was about the Remington. The one you sold the other day? The guy who bought it used it to shoot a friend of mine, and I want to find the sonofabitch."

"That's not... my fault..."

"I never said it was. But along the way, I managed to piss off these Red Dragon assholes. When I found out they do business with you as well, I thought I'd kill two birds with one stone."

He smiles. His mouth is filled with blood. "You'll never... get out of here... alive."

"Don't you worry about that. I'll think of something."

I place the barrel of the Browning Hi-Power against his left temple and rest my finger on the trigger. "Any last words?"

He turns his head slightly and looks at me. "Fuck... you..."

I smile. "Nice. Probably what I would've gone with too."

I squeeze the trigger and blow the side of his head clean

off. He falls away from me, landing heavily among the parts of his skull and brain that have exploded across the floor.

I stand and walk over to Soo Yung, who's out cold but not dead. I tap his foot with mine but get nothing.

I look around the apartment. The three half-naked women are still sitting on the sofa, alive, if only in the biological sense of the word. The one on the left is covered in the blood of... someone. I don't know who. They're giggling to themselves, seemingly unaware of what's been happening around them.

I should really try to help them get out of here... but I just can't find it in me to do it. They're a colossal waste of life. I'll let fate decide what happens to them.

I walk out of the apartment and into the hall. There's a sea of bodies—both Red Dragon and Turner's men—leading from the doorway down to the elevators and the stairs.

Jesus. It's like a goddamn slaughterhouse in here.

I navigate the minefield of corpses and stand at the top of the stairs. I look over the handrail, all the way down to the first floor. From what I can see, every floor is the same. I hear voices below. Sounds like some Triads are still alive, which means they'll be coming to re-group with their boss. I look at the Browning in my hand, which has maybe seven rounds left in it.

Hmmm... the numbers are against me. How the hell am I getting out of here?

Ooh, lightbulb moment!

I rush back to Turner's apartment. I step over Soo Yung's unconscious body and into the kitchenette. I quickly raid the cupboards, looking for something useful. I find two bottles of vodka and a pack of cigarettes with a lighter.

I smile. These will do nicely.

I tuck the Browning in my waistband at the back and move over to the oven, turning all the gas burners on. I grab both bottles of vodka in one hand and the lighter in the other and turn to walk out of the apartment. I glance over at the women on the sofa. Two of them have passed out, and the third is looking at me curiously. I make eye contact with her. "You might want to consider getting out of here."

She stares at me blankly.

"Yeah? No?" I shrug. "Suit yourself. At least I tried."

I head for the door, but Soo Yung grabs my ankle as I walk past. I look down at him and see he's trying to say something, but he can't get the words out because of his dislocated jaw.

I kick him in the face with my other foot. "Piss off."

I stand in the doorway, tuck one bottle under my arm, and open the other. I pour the contents on the floor just inside the room. I walk backward into the hallway and shut the door behind me. I continue all the way to the elevator, pouring a thin trail of vodka as I do.

I reach the handrail by the stairs and hear shouting below me. I quickly glance over the edge and see at least ten guys running up the stairs toward me—all Triad.

I empty the bottle and open the second one, pouring a small pool at the top of the stairs before trailing it back to the elevators. I place it on the floor and use my fingertips to force the doors of the elevator open. I slide them apart and look down the ten-story shaft, glimpsing the roof of the elevator below. I let out a heavy sigh.

Heights have never been a favorite of mine...

I haven't really thought this through, have I?

Behind me, I hear the men getting closer.

Well, no time for fear now.

I finish emptying the second vodka bottle by the doors.

Without thinking, I step out into the abyss, grabbing hold of the thick cables running down the center of the shaft. I grip them tightly and wrap my feet around them. Putting one hand underneath the other, I slowly move myself down. I stop when my head's level with the floor. I get the lighter and flick it on, watching the flame flickering in my hand.

I glance down and close my eyes briefly, steeling myself for what is going to have to be a quick descent. I open my eyes and throw the lighter through the open doors. I hear the faint *whoosh* as the vodka trail catches fire.

Time to go!

As quickly as I dare, I climb down the cables. My hands soon start to sting and burn, but I ignore it. I'm keeping count of how many sets of doors I pass, so I know how far down I am without having to look below me.

I've just passed the fifth floor.

I hear screaming above me. I've got just a few more seconds before the trail of alcohol leads the flame into the apartment currently filling with gas... With a bit of luck, the remaining Triad men will make it in there just in time— assuming they make it past the flames at the top of the stairs.

Third floor.

I hear the explosion above.

Fuck me!

The cables shake and I almost lose my grip. I look up and see a huge fireball enter the shaft.

Oh, shit!

I start to fall. Looking up again, the cable whips and lashes toward me, chased by a cloud of fire. The blast must have snapped it...

Thankfully, I don't have that far to fall, but it's still close to two floors. This is going to sting like a—

Ugh!

I land heavily on the roof of the elevator.

Oh, man, that sucks!

Pain instantly shoots through my entire body. I wince, but I know I have little time to get out of here. I scramble to my feet and stomp on the security vent on the roof. It takes me three kicks, but it eventually falls into the elevator. I quickly jump into it and dive through the open doors and into the lobby. I hear the cables crash down behind me. I turn and—

Jesus!

The explosion completely engulfs the elevator shaft. There's a loud roar as the flames rush over me. I cover my head with my hands, making myself as flat as possible. The heat scorches my skin, and the stench of burnt vodka and flesh stings my nostrils.

After a few seconds, it's over.

I push myself up and rest on all fours, catching my breath. My arms are burning from the workout of climbing down the cable. It seems I'm not as light as I used to be...

I look up at the front door as it opens and see the large twins standing with their mouths open, in complete shock.

Speaking of not being as light as we used to be...

They must've run when they saw the Triad approaching.

I stand up, dust myself down, and stretch to crack my neck and back. I draw Soo Yung's gold Browning and level it at the pair of them. "Okay, here's the thing... I'm having a *really* bad day. I've just killed Joseph Turner and most of the Red Dragon Triad—including its boss, Jak Soo Yung. Before that, they killed the majority of Turner's men. I've also just blown up probably the top three floors of the building to kill any stragglers. I can't be bothered fighting with you two, and trust me, you two don't wanna try fighting with me, either.

What say we all forget we saw one another, and you two live to see another day?"

They look at each other, then throw their guns down, turn, and waddle through the main door.

I breathe a sigh of relief and walk slowly outside after them.

13

I'm sitting in the conference room in the FBI field office, at the head of the table at the far end, with the TV behind me. Agents Wallis and Johnson are sitting on either side of me. At the opposite end of the table is Agent Chambers.

The mood is... tense.

I walked out of Turner's apartment building and saw bodies—and *bits* of bodies—littering the sidewalk. I looked up and saw the top of the building on fire. Must've been the top three floors easily.

I smiled to myself, walked back to the car, climbed in the back beside Johnson. We sped off as fire crews and local police began showing up.

We made our way back to the field office, and I was ushered into this room with little interaction from anyone. The three of them disappeared for a while and only came back a few minutes ago.

Chambers stands and leans on the desk, looking at me

with disappointment in her eyes. "Adrian, we trusted you. What the hell happened in there?"

I shrug. "It went south. It started out all right—Jak Soo Yung arrived just as I was conducting the deal with Turner. I managed to plant the file on Turner's laptop, and Soo Yung found it like I hoped he would."

"So, what went wrong?" asks Wallis.

"The Red Dragon came a little more prepared than I anticipated. They brought a goddamn army with them. Must've taken out nearly all of Turner's men and were coming for me. I had no choice but to fight my way out."

Chambers sits again and massages her temples. "Adrian, you killed one of the largest black-market weapons dealers in the country *and* single-handedly destroyed an entire Triad operation. The repercussions this will have on the streets don't bear thinking about. What have you got to say for yourself?"

I shrug. "I don't know... you're welcome?"

She shakes her head and leans back in her chair. The room falls awkwardly silent.

"Did you find anything out from Turner about Pellaggio?" asks Wallis after a moment.

I reach down and take off my shoe. I open the heel and take out the USB drive. I slide it over to him.

He frowns at it, and then looks at me. "What's this?"

"I found it on his laptop. Well, on an external server. It's a rather long shopping list of disturbingly high-quality weaponry and tech—including a Remington—from a few days ago, along with an address where Turner delivered them."

The agents exchange looks of excitement, then Wallis gets up and leaves the room.

Johnson rolls his eyes. "At least you did something right..."

I glare at him. "Hey, it was either that or die in there. Sorry I chose not to sacrifice my life for the sake of your bureaucracy."

Chambers slaps the desk with her hand. "Cut it out, the pair of you. This isn't the time. We need to focus on finding Pellaggio and stopping him before anyone else dies."

Wallis re-enters holding a laptop. He sits without a word and connects it via a cable that allows his screen to be displayed on the TV behind me. He plugs in the USB drive and opens up the file it contains.

Silence falls as the three of them stare at the screen behind me, reading through the list. I watch Chambers. I see her expression change, as mine did when I read it.

She sighs heavily. "I don't even know what half of this stuff is."

I gesture to the TV behind me with my thumb. "It's all bad, trust me. Especially in Pellaggio's hands."

They finish reading and look at each other. I see them worrying as the numerous possibilities of what this stuff could be used for crosses their minds. I know because I've been there already.

Chambers sits up straight in her chair. "Right, Johnson, I want eyes on that address. Get me a real-time feed, plus still images going back seven days at thirty-minute intervals. If he's there, I want to see what he's doing. If he's moved on, I want to know when and where to."

He nods. "On it."

He stands and leaves the room, breaking into a run as he crosses the office floor.

"Wallis, I want you to work on this list of weapons. Where could Turner have gotten his hands on all this in the first place? This is all military-grade, so start there. We want to know about any missing shipments, serial numbers—the works. If we can find out where it came from, we might be able to get some help from the real owners in getting it back."

He stands. "No problem."

He races out of the room like Johnson did.

Chambers turns to me and gives me another disapproving look.

I shrug. "What?"

"Oh, I don't know. Maybe I'm a little annoyed about the fact you blew up half a building and killed God knows how many people? How do you do such things so frivolously?"

I take a deep breath and sigh. "Grace, it's not like I do things like this for fun or take them lightly. I was defending myself, that's all."

She looks away, furrowing her brow. She'll probably never understand what it's like to have to deal with that kind of situation.

"Hey, on the bright side, at least you've got one less arms dealer in your city. Look at this as an opportunity."

"An *opportunity*? How can I possibly do that?"

"You talk about the repercussions on the street... when the Red Dragon was in charge, they dictated what happened, and you guys let them. But now there's no one in charge. Nobody was big enough to take over before, which means they won't be big enough to do it now. They'll fight among themselves first. This is your chance to step in and put them in their place, let them know there's nothing to take over—that the law is back in charge."

I smile. After a moment, she smiles back, albeit shaking her head. "Maybe you're right... You never cease to amaze me. Finding a silver lining in every cloud seems to be one of your many talents."

I shrug with light-hearted humility. "Years of practice creating the clouds."

Chambers takes a deep breath and leans back again, rubbing her neck. I can imagine how she feels. My instinct is to rush over there and put a bullet in Pellaggio's head, but there's no way it would be that simple. For one, I doubt he's still there. And two, it's probably more important to find out what he's done or intends to do with the stuff on that list.

I look at her. Even though she's tired, she still looks great. She wears little make-up but doesn't really need any. She stretches her arms up and arches her back. I feel bad for so many reasons, but I can't help but steal a quick look at her. The way her white blouse falls and rests on her body, clinging to the right places, showing off all the work she must put in at the gym.

I look away quickly. Which... yeah, which she definitely spotted. Shit! She smiles a little, but to her credit, she says nothing.

Change the subject, Adrian...

"When was the last time you got any sleep?"

She sighs wearily. "I don't remember."

"Grace, you're no good to anyone if you're running on empty. Go and get your head down for a couple hours. Wallis and Johnson can manage here, I'm sure."

She smiles, which I think is out of appreciation, but I know what she'll say. She'll say she won't rest until this is over.

"Thanks, Adrian. But we have no idea what's coming next from Pellaggio, and I will not stop until this thing is over."

Told you.

I nod, understanding completely, and stand up to stretch. My back is aching from my fall.

Talk about getting the shaft...

I smile to myself and walk over to the door.

"And where do you think you're going?"

That sounded half serious and—I think—half flirtatious.

I look back at her. "I thought I might catch up with Johnson, see if he's got a fix on that address yet. I wouldn't mind having a look at the place myself. If that's all right?"

Chambers thinks about it for a moment. "Fine. But play nice."

She smiles and looks back at the screen, re-reading Pellaggio's shopping list. I turn and walk out of the conference room, across the open-plan area, and into the corridor. I follow it along as it curves slightly and head left into the larger open-plan area, which is full of activity.

I stand in the entrance, scanning the busy office, looking for Johnson. I see him about halfway down. He's standing at a bank of desks with four computer monitors on it, leaning on the back of a chair and discussing something with the person sitting in it.

I make my way over to them, nodding politely to the people who stare as I walk past. Johnson turns to look at me as I approach. I expect he'll greet me with some sort of confrontational or sarcastic retort...

"Hey, check this out."

Huh. A pleasant surprise.

He points to the screen, which is showing a slightly grainy, black and white, top-down image of a warehouse.

I narrow my eyes. "What am I looking at?"

"This is a real-time satellite feed on the address you got

from Turner. It's a warehouse on a disused pier near the Alcatraz ferry way."

The feed shows a man standing alone, looking out over the water from the pier. In front of him, tied up, is a small speedboat. It looks like he's pacing back and forth, smoking a cigarette.

I point at the screen. "Is that him?"

"We don't know. We can't get a good enough look at him to allow the facial recognition software to complete a scan."

"Can't we view it from a different angle?"

The agent working the computer turns to look at me and launches into a technical and detailed explanation about why that isn't possible.

I won't lie, I zoned out shortly after the guy said, "Well, to put it simply…"

Whatever he's saying doesn't even sound English to me.

God, I wish Josh were here.

I picture him lying unconscious and oblivious to everything that's happening. If I could just—

"Adrian!"

Huh?

I spin around to see Chambers standing across the office. She's holding her cell phone and looks worried. "Adrian, it's him. And he's asking for you."

I rush over, with Johnson close behind. I take the phone off her and put it on speaker. "I'm here."

"Good," replies Pellaggio.

His voice is different this time. He's not distorting it in any way. I pick up on the hint of old Italy in his surprisingly deep tone. He sounds just like his old man.

"Are you taking me seriously now?"

"No. You're still a worthless bastard, *Danny*, and you're still gonna die."

He laughs. "I'm so glad you finally figured out who I am. I left you enough hints. So, tell me, how's your little friend?"

I clench my jaw muscles and take a breath to compose myself. "He's fine. Unlike you, he's not a pussy who cries from a bullet wound or two. He's sitting in bed watching *Downton Abbey*, or whatever it is British folks watch. You shoot like a little bitch, you know that?"

He laughs again—a little longer this time. "Adrian... Adrian, Adrian, Adrian... Ever the macho asshole. I know full well he's in a coma and not likely to survive. Your false bravado won't do you any good now. You think my last attack was bad? You ain't seen nothin' yet."

I exchange glances with Chambers and Johnson, who look increasingly more concerned. Before I can speak, Wallis comes running down the corridor toward us. He immediately senses the mood and holds back, gesturing he'll remain quiet.

"So, what, you just rang to brag about it? Is this all part of your twisted little game? If you've got a problem with me, why don't you come and get me, and we'll settle it like men?"

"Typical Adrian, thinking this is all about you." His voice darkens. "Have you not figured it out yet? I fucking hate you, and I intend to watch you die, but if you think I went to all this trouble just for little ol' you, then you're much stupider than you look."

"So, what's your endgame, Danny?"

"You know where I am, don't you? Why don't you come and find out?"

The line clicks dead.

Christ.

I look at Chambers. "We have a serious problem."

"Yes, we do," interrupts Wallis.

Chambers looks at him. "What have you got?"

"Two things. The first is a report detailing a missing shipment of weapons coming in from Afghanistan, which was originally scheduled for delivery to Hawthorne Army Depot in Nevada, where they were to be decommissioned. They never made it there. The full inventory is quite extensive, but it includes everything on Pellaggio's shopping list."

"Okay, so now we know where Turner got the weapons. I normally wouldn't want to ask the military for help, but under the circumstances..."

I briefly consider pointing out the hypocrisy of being criticized for *my* male pride, then having to listen to them worry about saving face with other agencies, but I decide against it.

"Already taken care of. I've contacted Hawthorne and explained we have reason to believe those weapons are in play with an ongoing investigation. I said I was letting them know as a courtesy, if they wanted to help clean up their own mess."

"Nice," says Johnson.

"What did they say?" asks Chambers.

"They're going to send a liaison over, who should be here in the morning."

"Well, that's something. What else have you got?"

"I've got two dead naval officers. A Petty Officer Higgins and an Ensign Lyman. Both found dead within the last week."

"How's that related?" asks Johnson.

"Both bodies were found within seven blocks of Pellaggio's warehouse. Both were on active duty in the area. Both were shot at close range with a silenced Beretta 92A1."

I frown as I feel all eyes turn to me. I hold my hands up.

"Hey, it wasn't me. You know that. You've got my guns here. Wallis, was that weapon on Turner's list?"

He checks his notes. "Yeah."

"Right, so this is another sick little message for me. Question is, why kill two active Navy personnel?"

"Could they just be random, like the shootings at the Transamerica building?" asks Johnson, thinking out loud.

Chambers shakes her head. "No. They weren't random the first time, and this doesn't feel random, either. A petty officer and an ensign, shot at close range..."

She looks at me. Her face is a mixture of confusion, resignation, and despair.

I nod. "They were executed. No doubt. We just need to figure out why."

"We do. But right now, we have to focus on the things we can actively work with." She turns to Wallis. "That's great work. When the liaison from Hawthorne gets here, I want you to work with them on that lead. They might be able to offer some extra insight."

"Got it."

"Johnson, you're with me and Adrian."

I raise an eyebrow. "And... what are we doing?"

"We're going to follow up on the only solid lead we have."

"We're... going to the warehouse?" asks Johnson.

I note the apprehension in his voice.

Chambers nods. "Yes. Even if he's not there anymore, we might find some clue about where he's gone."

I quickly rub my hand over my neck, loosening myself up. "Well, you know it's gonna be a trap, right? He wouldn't invite us down there if there were any real chance of us actually finding him."

She smiles. "I know. It's almost certainly a trap of *some* kind. That's why you're going in first."

I smile back. She's starting to think like me, the poor woman. But she's also starting to see what it takes to win these types of games...

I nod. "Works for me."

14

It was funny noting the contrast between them. Chambers armed herself with her Glock and Kevlar vest quickly and professionally. Johnson did the same but in the way a child would do their chores—like it was necessary, but he could think of a billion things he'd rather be doing instead. Wallis, on the other hand, was visibly unhappy not to be included, as if sitting behind a desk was his idea of hell.

I was surprised how easy it was to convince Chambers I should have my guns back. All I had to do was ask.

We're huddled together around a table in the smaller office area by the conference room. The whole team of agents is here, game faces on. I look around the crowd as Chambers prepares to explain what's about to happen. I notice at the back is Agent Green. I've not seen him since he arrested me a couple days ago outside City Hall. I stare at him for a moment, but he doesn't acknowledge me.

"Special Agent Johnson, Adrian, and I are going to check

149

out the warehouse," Chambers announces to the room. "We want to keep this discreet, just in case Pellaggio *is* still there. The last thing we want to do is give him more notice to run. We'll carry out a preliminary search of the property, then call it in. We'll have a second team on stand-by, ready to carry out a full analysis. We'll need forensics in there too. Hopefully, we can find something that will tell us what Pellaggio's next move will be."

There are a few murmurs from the crowd—a mixture of agreement and concern.

"Okay, let's get to it."

She looks at Johnson, then me, and gestures for us both to follow her.

The crowd disperses with practiced efficiency. They all return to their own workstations as Chambers, Johnson, and I walk out of the office area and through the small network of corridors toward the elevator. We ride it down to the lobby and walk out to the street. There's a sedan parked out front. Johnson slides in behind the wheel. Chambers takes shotgun, so I climb in the back and sit in the middle.

Johnson guns the engine and pulls away from the curb. The traffic is light, considering it's mid-afternoon and approaching rush hour, but it's picking up. Johnson navigates the increasingly busy streets with ease as we make our way over to The Embarcadero, which runs the full length of the coast. It's where all the piers are located and where the ferry ways converge.

Chambers turns slightly in her seat to face me. "Are you ready for this?"

I nod. "For once, we're doing something I wouldn't do any differently on my own. Just get me to that warehouse."

She cocks her head slightly. "I'm glad you approve of the operation. But just remember—this is still our show. We work as a team. You don't go off on your own and start blowing things up, okay?"

I can't tell how serious she's being, so I play it safe and simply raise an eyebrow to silently acknowledge her request.

After ten minutes or so, we turn left at Embarcadero and Broadway. Johnson points to our right. "It should be just along here. I think it's the third pier up from where we are."

I look behind us and see Pier 7 on the other side of the junction. "Yeah, that'll be about right. He was right at the far end, wasn't he?"

"Yeah, Pier 17. We can drive straight down."

"I suggest we park halfway down and approach on foot," says Chambers. "It'll make our presence less obvious, if anybody *is* there."

I nod. "Agreed."

There's only one way in or out of the warehouse, which I don't like. If I'm infiltrating somewhere, I look at all entrances and pick the hardest one to get in. That's always the one least protected. But in this instance, we have no choice, and I hate being so exposed.

Johnson pulls over to the parking lot and eases the sedan to a stop by the entrance to the pier. "We're here."

I look around. A handful of parked cars line the side of the street. The sidewalk isn't busy, but there are some people walking back and forth. The parking lot is half-full, and the entrance to the pier is open. There are other businesses that occupy the warehouses nearest to us, and there's some hustle and bustle as they go about their day.

Chambers lets out a taut breath, like she's steeling herself for what happens next. "Okay, let's make a slow approach."

Johnson set offs again, turning cautiously onto the pier.

The sun glares through the windshield, reflecting off the bay and partially blinding us. Both Johnson and Chambers pull their visors down and squint as we make our way along.

We pass an open loading bay on the right, where two guys dressed in dark blue coveralls are unloading something from a truck. I lean forward to get a clear view of what lies ahead. The sun glistens on the bay, making for a picturesque scene I wish I had more time to appreciate.

Chambers points to a space outside a warehouse roughly halfway along. "This will do. Pull over here. We'll cover the rest on foot."

Johnson slows to a stop and we get out. I stretch and look around, seeing nothing that jumps out at me as strange.

Chambers draws her weapon and sets off walking toward the last warehouse of the pier. "On me."

I look up, knowing the FBI is watching in real-time through the miracle of technology. I draw one of my Berettas and follow her.

Johnson gestures to my gun. "You got a permit for that?"

I'm not sure if he's joking or not. It's not easy to tell with him.

I raise an eyebrow. "Seriously? Is now really the time?"

He smirks and walks on, moving in front of me and falling in behind Chambers.

I think that was his attempt at light humor...

We walk past another truck parked in front of the warehouse just before Pellaggio's. It's empty, and there's no one else around.

Pellaggio's going to be long gone. We're all thinking it. I just hope we find something useful inside. Ever since I spoke to him, like everyone else, I'm worried about what he might have planned. Since the beginning, we've assumed this entire thing has been about taking revenge on me. And

I think it still is, to a point. But if the game he's playing with me is just a small part of something bigger, then we've been purposefully distracted, so we wouldn't figure things out sooner.

Ahead, Chambers raises her arm, signaling for us to stop. We've reached the entrance to the warehouse.

She puts her first two fingers together, like a gun, and whips them repeatedly forward, commanding Johnson to run on ahead and cover the far side of the entrance. I fall in behind her, no stranger to the tactics of breaching a building. Chambers and Johnson lean against the wall on either side of the large metal roller, which has a smaller door cut into it. Their guns are held out low in front of them, arms locked. I kneel behind Chambers, a few paces back, holding my Beretta firm but with my arms loose.

She gestures to the handle. Johnson leans forward and grabs it.

"On three," she whispers.

She counts up on her hand. When she hits three, Johnson thrusts the door open for me.

There's no way Pellaggio is still here...

I walk in casually, gun by my side, my arm relaxed. Johnson follows and heads right. He takes a few steps inside, then crouches to cover. Chambers is last in and does the same but to the left.

I look at them both. Their operational tactics are sharp and accurate. Textbook, almost. But I fear it's unnecessary.

I look around the vast expanse of the warehouse. There are no partitions or makeshift rooms. It's just one big, empty building. The far wall is old brick, except the top few feet, which is a large, dirty, plastic window. The sun is beaming in through the grime, bathing half the floor in natural light. There's nothing except the odd piece of old timber, large puddles, and a pile of old wooden boxes in the far corner that have probably been there for years. I can smell the damp and decay that's been eating away at them over time.

In the middle of the area is a workbench. Three tables are arranged into a loose U-shape, with a few sheets of paper scattered across them. My eyes rest on the large pile of wooden crates just to the right of it. They're new. And they're open.

I call back over my shoulder. "Guys, check this out." I point to the middle of the room. "Looks like we're too late."

They both stand, breaking formation, and move next to me. They take a quick look around, presumably coming to the same conclusion as me. This is a bust.

Chambers lets out a low growl of frustration. "God-dammit. We missed him."

I shrug. "We expected as much. Don't take it too personal."

I walk over to the workbench. They both follow me, and we all stand in front of the table running horizontally between the other two.

I look down at the papers. "Looks like a blueprint for chaos."

Chambers picks it up and looks at it briefly. It's a detailed sketch of the California Academy of Sciences, with markings that clearly detail where the bombs were.

She takes out her phone and paces away to the side as she dials a number. Johnson moves over to inspect the crates. The top one is about chest-high and the lid is resting open. I watch him slide it off fully, pushing it to the floor. He looks inside and his eyes go wide with obvious horror.

I frown. "What is it?"

"We've got a major fucking problem!"

I rush over and look inside. There's a large bomb resting

on a bed of wood shavings. It's got multiple wires coming out of it and an LED timer that's counting down...

It's showing nineteen seconds...

My eyes grow wide. "Oh, fuck!"

I turn and start running. Johnson is right behind me. I look over at Chambers. "Grace, we gotta go! Now!"

She turns, sees us, and follows without question. We cross the warehouse floor at full speed. I was trying to keep count of how long we have, but I've lost track. Shit!

We reach the entrance and file through the metal door, out onto the pier.

I gesture wildly ahead of us with my arm. "Run! Get as far away as—"

A deafening explosion goes off behind us, tearing through the warehouse and drowning out my voice. The force from the blast sends us all flying off the edge of the pier and into the bay below. I take a large breath as I'm falling. My survival instincts kick in, protecting me while my brain freezes, trying to understand what's happening.

When going underwater, the best thing to do is take a deep breath *before* you go under. If you simply hold your breath, it means that you have to breathe in as you resurface, which causes you to inhale all the water that splashes up with you. If you have a lungful of air already, you simply breathe out and avoid choking.

I plunge into the water back-first. I turn and move quickly, looking around to make sure the other two are okay. I see them thrashing, dealing with the surprise of what's happened and the shock of the water. They'll be fine.

I think for a brief moment how insane it is that I can be so used to things like *this* happening... I get blown up way too much!

Above us, the cloud of fire from the explosion is still

billowing out over the water. I look again at Johnson and Chambers, who have managed to compose themselves a bit more and are looking around for me. Our eyes meet. I give them the *okay* signal with my hand, which they return. I point up and swim to the surface.

My head breaks the surface. I exhale a long, painful breath, then take some quick ones to regulate my heartbeat. The others do the same.

I swim over to them. "Well, I'm no expert, but I think *that* might have been the trap we were talking about."

Johnson rubs his face, clearing water from his eyes. "Jesus Christ!"

Chambers hasn't said anything. She's pale and her eyes are wide, darting around rapidly. It looks like she's going into shock.

"Grace, talk to me. Are you all right?"

She's taking in quick, deep breaths, but she manages a nod.

I focus on my breathing for a moment to compose myself.

Yet again, someone has found a new way to piss me off. The door keeping my Inner Satan at bay was blown off its hinges with the school bus full of kids. Now, Pellaggio has just walked inside and slapped my Devil across the face.

Enough is enough.

"Okay, listen up. Your official methods got us this far, and it's been a great team effort to figure out where this bastard was hiding. But I only stick with a plan until it gets me blown up. Now we do things my way."

Johnson spits some water out. "Adrian, this is still an FBI invest—"

"I'm not asking. I'm gonna get out of this water, hunt that sonofabitch down, and put a bullet in his fucking head.

That's what's going to happen next. Whether I end up in prison afterward or not is up to you. But I'm done playing nice."

Johnson looks over at Chambers, like he's expecting her to back him up, but she's too busy trying to control her breathing and deal with the shock. She simply shakes her head.

I swim over to the nearest wooden strut, which has some rope netting tied around it. I climb up and heave myself back onto the pier. I glance down to make sure they're both behind me.

I'm on all fours, taking a necessary moment to rest and catch my breath.

I'm getting too old for this shit...

I look over at what's left of the warehouse. The blast has blown the roof almost completely off, as well as most of the wall facing the bay. Debris is scattered everywhere, and the heat coming from the building is intense.

I look back up the pier to see if there's been any collateral damage to neighboring buildings. That empty white van is still parked outside the next warehouse over.

Wait a minute...

It's not empty. There's a head poking out the passenger side window, staring at me. I can't quite make out the exact features because of all the smoke around, but I can see the smile. It's a sick, evil smile.

Danny Pellaggio.

15

I scramble to my feet and set off running toward the van. I reach behind me to draw a Beretta. "Hey! Pellaggio, you piece of shit!"

He laughs as he disappears back inside the van. It quickly reverses, performs a J-turn, and speeds off. Its tires screech as people who have gathered at the entrance to the pier scatter to avoid getting run over.

I slow to a stop, gasping for breath. "Fuck!"

Chambers and Johnson appear next to me, shaking in their wet clothes, looking confused.

I point to the van, speeding away from us. "That was... him. That was... Pellaggio!"

Chambers seems to snap out of whatever shock she was in. "Come on! I'm not letting him go now!"

We all run back to the sedan as best we can in our wet and heavy clothes. I climb in the passenger side—I much prefer shooting than driving. Johnson takes the wheel and

Chambers clambers into the back seat behind me. We speed off in pursuit, following the van up the Embarcadero and left on Lombard Street. Johnson hits the sirens built in behind the front grill. I lean out the window, yelling and gesturing at people to move out of the way as we speed past.

Behind me, Chambers reaches for the cell phone stored in the console between the seats and calls for backup. "See if we can get close enough to ID the plates."

Johnson grits his teeth, wrestling with the wheel as he navigates the busy streets at high speed. "Do my best..."

The van is only a few cars in front of us.

Chambers taps me on my shoulder. "Adrian, did you get a look at him?"

I turn my head slightly toward her. "I didn't get a good look, no, but I know it was him."

Johnson moves sharply, narrowly fitting into a gap in the outside lane. Nearby drivers beep their horns.

I look over. "Jesus, Johnson! Who taught you how to drive?"

He sighs. "Just trying to get you near enough to shoot the bastard, all right?"

He throws me a sideways glance. I see he's not happy about it, but he knows what has to be done.

I nod, then turn back to Chambers. "We've got another thing to consider. Pellaggio was in the passenger side."

"Shit. So, who's driving?"

I sigh with frustration. "Hang on, I'll go ask..."

We've gained a few places thanks to Johnson's adventurous driving, and we're only three cars behind him now. We're driving through the Russian Hill district and gaining ground on Pellaggio as we hit the 101.

I tap Johnson on the arm. "You've almost got him."

The van is just ahead, but he runs a red light, which

causes two cars coming across the junction to crash. Johnson manages to swerve and avoid the collision, but we fall behind again, stuck behind a car that's slowing down to stare at the accident instead of making room for the sirens.

Johnson slams his fist on the horn. "Get out of the goddamn way!"

We manage to get through the congestion and back on the trail, but he's way out in front. We converge on Richardson Avenue and follow the 101 as it merges into the Presidio Parkway.

Chambers's arm appears next to me as she points ahead. "Christ, he's heading for the bridge! If he gets on there, we won't be able to stop him without causing complete chaos on the roads and endangering a whole lot of innocent people."

I lean out the window again. We're doing fifty, which is no mean feat in this much traffic. But we're still not gaining enough ground to catch him.

It's time for a more direct approach...

I look at Johnson. "Line us up behind him."

"What for? There are seven cars between us!"

"Just do it!"

He takes another tight gap and gets us in the same lane as Pellaggio, albeit some way back. With my Beretta in my right hand, I reach over with my left and grab the edge of the roof. I pull myself further out the window, until I'm practically sitting on the doorframe.

"What are you doing?" yells Chambers.

I ignore her. I don't have an answer she'll want to hear.

I'm lucky there are only cars in between us. It gives me an unobstructed view of the larger, taller van.

I use my left hand to steady myself, then take aim and fire with my right. The first two shots miss their mark, but the third hits the passenger door mirror. The van swerves sharply, then fishtails back and forth until the driver eventually regains control. That's allowed us to make up some ground—we're only one car behind them.

I frown. What the...

The rear doors of the van have opened, and Danny Pellaggio is standing there, holding onto the roof with one hand for balance. I don't remember anything about him from when I shot him a year ago. He was just another target back then. But now, as I stare into his empty brown eyes, I can see exactly who he is. He's quite thin, almost gaunt, but wiry with some muscle on his small frame. He's wearing a dark gray jumpsuit and black boots. His skin is a light olive color.

I flash a quick look ahead of us and see the tollbooth for the Golden Gate Bridge approaching fast.

I look back at Pellaggio.

Is that...

Oh, shit! Yeah, it is!

He's holding an M4 carbine assault rifle in his other hand, and he's aiming directly at us.

He flashes me a wicked smile and opens fire.

"Look out!"

I quickly duck back into the car as a hail of bullets pepper the hood. I crouch as low as possible behind the dashboard. I look to check on Chambers—she's flattened herself across the back seat. Johnson's doing the best he can, but he has to keep looking where he's driving, so he can't afford too much cover. I stick my arm out the window and fire a few rounds blind in an effort to deter Pellaggio from shooting at us.

The staccato roar of the machine gun continues.

It's not worked. Shit.

I stay low but sit up in the seat, so I can see what's happening. I need to—

Holy shit!

The car in between Pellaggio and us just caught a burst of gunfire. It swerved up onto the sidewalk and into a building.

Jesus, this guy is insane! He has no regard whatsoever for innocent life. I've got to stop him.

We weave back and forth, trying to make ourselves harder to hit, but we're so close that it doesn't really make any difference.

I look over at Johnson. "Try and draw nearer to his right side!"

Without question, he does. He hits the gas and approaches the rear of the van on the passenger side. Pellaggio is still firing. He's holding an assault rifle in one hand, and his arm is extended almost level in front of him. The strain on his muscles is going to be intense, and he doesn't look that strong. Sooner or later, he'll either need to hold it with both hands—which he can't do, as he'd fall over if he lets go of the roof—or stop firing altogether.

More bullets spray the driver's side of the car, shattering the window next to Johnson.

He struggles to control the vehicle. "Fuck!"

He's doing a great job, considering we're doing nearly sixty right now.

I lean over him and return fire, this time accurately enough to make Pellaggio stop shooting and retreat into the van.

I sit back and look at Johnson. "Hey, you all right?"

He nods. "Yeah, thanks."

I look over my shoulder at Chambers. She's been showered with glass and has lots of small cuts across her hands and top. "Grace, you good?"

She winces a little. "I'm fine. Just focus on stopping him."

She speaks on the phone again, giving details of the van's license plate, as well as a sitrep. Hopefully, that means the cavalry will soon be on its way.

I look ahead of us and see the traffic's slowing as we approach the tollbooth. It doesn't seem to deter the van driver, worryingly. It speeds on, smashing into the back of a car, spinning it out of the way and into some others, causing a pile-up that spreads across the opposite lane.

I need to take this guy down before he kills someone.

I point to the van. "Johnson, keep behind him. He's making a path for us through the traffic. Hang back and follow him until we reach the bridge. Once we have a straight run, I can take him down."

He nods. "Got it."

He drops back and tailgates the van as it plows recklessly through the lines of vehicles and reaches the tollbooth. It clips the rear end of a car, spinning it away as we shoot through the booth and hit the Golden Gate Bridge. It skids sideways, but the driver regains control and they speed on. We're just a few feet behind them.

"We've got a chopper inbound," announces Chambers from behind me. "ETA—five minutes."

I glance back at her. "That might be too long. This guy's insane and a really shit driver. I've gotta try to stop them now."

On cue, Johnson pulls to the side, faking right, then going left, trying to get alongside the van. I lean out the window and fire three rounds. The first two hit the wheel arch and the driver's door. The third blows out the front tire.

The van slides out of control and does a three-sixty spin in front of us.

Shit...

"Johnson, fall back!"

He sees it a fraction too late...

Uh! Shit!

The van slams into the front of our car. I see the driver of the van fighting for control.

Johnson grips the wheel tightly. "Hang on!"

The collision sends us spinning into the barrier along the edge of the bridge. The van spins away from us and skids to a halt farther along the road. We manage to keep control of the car, but the front end's been smashed beyond repair. The hood has crumpled up, and pieces have flown off into the road. Chambers grunts in pain as she flies into the back of my seat. I'm catapulted against the dashboard, smashing my ribs just before the airbag inflates.

The screeching of tires and the sound of crushing metal stops, leaving an eerie silence broken only by the occasional horn of a car and distant sirens.

I sit back, wincing as pain shoots through my ribs with every breath I take. I look over at Johnson, whose head is resting on the wheel. I tap his arm. "Hey, you with us?"

He groans and sits up slowly, revealing a deep, nasty-looking gash across his eyebrow. A thin line of blood is trickling down the side of his face. He smiles weakly. "Whoops..."

I smile. "Hey, you did good, Johnson. But we gotta get out of here."

I look over at the van, which has spun around and is now facing us. The grill and hood look as damaged as ours. I can't see any movement, but I'm not taking any chances.

I hustle out of the car and make my way cautiously over

to the van, gun in hand, ready to shoot. The broken glass crunches underfoot with each step I take, sounding loud in the silence and growing louder as Chambers and Johnson exit the car and follow me.

I approach the passenger side door in a wide arc, gun raised and ready. I smell the burnt rubber from the tires and a faint odor of gasoline. Inside the van, the driver is resting against the wheel, as Johnson was. Except this guy's not moving.

There's no sign of Pellaggio... He must've gone out the back, which means he might have that carbine locked and loaded.

Shit.

I hold back, edging farther round, trying to get the angle to see.

"Erm... Adrian? I think we've got company," says Chambers behind me.

I look over my shoulder at the others and see them standing, guns drawn, looking down the bridge, back toward the tollbooth we just came through. I follow their gaze and see two more vans, similar to Pellaggio's, speeding toward us.

I look back just in time to see Pellaggio walk around from behind his van, carbine in both hands, aimed right at me. He smiles that evil smile of his. "Put your fucking gun down, Adrian."

I quickly look back behind me and see the two vans slowing to a stop, side-on to us. Four men get out of each, all carrying similar-looking assault rifles.

Shit...

I turn and look at Pellaggio, sighing heavily.

Double shit...

I relax and let my Beretta hang loose by the trigger guard from my index finger. He walks over, takes it from me, and—

Uh!

He snapped a short elbow into my face. I stagger backward a few steps but don't go down.

He throws it to the ground. "And the other one."

I do the same with the one still at my back. He tosses it aside. "Now tell your FBI friends to drop their guns too."

My jaw muscles clench as a fresh wave of anger hits me. Every cell in my body is urging me to rip this bastard's throat out, but I know he's got us beat.

"Guys, do as he says. We've got no move here."

"Now get over there with them," he orders.

I turn and walk over, standing between them, facing the eight guys who have just arrived.

Pellaggio walks in front of us, eyeballing each one of us in turn.

"Who was driving?"

I say nothing, hoping the other two will do the same. Straight away, I know where this is going. I look around quickly for inspiration, for any sliver of hope that will allow me to stop this from unfolding exactly how I know it will. But I've got nothing.

Triple shit.

Johnson takes a step forward. "I was."

I close my eyes and look away, down at the ground.

Why the hell did he have to open his mouth?

That stupid...

I sigh.

I'm getting angry but not at him. Not really. I'm angry at myself because I've allowed myself to be put in this position, where I'm completely helpless and can't do anything to stop what's happening.

I hate it.

Without a word, Pellaggio raises his rifle and opens fire, riddling Johnson with bullets. He aims low and raises the gun as he fires. The sickening, dull squelch of the bullets pounding into Johnson's body is muted by the violent roar of the carbine. He's hit in his thighs, his stomach, his chest, and eventually, his face. His body spasms and jerks around in a crazy dance. His arms flail up and down as he flies backward from the impact and lands a few feet from our car. He rolls and finishes on his front, with what's left of his face looking at us. His remaining features are contorted from the agony he endured in his final breath, and his eyes are wide in a vacant gaze.

Chambers keels over like she just got punched in the gut. "No!"

I quickly put my arms around her to stop her doing anything stupid, like running at Pellaggio. That was my instinct too, but I know better than to let any emotions cloud my judgment now.

Pellaggio looks at Chambers and me in turn, then rests his gun over his shoulder and smiles. "Now... to business."

16

I let go of Chambers. We stand side by side, facing Pellaggio and his eight hired guns.

There's a cool breeze coming across the bay, whirling the lingering smell of gunpowder around us. The sun is high and there's few clouds in the sky. I glance over at Johnson's body, slowly drowning in a pool of blood on the road.

The area around us is strangely deserted. I assume authorities are on their way in force. I hear the faint sound of sirens in the distance, but the traffic's managed to stop all on its own. People and cars are giving us a wide berth.

Pellaggio is standing about fifteen feet away. He's aiming his gun loosely from his hip in our general direction. He's looking at me quietly with a bemused expression on this face.

My eyes narrow as my mind ticks over, visualizing all the ways I could end his twisted little life. And believe me—I *am* going to end his life. Maybe not now, but I will. He's earned the privilege of dying by my hand.

I look past him at his backup. No chance of avoiding getting shot if I make a move. I'll have to bide my time…

I feel Chambers grab my hand and squeeze tightly. She's an exceptional FBI agent from what I've seen, and a smart and capable woman. But now she's absolutely terrified. Her hand is trembling in mine, and she's staring vacantly at the ground. And I can understand why. Nothing can prepare you to see someone you know murdered in cold blood in front of you, knowing your life is in danger and being helpless to do anything about it…

"You're going to come with us, Adrian," says Pellaggio. "We're going to go somewhere a little more private, so you can have a front row seat for the grand finale."

I know that chopper's on its way… I just have to buy a few more minutes.

I take a small step forward, still holding Chambers's hand. "Tell me, Danny Boy. After Heaven's Valley, did you ever suffer from that—what's it called?—survivor's guilt?"

His expression darkens. His jaw muscles clench, but he remains silent.

I continue. "You know, because you lay there bleeding, looking on as your entire family was slaughtered right in front of you. You did nothing as I put a bullet between your old man's eyes. Do you not feel bad about that?"

In the blink of an eye, he rushes toward me. He brings his gun up and—

Oof!

Ah, *shit!*

He slammed the butt hard into my stomach, which knocked the wind out of me. No choice but to drop to one knee and double over.

Sonofabitch.

Still... I touched a nerve there, I think.

I laugh out loud, which is harder than it should be. "My only regret is not going back to finish you off in the hospital when I heard you'd survived."

He raises the gun once more but refrains from smashing it into my face. Instead, he smiles and walks back to where he was originally standing. He turns to face me and taps his temple with his finger. "I'm smarter than you are, Adrian. You and your famous mouth are trying to taunt me, and it won't work. I've spent a year planning this, and I'm too close to the end to let you ruin things now."

In the sky, behind him and his crew, I see the small outline of a helicopter appear.

Bingo. I just need another minute...

"So, tell me, what *is* your endgame here? If all this wasn't for me, what *was* it for?"

He smiles. "Oh, you'll see soon enough."

I see him catch my gaze as I glance at the chopper again.

Shit!

He turns and looks up, seeing it for himself. He looks back at me and laughs. "Ah, you think your rescue is coming, don't you?"

He turns and walks over to one of the two vans that just arrived. He disappears into the back for a moment, then re-appears holding an RPG-7 launcher.

Something else off his shopping list.

"Oh my God..." whispers Chambers beside me.

My eyes go wide. I'm not panicking. It feels more like involuntary shock at what I know he intends to do. "Danny! Leave them alone. They're innocent. Let us call them off at least, then we'll come along with no more fuss. You have my word."

He laughs again, which prompts his men to laugh with him. "Your word, eh? Well, I appreciate that, and your sentiment *is* touching. However, you'll be coming with us anyway, so your proposal is meaningless."

He walks to the middle of the bridge and lifts the launcher up onto his shoulder. The weapon is roughly three feet long and weighs around fifteen pounds. It fires a single high explosive, anti-tank warhead, known as a HEAT missile. It's good for a thousand yards before it self-detonates. It'll destroy that chopper easily.

Every fiber of my being is begging me to run at him, but I know I'd never get close, and I'd die for nothing. I grit my teeth, glaring at him with an anger I wish I didn't have to restrain.

"Danny, don't do it!"

Next to me, Chambers is squeezing my hand so tightly that she might break it. Her fear seems to be subsiding, and I sense her getting angry—a feeling I know all too well.

I'm certain Pellaggio wants us alive, at least until he's executed his plan, so I think it's unlikely he'll kill us just yet. But then, having said that, I have no doubt that he would if I push him too far. Plus, he has eight of his men surrounding us.

We've got no choice but to stand and watch.

The chopper approaches. Pellaggio takes aim. It's still about a mile out, closing fast. It'll be in range of that missile any moment.

"Please, don't!" pleads Chambers.

She instinctively steps forward. I hold her hand firmly, stopping her as all eight guns turn and take aim at us.

I glance sideways. "Grace, don't. I hate this too, but there's nothing we can do unless you wanna die here on this bridge."

She looks at me with tears in her eyes. "How can you be okay with this?"

"I'm not, goddammit! I don't want to watch innocent people die any more than you do, but we die right here, right now, if we try to stop him. Whatever's happening is bigger than us *and* that chopper."

"So, this is what you do, is it? Your life, your job—it's made you into a monster, Adrian, whether you admit it or not. You disgust me!"

I take a deep breath. It hurts to hear her say that, but this isn't the time for sentiment. I look back at the chopper. It's almost within range.

"No more playing games!" shouts Pellaggio, his eyes glued to his target.

A silent, tense moment passes... then he fires.

The missile makes a thunderous *whoosh*, and Chambers jumps in fright.

He laughs like a frat boy at a college party. "Oh, yeah! Woo!"

I watch in horror as the missile flies with deadly intent through the sky, toward the chopper. The pilot tries to bank sharply, away from the bridge, but he isn't quick enough. I see the impact a split-second before I hear it. The chopper disappears in the explosion. It sounds like an eruption. Seconds later, the flaming wreckage plummets toward the ground, leaving a black trail of smoke behind it.

The chopper's burning carcass hits the edge of the bridge and snaps in two. The tail slides across the blacktop and hits a couple of abandoned cars a way in front of us. The cabin section drops over the edge, into the bay below.

Pellaggio watches the scene unfold almost perversely. He turns to us and drops the launcher on the ground next to him. "Now... get in the fucking van, both of you. There's someone you need to meet."

I gesture to Chambers with a slight nod. "At least let her go. Your issues aren't with her. It's me you want."

He smiles and raises his arm, signaling with his hand to the guys behind him. Four of them walk over, purpose and menace in each step. Two move behind us, and the others stand on either side. They prod us with the muzzles of their rifles and usher us over toward the two vans. Two guys climb in the back of the nearest one first, and we're ushered in behind them. There are two wooden benches running the length of each side of the interior, behind the cab. Chambers and I sit opposite each other. Finally, two more guys get in and slam the door shut behind them.

She stares at me with a mixture of emotions on her face.

I stare at the floor, feeling ashamed of myself. I can't even look her in the eye. "Grace, I'm sorry..."

The engine starts up and we drive off.

She lets out a heavy breath. "So am I, Adrian. So am I."

15:58 PDT

I try keeping track in my head of how long we've been traveling, but I soon lose count. It can't be more than twenty minutes or so. Most of the journey has been spent in silence.

Chambers looks distraught and pissed off. I'm not sure whether her anger is directed at me personally, or if it's just a general feeling after being forced into such an awful situation and being so helpless. I think she knows it was the right decision to stand down on the bridge, but I know from experience that doesn't make it any easier to deal with. She's staring at the floor, barely blinking.

In theory, I could take out these four guys with minimal fuss. It's not like I'm restrained in any way...

No... I better not. There's nowhere to run. Plus, a stray bullet in such a confined space could be disastrous.

It's not worth the risk.

I nudge Chambers's foot with mine. She looks up at me. Silently, I gesture to ask if she's all right. She doesn't acknowledge me; she just stares at me blankly for a moment before returning to looking at the floor.

I'll leave her in peace for now. I think she's strong enough to avoid going into shock, but no one can tell you how you should act in a time like this. You've got to get there on your own.

We seem to have been keeping a steady speed for most of the journey, but I can feel us slowing down now. I figure we've turned into a side street or something. A few moments later, the tires crunch on gravel as we gradually slow to a stop.

I hear the cab doors open and close, followed by footsteps. Then the back doors open to reveal Pellaggio standing next to the guy I assume was driving. Neither of them has a weapon. The two guys in the back with us nearest the doors jump out, turn, and aim their weapons at Chambers and me. The guys on the other side of us stand and usher us both out.

I jump down and make a point of stretching my arms and back. I casually glance around but don't recognize where we are. It looks like an old industrial estate of some kind. I stand with my back to the van. The other four guys have parked a few feet behind us and are milling around, weapons loose. There is a large warehouse close by, with four big loading bay doors in a line. The shutters are down on all of them. I scan the skyline, trying to find something identifiable that gives me some idea of where we are, but see nothing of any use.

I look at Chambers, who still has a glazed look on her face. She doesn't look at me, she just keeps her eyes to the ground. I think she's trying to numb herself to the situation, which isn't a bad idea.

I've got a feeling things will get a lot worse before they get better.

But they *will* get better. I just have to bide my time for the right opportunity.

I turn to Pellaggio. "Nice place. Could do with a little work."

He laughs. "Your mouth really doesn't have an off switch, does it?"

I shake my head and smile. "If it does, I haven't found it yet."

"Allow me."

Ow!

He walked over and launched his fist into my face. He connected squarely on my cheekbone. It was a lovely shot. There's no denying that. Hurt like a bitch too.

I take a step back to re-balance myself. I look back at him and laugh. "That all you got? You hit like a girl scout."

I have to keep pushing his buttons and wait for the mistake. If you make anyone angry enough, they will always make a mistake. And that's when you make your move.

Antagonize and capitalize.

He doesn't bite. He simply stares at me with evil eyes and walks away. His group of armed minions follow him, ushering us along with them. We head toward the loading bay doors. I keep looking around, memorizing my surroundings, planning my escape route for later. I just need to let all this play out long enough to learn what's really going on.

As we approach, the shutters on one of the loading bays rumble and splutter into life, slowly moving up. There's a small platform to climb up in front of the doorway. We step up and inside the warehouse.

The interior is spacious. It's one enormous warehouse, not four separate ones like I thought it might be from the outside. It resembles an aircraft hangar. The roof isn't anywhere near high enough but looking at the vast floor space, I would almost expect to see an airplane parked here. Along the walls and in the middle of the floor are tall racks of metal shelving, rusted and long abandoned. Toward the back wall, someone's used plywood to section off a few rooms, creating a makeshift office area.

We walk halfway across the warehouse floor and stop. The men with guns move and form a loose, wide circle, surrounding Chambers and me. Her glazed-over look gives way to alertness and concern, her eyes flicking left and right at the circle of assault rifles pointing at us.

Pellaggio's in the circle with us, smiling his wicked smile. My eyes narrow as I stare at him, remembering everything he's put me through in such a short space of time. Not to mention the innocent lives lost in the process and the injuries he inflicted upon Josh.

I can't wait to kill him.

He holds his arms out to the sides. "So, Adrian. Here we are... *finally*! I've waited a long time to get you all to myself. Patience isn't one of my virtues, so it's a relief for all the games to finally be over."

I glance around the circle, gesturing to all the armed men. "I'd hardly say you have me all to yourself, Danny Boy.

Looks like you're sharing me with all your boyfriends. What say you send them all away and we settle this like gentlemen, yeah?"

In an instant, his expression darkens, and his face changes to one of pure evil. He lunges forward with lightning speed, producing a knife from behind him as he does. He takes me by surprise; I didn't expect him to be capable of such speed and precision. He grabs Chambers by her arm and drags her toward him.

Shit!

He pulls her close, turning her so that she's pinned with her back pressed against him. He moves the knife to her throat and presses the sharp metal against her flesh. His face is contorted with rage.

"Fuck you, Adrian!" he screams. "You're going to suffer, and you're going to watch everyone die before I end you! You took everything from me, and now you will feel the full extent of my wrath!"

I take a step back, dropping into a loose fighting stance, reflexively. I'm unarmed, surrounded by eight men who aren't. I'm sure I've been in worse situations, though none spring instantly to mind. I think back to my first morning in San Francisco, when the FBI had me in the exact same situation in front of City Hall. These guys probably won't exercise as much restraint with their trigger fingers.

I look at Chambers, who seems to have put her opinions of me to one side and is staring at me with frightened, pleading eyes. It's ironic that the closest thing I have to an ally right now is an FBI agent. It makes me realize how dependent I am on Josh and his ability to give me information that can save my ass. I've not been doing so great without him. He'd better pull through, or I'm screwed!

Come on, Adrian. You need to turn this around.

"Danny, let her go."

"Why should I? What do you care about one more victim?" He presses the blade harder against Chambers's throat. "You're Adrian Hell, master assassin! You've got more blood on your hands than anyone here. How can you plead for someone's life when you've taken so many yourself? What gives you the right?"

"Hey, I only take contracts to kill people who deserve it. Bad people who've done bad things. You know, like your old man?"

A primal anger erupts in his eyes. He points the knife at me, giving Chambers a moment's reprieve. "You don't get to talk about him!"

Jesus, this guy's losing it. It's almost like he has a split personality. He can flip and go from zero to crazy in a heartbeat. I need to be careful. I might have underestimated exactly how pissed off Pellaggio is.

I raise my hands defensively. "Okay, fair enough. Let's talk about *you*. Why call yourself the Shark?"

Pellaggio visibly calms down, and his chest swells a little with pride. "Because the shark is a beast... a *predator*... honed to genetic perfection through evolution. It's immune to all known diseases, it can smell blood from miles away, and it strikes without conscience or fear. It's nature's ultimate killer!"

"Fuck me, you're insane! It was definitely a mistake not going back to finish you off when I had the chance. I would've been doing the world a favor."

"I'm gonna—"

"Danny, stop playing with him. You're wasting time."

The voice came from the back of the warehouse. It was calm and calculated. The outline of a figure emerges from the plywood office area at the back. There isn't much light coming from back there, so I can't make out features, but the voice sounds oddly familiar.

Pellaggio smiles and turns to greet the silhouetted figure as they approach. The light is slowly washing over them, revealing them piece by piece from the bottom up. I see shiny, black shoes, a light gray suit...

Just as the light is about to reveal their face, I feel a sharp explosion of pain in the back of my—

17

??:??

"Hello, Adrian."

I open my eyes. The bright light forces me to squint, so I close them again. I frown as I feel a dull ache throbbing at the base of my skull, growing worse now that I'm aware of the buzzing from the fluorescent lighting overhead.

Okay, let's leave the eyes for a moment.

How long have I been out?

I'll try moving instead.

I twist my shoulders but feel my arms bound together behind me at the wrists.

Shit.

I try to stand, but my ankles are tied to whatever I'm sitting on.

Double shit.

Fine, let's try the eyes again.

I open them slowly, letting them gradually adjust to the light.

"Wakey, wakey, Adrian."

There's that voice again.

Who *is* that? I recognize it from somewhere...

I blink rapidly to clear the last of the fuzz and look around. The first thing I see is Jimmy Manhattan sitting in front of me, perched on the end of a desk.

And... triple shit!

I knew I recognized the voice. Great.

I frown again as I try to process the fact he's here and figure out why. I look around the rest of the room. I'm guessing I'm in one of the makeshift offices at the back of the warehouse. The space is small—I'd say no bigger than fifteen by fifteen. The door must be behind me because I can't see it from where I am.

I look down and see I'm sitting on an old, wooden chair in the center of the room. In front of me is a desk—the surface of which is clear, except for Manhattan, who's sitting on it and staring at me.

Jimmy fucking Manhattan.

He's the last person I expected to see again, although the more I think about it, it does explain a lot—namely, Pellaggio's bankroll and the intricate planning of his attacks.

I stare at him and raise an eyebrow. "What the hell are you doing here?"

He smiles. It doesn't reach his eyes. It's all business, with no humor in it. "I'm helping young Daniel get revenge for the death of his family."

I nod slowly. "Ah, okay. So, what are you *really* doing here?"

He smiles again, like we're old friends sharing a joke... like he didn't really expect me to buy his first answer. "I've always said you were smarter than you look."

"Not *that* smart. I've no idea how you managed to track

me down in the first place. I took the San Francisco job on a whim..."

"I know you did. I was worried I wasn't subtle enough at the start, but once your little British friend was out of the picture, I knew you'd have too much going on to notice..."

He lets his words trail off, and my brain starts ticking over.

What does he mean?

My mind's racing in a thousand different directions at once, and I can't focus on any one thing. I have to figure out how to get out of here without getting killed—which seems to be getting harder and harder to do. I'm also worried about Chambers. I have no idea where she is or what's happening to her.

I take some deep breaths, calming myself.

Focus, Adrian...

They've been playing me from the start, setting me up so that I'd be right where they wanted me when they wanted me there. But how?

Wait a minute...

Oh, you sonofabitch!

I shake my head, angry at myself. "The Richard Blake job was a set-up, wasn't it?"

Manhattan smiles again and nods but remains silent, like he's letting me come to the conclusions myself.

"There was no gangster. You're Nathan Tam, aren't you?"

Nathan Tam. Hang on...

"...which is an anagram of Manhattan. Goddammit!"

He laughs. "Well done, Adrian. All on your own too. As I say, I was worried I hadn't been subtle enough, but it's all worked out perfectly."

"So, who was Richard Blake? And why did you want him dead?"

"Well, he wasn't a drug user, obviously. He was on Roberto's payroll and then found himself on mine. He'd served his purpose, so I killed two birds with one stone, so to speak."

"Sonofabitch. And how have you managed to stay one step ahead of the FBI all this time?"

"Ah, now that would be telling, wouldn't it?"

"Yes, it would. Which is kind of why I asked, asshole."

Manhattan stands. "All in good time." He leans over the desk and reaches to open a drawer on the opposite side. He retrieves a small box, which he places on the surface in front of me. "First, you and I have some unfinished business."

Hmmm.

Jimmy Manhattan. A small box. Me tied to a chair.

We've been here before...

The two-inch-long scar below my eye itches—a psychological reaction as I recall the last time I was in this situation, back in Heaven's Valley last year.

Manhattan opens the box and takes out a surgeon's scalpel.

I roll my eyes. "Oh, come on! Really, Jimmy? At least try something original, please."

He shrugs. "I like to stick with what works."

He moves toward me, pointing the scalpel at my face. The lights above reflect off the blade, shining into my eyes and forcing me to squint. He leans over me, his face inches from mine with the blade between us.

"Now the privilege of killing the mighty Adrian Hell belongs to Daniel. But I think I owe you some payback nonetheless."

I keep my eye on the scalpel, trying to move my head away from it. "How'd you figure that? The last time we spoke, I saved your life."

"The last time we spoke, you hit me in the face with your gun and left me on the floor of a portable cabin, surrounded by a group of heavily armed Russian terrorists."

"Well, if you're going to argue over the details..."

"And then you had me arrested for a murder I paid *you* to commit."

"Oh, that was just a joke between friends. C'mon..."

"And now I get to say to you the one thing I've been dying to say for almost a year."

"Do I wanna know?"

Manhattan stands up straight, tosses the scalpel in the air, and watches as it spins around. As it falls, he catches it by the handle and jams it deep into my left shoulder, just above my pectoral muscle.

Ah!

I grit my teeth, trying to suppress a yell of pain.

Fuck!

He holds it there and leans forward. Our noses are almost touching. His eyes are burning with rage. "Now we're even, you sonofabitch!"

I feel blood start to run from the wound. I take quick, deep breaths to counter the pain and focus.

He regards me for a moment, the anger seeming to leave as quickly as it came. He walks past me and out of the room. I'm sitting here with a goddamn scalpel sticking out of me, tied to a chair.

Shit!

Think, Adrian—think!

I doubt I'll have long to wait before Manhattan or someone else comes back. I have to get out of here. I look around the room and see nothing that's any use to me. I jerk my whole body up, but I'm held in place to the chair. It achieves nothing besides making the chair squeak a little.

Wait a minute.

I'm tied to an old wooden chair.

Hmmm...

I rock forward, so I'm essentially standing up but still positioned like I'm sitting down. I don't have much mobility in my legs, but I bounce up and down on my toes, trying to build a little momentum. After a few moments, I jump as high as I can and dive forward, twisting in the air so that I land on my back. The impact hurts like hell, especially in my arms, but the chair shatters under my bodyweight.

I'm glad that worked. Otherwise, I would've looked really stupid!

Now that I'm free of the chair, I bring my knees up to my chest and move my arms down the back of my legs and over my feet, so they're in front of me. I reach up and quickly yank the scalpel out of my shoulder, ignoring the bolt of pain that shoots through my arm and chest.

I turn it in my hands and hastily cut through the ties on my wrists and ankles. I lie on the floor for a moment, slightly out of breath, processing the pain that's pulsating through my entire body.

I'm definitely getting too old for this shit.

It feels like I'm saying that a lot lately.

Fuck it. I don't have time to hurt right now. I'll do it later. Maybe.

I drag myself up and inspect the wound in my shoulder. It's deep, but since it was a narrow blade, the overall damage is minimal. I can certainly live with it. I throw the scalpel on the desk and instinctively reach behind me for my Berettas.

Shit. They're both on the Golden Gate Bridge...

I pick the scalpel back up. It'll have to do for now.

I hear a long, high-pitched scream from somewhere nearby.

Grace!

I burst out the door and step out into a narrow corridor between the two rows of crudely constructed plywood offices. Quickly, I scan left and right. There's no sign of anyone, and I can't tell which direction the scream came from.

When in doubt, go left.

I hold the scalpel in my hand, upside-down by the handle to conceal the blade against the underside of my forearm, ready to strike should anyone discover me.

This is how a professional holds a knife—so you never see the blade until it's too late. If you see someone holding it like a popsicle, waving it around in front of them, don't worry about it. They have no idea what they're doing, and you'll be able to disarm them easily enough.

I move as quietly as I can and as quickly as I dare. I pause at every closed door, listening for movement behind. Every small room looks the same—the doors cut from the same plywood as the walls. A rush job of simply cutting a hole in the wall and then re-attaching the piece with hinges.

There's no sign of life so far. I press on and soon reach the end of the corridor with no success.

I should've gone right—dammit!

I turn back. The door nearest me opens. One of the eight armed minions who brought me here walks out. His M4 carbine is slung over his shoulder, hanging loose by its strap. He has some papers in his hand.

He looks at me.

We both freeze, like deer caught in a set of oncoming headlights.

It feels like I've been staring at him for hours. I should probably kill him.

My brain re-engages and my killer instincts take over. I

rush forward, catching him off-guard. I clamp my hand over his mouth and jam the scalpel into the side of his stomach. I feel it pierce through his flesh. I push it until it can't penetrate him any further, then yank it out and jam it into his neck, just next to my hand. Blood spurts out in a thin fountain. He makes a brief noise, but my hand muffles it.

His death is quick and reasonably painless. I feel his lifeless body sag against me. Leaving the scalpel in his neck, I take his weight in both arms and guide him gently to the floor, trying to keep any noise to a minimum. I lay him down and step over his body, opening the door he's just closed. I prop it open with the back of my foot, bend down, grab his ankles, and drag him into the room. I take the carbine from his shoulder and check him for spare magazines. I quickly leave the room and close the door gently.

I take a deep breath, wincing as my shoulder wound throbs, reminding me it's still there.

That's one down and—including Pellaggio and Manhattan—nine to go.

I look at the M4 assault rifle in my hands.

The next one won't be going as quietly...

I make my way back up the corridor, keeping as low as I can. Just past the room Manhattan had me in is a crossroads. There are more offices straight ahead, arranged exactly like the ones behind me. If I go left, it'll take me back to the main warehouse floor, whereas going right seems to lead to an exit out the back, which is worth noting for later.

I press myself against the wall and peer around the corner. I see a group of five men standing in the middle of the large space, in line with the shutter, but I'm too far away to make out any features. From the outlines, I'm sure none of them are Pellaggio or Manhattan.

I can probably get the drop on them and take them out

with minimal fuss, but this isn't my first rodeo. A full-frontal assault is time-consuming and noisy. Yes, I'll inevitably dispose of these five, but I leave myself open to the four guys I've not found yet—who are likely somewhere ahead of me. The first sign of noise, they'll outflank me, and I'll be dead. I'll save them for last when there's no one to help them.

I quickly cross over the gap, ensuring I remain unseen, and carry on along the corridor. Up ahead, I hear voices. I pause halfway and drop to one knee, raising my rifle. The door on my left is slightly open. There's a bright, fluorescent light shining out through the narrow gap. I listen closely...

"Get the hell off me!" says a woman's voice.

That's definitely Chambers.

My jaw muscles tighten, and I get short of breath as I feel my anger start to rise. While there's always an exception to every rule, I generally don't condone violence against women. If they're trying to kill you, then fair enough. But you don't hurt them just for the sake of it.

I hear Manhattan talking to Pellaggio. I strain to pick out the words.

"Danny, stay focused. You can have your fun when all this is over, but for now... we carry on as planned. Understand?"

"Yeah, I understand, Jimmy. But Adrian and this FBI bitch stay here. I've got big plans for them when we're done with this city."

Well, *that* doesn't sound too promising...

I have to avoid firing my gun until I'm ready to engage the large group on the main floor. I'll be a sitting duck if they decide to come running right now. But at the same time, I have to get in there and rescue Chambers. With Manhattan and Pellaggio in the same room, I can't pass up the opportunity to take them both out and put an end to all this. Rushing in there is a stupid plan, and it'll likely end up with either Chambers or me being killed... or both of us.

Think, Adrian—think!

If only I could ring Josh...

Well, I can't, so I'll have to just stick with what I know.

Fuck it!

I stand and kick the door open.

In my mind, the entire scene slows down. I scan the room, which looks identical to the one I woke up in—even down to the desk and wooden chair, which Chambers is sitting on. She has her back to me. Manhattan and Pellaggio are standing behind the desk in front of her. Both are unarmed. As I enter, I see one of the minions, who *is* armed, stood with his rifle aimed at her.

Everyone looks up, their faces a mix of shock and confusion. The guy in the corner swings his gun lazily toward me, but I snap to him, drop to one knee, and fire a three-round burst into his chest. The force of the impact pushes him backward and he hits the wall. He slides down to the floor, leaving a crimson stain behind him.

I stand up again quickly and take aim at Manhattan and Pellaggio.

Everything resumes normal speed.

"Hey, fellas. Miss me?"

Pellaggio snarls. "What the fuck? How did you get free?"

Hmmm, what would Josh say right now?

I smile. "A magician never reveals his secrets."

I see his hand move behind him. I quickly adjust my aim. "Both hands front and center, asshole."

He reluctantly complies.

I move round to my right, drawing level with Chambers. "Grace, you all right?"

She nods. "I'm fine. Just get me out of here."

I look up at Manhattan. "You heard the lady. Untie her."

I hear commotion close by, outside the room. I assume the five guys from the warehouse are coming to see what's happening...

I emphasize the fact my rifle's pointing at him by nodding at it. "Today would be nice, shit-for-brains."

Manhattan takes a deep breath and opens the top drawer of the desk, pulling out another blade. Not a scalpel this time but a combat knife with a leather grip and a long blade that has one serrated edge.

I raise an eyebrow. "Shit, Jimmy, do you keep knives in every desk you have? Christ!"

He holds the blade in his hand for a moment, seemingly weighing up what options he has.

I take a step forward. "Hey, hey, hey—nice and easy, you old bastard..."

Manhattan's smiling, but he complies without incident. He moves behind Chambers and cuts the ties on her wrists, then crouches to do the same with her ankles. I step back, almost behind the door, so I can cover the room and everyone in it with ease. He stands slowly. His narrow, unblinking eyes stare a hole right through me. His entire body is visibly tense, the rage seeping from his pores. But he doesn't move.

Chambers stands, rubbing her wrists to get the blood flowing. She turns to look at me. She doesn't smile, but it looks like she's past hating me. Her eyes betray her feelings —a mixture of regret, sorrow, anger, and determination.

She marches over to the dead minion and picks up his carbine. She turns to face Manhattan. Without a word, she slams the butt of the rifle into the side of his head. He drops almost instantly to his knees.

She glares down at him as he reels from the blow. "Bastard!" She quickly raises the gun, aiming it at Pellaggio. "And you, you deluded prick—start talking right now. What the hell's going on here?"

Pellaggio looks at me, apparently surprised at her approach to interrogation. I simply raise an eyebrow, smile, and shrug, as if to say, *you're on your own*. I look at her admiringly. Now I've seen her in action, I like her even more.

I swap sides, so my back's to her, allowing me to cover the door. I can still hear the guys outside. I assume the reason they've not yet rushed in, guns a-blazing, is because they know their bosses are in here.

At my feet, Manhattan's trying to stand. I kick him in his side, and he collapses on his front, groaning in pain. If I thought *I'm* too old for this shit, he *definitely* is!

"C'mon, talk, Danny..." urges Chambers. "Why are you doing all this?"

I look over my shoulder at him. "And don't feed us the bullshit about this being all about me—we all know there's more to it than that."

He smiles at us. A sickening smile filled with far more confidence than his current situation deserves. "Fine. You wanna know what I'm doing?" He pauses for effect, like an asshole. "I'm going to start a war!"

18

??:??

Manhattan's lying on the floor, trying to tell Pellaggio to keep quiet, but he doesn't have the energy. His words are coming out as a dull groan. He gives up and focuses on trying to get to his feet again.

Pellaggio's statement was dramatic and cause for great concern, but I don't understand it.

Chambers steps toward him, adjusting her aim. "Details. Now!"

I'm aware time's running out for us, so whatever we're going to get out of Pellaggio, we have to get it fast.

He sighs wearily. "In a way, this *is* all about you, Adrian. About your actions in Heaven's Valley."

I frown. I don't take my eyes off the door. "Make your mind up, jackass. I thought you said this *wasn't* about taking revenge on me?"

"Oh, I *will* have my revenge for you killing my entire family. But this isn't just personal—it's business. My father lost millions of dollars and a significant amount of assets because of the betrayal of his business associates and the actions of a small few."

Chambers half-turns to me, keeping one eye on Pellaggio. "Adrian, what's he talking about?"

I run what he's just said through my head. Starting a war... loss of money and assets... actions of a small few...

There's only one logical explanation.

"He's referring to Dark Rain. My guess is, he blames them for his daddy's business deal falling through because *they* were given the land *he* wanted."

Manhattan has managed to crawl over to the desk and is using it to drag himself to his feet. He looks exhausted from the effort. As he shuffles to get comfortable on it, he glares at Pellaggio. He looks pissed at him for opening his mouth. He's breathing heavily through his nose; his lips are clamped shut, forming a thin line of frustration. He looks like he wants to say something but keeps stopping himself. I doubt he'll be thinking of a way to talk himself out of this. He's smart enough to know when he's beaten.

I watch his personal dilemma. "Something to add, Jimmy?"

Manhattan lets out a heavy sigh. "Roberto blamed GlobaTech and Dark Rain for his losses, which were... considerable. They took the land he was supposed to buy, and then you came along and took it from *them* before giving it away. He was planning how to recoup those losses when you... ah... paid him a visit."

"I ain't here for the re-run, ass-wipe. What's happening here and now?"

Pellaggio steps in front of Manhattan before he can say anything else. "We're gonna devastate this city and make sure those Russian bastards take the blame!"

I see the venom in his eyes—the unwavering belief in what he wants to do.

Chambers and I exchange a worried look.

What else can he possibly intend to do?

Actually, I've just remembered his shopping list. He can do pretty much whatever he wants.

I keep my gun aimed at the door but glance over at him. "That's the most ridiculous thing I've ever heard. You do realize Dark Rain were just as pissed with Russia as they were with everyone else? And everybody knows that—including the U.S. government. Framing the Russians and hoping the U.S. will retaliate against them won't achieve anything. It's causing chaos for nothing!"

His eyes grow wide with an insane anger. "I've lost everything!"

Even Manhattan's looking on with curiosity. It's almost like he's never been fully aware of Pellaggio's torment until now.

"Because of you, I have no one. But it doesn't start with you. If you trace it all back to the beginning, it's because of those Russian bastards that the whole thing happened the way it did. And you're all gonna pay!"

Manhattan holds up a hand. "The, ah... the events unfolding now... they've been meticulously planned for almost a year. The things that are in motion won't be stopped—by you or anyone else."

Chambers shakes her head. "Call your men off. This is over. There's no need for any more bloodshed."

I admire her optimism and her ability to remain professional under the circumstances, but things are far from over. We're still outnumbered, and we still have no real idea what Pellaggio intends to do next. But I know they won't be coming along quietly.

I move over to her and nudge her arm with my elbow. "Grace, we have to move. Can you cover these two?"

She sighs and nods. "Yes."

No doubt, no fear... just a job that needs to be done.

"Good. We're leaving. Stay behind me."

She organizes her prisoners, keeping them both covered with the rifle, and stays a few steps behind me.

I notice we require little interaction to function as a highly effective team. It's nice. I remember how I got it wrong the last time I found myself in a similar situation, but things are different with Grace. I'm not dealing with another killer, like me. I'm dealing with the law. And I know she's got my back—not because she agrees with working alongside a *bad guy* but because it's simply the right thing to do to get the job done.

I open the door slowly and edge out, trying to see where the other guys are. I have two dead and two in custody, which leaves six still active. Five are about to die. My guess is the remaining minion is outside by the vans.

I keep low and make my way slowly into the corridor. There's no sign of life, but I know they're here.

I hold up my hand and gesture like I'm patting a dog. "Stay low. And that means all of you. I don't want either of you getting shot in any crossfire." I turn to look at them both. "But make no mistake—step out of line, and she'll put a bullet in you."

They both look at Chambers and she smiles in return.

I make my way to the crossroads in the corridor, press myself against the wall, and peer around the corner into the main warehouse.

The plywood splinters inches from my head as a hail of bullets comes flying toward me.

"Shit!"

I dive back around the corner for cover. I look behind me down the corridor. Chambers has stepped away from Manhattan and Pellaggio; she's covering them tightly but from a small distance. From the position she's in, she has all the angles covered and enough distance that they can't surprise her.

Despite the gunfire, I manage to smile. She never ceases to impress me.

I point my carbine around the corner and fire blind, trying to buy myself some time. I peer around the corner again. I can see four out of the five guys, all taking cover behind boxes or shelving, poised and ready to shoot on sight. The fifth guy must be closer to me, likely against one of the front walls of the office area, just around the corner at the end as I'm looking now.

I can't take them all out in one move because they're too spread out. Plus, I have to make sure Manhattan and Pellaggio remain unharmed until I can figure out how to get them out of here.

I consider my options. I can either stand here trading potshots with them, hoping I kill them before I run out of bullets, or...

I stand and look Chambers in the eye. "I need to ask you to trust me."

She regards me for a moment, her hard, gray eyes unblinking. "I do. Do whatever you have to do to get us out of here."

"Okay."

I walk over to them, take hold of my rifle, and slam the butt into both Manhattan's and Pellaggio's faces in turn. They fall to the floor. Pellaggio is dazed but awake. Manhattan's out.

"Wait here."

Chambers stares at me, bewildered. "Well, I could've done *that*..."

She sounded a little dejected that she didn't get a chance to hit either of them herself.

I walk back to the corner and slowly peer round at the large space in the center of the warehouse. Then I lean around and slide my rifle across the floor as far as I can toward the group of men.

"Adrian! What are you doing?"

Her voice was hushed and serious. I wink at her and smile. "I told you to trust me."

"You're insane."

"Yeah, so people keep telling me."

She tuts. "I wonder why?"

I poke my head around the corner. "Okay! You guys win! I'm unarmed and I'm coming out."

I take a deep breath, stand up, and walk out onto the main floor.

The sun is shining in through the raised shutter. Outside, I see the two vans parked near the bay doors. There's a light breeze circulating around the warehouse. I can't tell if it's just drafty in here, or if it's blowing from out there.

I've got my hands up, elbows bent, palms open, facing the front—my body language gives a clear message of surrender and compliance. The first of them emerges from cover and points his assault rifle at me. A moment later, his friends appear and do the same.

I look at them in turn. "Hey, take it easy, fellas. I've got no weapon. Your boss has my friend, and I know when I'm beat."

They congregate in a wide circle around me, similar to when we first arrived, except slightly smaller as there's only

197

five of them left. They're holding their weapons loose at their sides, sensing no threat from the surrounded, unarmed man.

Like I hoped they would.

As they move in closer, their formation becomes more rigid. I stand facing the loading bay door. I quickly assess the group and plan my next few moves. I think of their positioning like a clock face, and in my head, I assign names accordingly.

I've only got one shot at this and I need to be fast. I'm using every trick in the book to make sure I live, and they don't. This way, I only need to look at them once to remember where they are, so I don't need to constantly remind myself while I'm working out my attack.

I have two guys just behind me. I'll call them Four and Eight. There are two more just in front of me. They're Ten and Two. The remaining guy is dead ahead. Hello, Twelve.

I lower my hands and hold them out in front of me as a further gesture of submission. I smile. "Be gentle, boys."

As expected, Twelve steps forward to restrain me. As he approaches, I discreetly slide my foot behind me about three inches. I bring my heel up so that all my weight is on my toes, giving myself some extra leverage. I let him get within a few feet of me...

I push off with my back foot and explode forward. My forehead connects right between his eyes. Bone crunches under the impact as I shatter his nose, flattening it into a crimson mess which erupts across his face.

He starts falling. I have to be quick...

I use my momentum to fall forward into him and grab the barrel of his gun. I push with my body weight and swing him around by his rifle, spinning him so that we swap places —his body is now shielding mine. As he turns, I slide the rifle off his shoulder and hold it by its barrel, like a baseball bat.

No one's reacted yet, and I'm taking advantage of every valuable second of surprise I have left.

I grab him by his collar and push him as hard as I can to my left while stepping to the right. He collides with Two and they fall to the floor, both temporarily neutralized.

I make my way counterclockwise and swing the rifle like I'm aiming for the fences. I connect with Ten, smashing the butt into the side of his head. Maintaining my swing, I follow through and around, spinning in a full circle as I duck low. I come around a second time and hit Eight on the outside of his knee. The impact takes his legs out from under him, dropping him hard.

I come to a stop on one knee and flip the rifle around in my hands, ready to shoot. I fire two short bursts at Four before he has time to process what's happening and react. I hit him in both legs, and he goes down screaming in pain.

I stand and look around. Two is just getting to his feet, pushing his semi-conscious colleague off to the side. I walk over as he's standing and thrust my knee forward, catching him sweetly on the side of his face, right on the bend of his jaw. He's out before he hits the floor.

I turn a slow circle, taking deep breaths to control my adrenaline. I look down at each of the five bodies. Satisfied it's over, I look back at the corridor. Chambers is standing at the crossroad with her mouth open, staring at me. We lock eyes for a moment, but I turn away. She's not going to like this, but it's not over quite yet.

This is war.

I level the carbine and fire a three-round burst into each guy's chest. Their bodies twitch as the bullets drill into them.

I look at each of them again, confirming they're dead.

Now it's over.

I hear a noise behind me. I spin around to see Chambers on all fours, holding the back of her head. I start running toward her and hear a gunshot from somewhere out of sight. Pellaggio appears, pausing to stare at me and smile.

I pick up the pace. "Hey! Don't you even think about it, asshole!"

I try to aim with the carbine, but I can't get it in position for an accurate shot while I'm running, and I don't want to risk hitting Grace. I make it to her just as he turns and runs down the corridor that leads out back.

"Shit!"

I crouch beside her to make sure she's okay. I look left. Manhattan is lying flat on his back with a bullet hole in his chest. I look over at the exit.

Should I go after him?

I put my hand on Chambers's shoulder as she groans from what I assume is the beginning of a moderate concussion.

No... I found him once. I'll find him again.

I help Chambers to her feet. "What the hell happened? Are you all right?"

She nods carefully, still holding the back of her head. "It was... Pellaggio. He got the drop on me. I'm sorry."

I shake my head and smile. "Don't worry about it."

I grab her hand and squeeze gently, trying to offer some comfort and reassurance. She looks up at me and smiles groggily.

I nod over at Manhattan. "What happened to him?"

She shrugs. "I don't know. I must've blacked out for a moment when Pellaggio hit me on the head."

"I don't understand..."

She sighs. "Adrian, it wasn't me. It was Pellaggio. *He* shot Manhattan."

Outside, I hear the faint sound of doors slamming.

Pellaggio must've made it to the vans...

I look at Chambers, who's staring toward the main doors, clearly having heard the same thing I did. She waves me away dismissively.

Gun in hand, I turn and sprint across the warehouse toward the loading bay doors. At full speed, I exit and jump down the small ledge just as the van is pulling away. Pellaggio leans out the passenger window, produces a pistol, and fires in my direction. I skid to a halt on the gravel and drop to the ground in one movement to avoid the bullets. The second he stops firing, I'm straight back up. I level the gun and take aim, but the van's too far away for it to be worth my effort.

Pellaggio is in the wind again, at least for now.

I look up to the sky and close my eyes, screwing my face in frustration. "Fuck!"

My voice echoes around the deserted industrial complex.

I walk back inside and over to Chambers, who's managed to get to her feet. "You okay?"

"Yeah, I'm fine. No luck?"

"No, he'd already got away."

She looks down at Manhattan. "He's still breathing. We should get him to a hospital."

"Or we could leave him here to die. Saves me a bullet later."

"Adrian, he's got valuable information on Pellaggio's plans. Now that he's just been shot by his little protégé, he might just be a bit more willing to tell us about it."

"Huh... fair point." I take my phone out of my pocket and hand it to her. "Here, make the call."

I leave her and walk down the corridors at the back of the warehouse. I may as well explore each room—I might find something useful.

I spend a few minutes and try all the rooms on this corridor, except the one I found Chambers in. I know there's nothing in there.

No luck.

I head down the opposite corridor, starting in the room across from the one I woke up in. It's where I dumped the first guy's body. I step inside and over his corpse. I'd left without looking around, but it looks like I've hit the jackpot here. He was holding some papers when I killed him. There are more scattered over the desk in here too. I gather them all together and have a quick look over them. They don't mean much to me, but I'll take them for Wallis. He might find something useful in them.

I fold them up and tuck them inside my jacket. I leave the room and head back to the warehouse floor to find Chambers.

She turns as I approach. "An ambulance is on its way. I called the field office too. Wallis and the military liaison are going to meet us at the hospital. They have an update for us, which sounds positive."

"Well, I just found some documents that might be useful —diagrams and receipts, mostly. I'll let Wallis look over them."

We fall silent for a moment.

I glance at the floor. "Did you... ah... did you tell Wallis about Johnson when you spoke to him?"

She shakes her head. "I couldn't do it. I'm a coward."

I should maybe try to comfort her. I take a step forward,

but she rushes close to me and throws her arms around me, burying her head in my chest as the tears start to flow. My arms are out to the sides as she holds onto me. I wasn't expecting this. I'm not entirely sure what's appropriate here. I mean, sure, it's been a stressful day. I've grown accustomed to car chases, being shot at, getting blown up, and seeing innocent people die. But Grace? I think it's all a little too much. I imagine seeing her colleague gunned down tipped her over the edge. That's when she fell silent on the bridge. I initially thought it was anger toward me, but looking at her now, it's clear she's in the early stages of shock.

I slowly put my arms around her and hold her as she sobs. No amount of training or experience can prepare you for days like today. I look over at Manhattan, lying on the floor, wounded by his own man, and it sets my spider sense tingling.

The worst is still to come...

19

The ambulance didn't take long to reach us. Chambers called her office first, and they triangulated our location from her cellular signal. We traveled in the back while EMTs worked on Manhattan. He's apparently going to survive, but he's in bad shape.

We arrived at San Francisco General and found Wallis waiting for us at the main entrance. Chambers talked him through what happened, which he understandably struggled to wrap his head around. Then he'd asked where Johnson was. Chambers took him to one side, presumably to break the news to him. They were partners and the news will hit him hard. That's not a conversation I'd want to have.

I intended to stay with Manhattan, but the nurses wheeled him away for surgery. So, with nothing else to do, I figured I'd go and see how Josh is getting on. A nurse approached me as I went to enter his room and asked who I was. I told her I'm family. She smiled sympathetically and explained that his vitals are improving steadily, but he isn't out of the woods just yet. They've brought him out of the coma, but they're keeping him sedated. She checked his charts and his various drips and machines, then left me alone.

I'm standing at his bedside. He's still unconscious. I look down at him. He's wearing an oxygen mask and has wires connected to small pads stuck to his chest. There's an IV feed in his hand and a small crocodile clip on his index finger. The machine next to him is still beeping away, steady and stubborn.

I can't help but think about how everything would've played out if he'd been there, helping me like he always does. I couldn't have avoided getting blown up on the pier. Could I have prevented what happened on the bridge, had Josh been in my ear? Maybe. But I've learned from experience there's no point beating myself up about all the things I could've done differently. Things have played out the way they've played out, so that's what we have to work with. End of story.

What's that saying Josh sometimes comes out with? *There's no use crying over spilt milk.* I smile and think about how annoyingly upbeat and British he always is. I could definitely do with some of his trademark enthusiasm right now.

A short knock on the door interrupts me. I turn to see Chambers standing there, with Wallis by her side. Without a word, he walks up to me and extends his hand. I shake it without hesitation. "I'm sorry about Johnson. He might have been an asshole to me, but he was a good agent and a decent guy. He didn't deserve what happened."

Wallis nods his appreciation. He glances at Chambers, who's still over by the door, and then back at me. "Way I hear things, as bad as it was, it could've been worse if it wasn't for you."

I flash a smile. I have no wish to receive any praise for my actions during the last twenty-four hours. "Agent Chambers said you have an update?"

"Ah... yeah... I've been working with the liaison from Hawthorne on the weaponry Pellaggio bought from Turner. They also had a look at the case and have come up with some good theories. I'm hoping the papers you brought from the warehouse will back some of them up."

I reach into my jacket pocket and hand all the documents over to him. "Knock yourself out."

Wallis takes them and leaves, presumably heading back to the field office to begin his analysis.

I look at Chambers. "How are you holdin' up?"

She shrugs and shows me a tough smile. "I'll live. The doctor already gave me a once-over." She nods at my shoulder wound. "How are you?"

I look down at it and raise my eyebrow. "Oh, yeah... forgot all about that, to be honest. I'm fine. I'll get someone to look at it before I leave here."

"Make sure you do."

We regard each other for a moment in silence. "Hey, this liaison sounds like a team player. Bet you're glad they're cooperating with the FBI so willingly?"

"Actually, they said they were doing it as a favor to you."

I frown. "A favor to me? I don't understand."

"And I know how much that must piss you off!" says a man's voice from outside the room.

Huh? The voice is familiar, but I'm too confused to place it.

I look over just as Robert Clark walks into the room and stands beside Chambers. "Hello, Adrian."

Robert Clark is a high-level employee of GlobaTech Industries. He got promoted when I executed Ted Jackson in Heaven's Valley last year, who held his position at the time. He's the one who figured out GlobaTech's involvement in that whole affair and put an end to it, helping me take out Roberto Pellaggio *and* stop Dark Rain from killing a lot of innocent people.

Josh has kept in touch with them to keep the relationship alive, thinking they could prove a valuable ally. I've not personally seen or spoken to Bob since I left him on that highway, shortly after blowing half of Nevada into space.

I get over the surprise and refocus. "Hey, Bobby. What are you doing here?"

He's still smiling, probably at the shocked look on my face. "I was asked to work with the FBI on behalf of Hawthorne Air Base."

"So, *you're* the liaison? I was expecting someone... you know, from the military?"

Clark shrugs. "GlobaTech works closely with Hawthorne because a lot of the weapons we make go through there. Our R&D boys made some of the stuff that Pellaggio, Jr. now has in his possession, so we have a vested interest in getting this whole debacle resolved. How's that going, by the way?"

I look behind me at Josh, then back at Clark without saying a word. He simply nods in understanding. "How's he doing?"

"I just spoke to the nurse, who said he's improving, slowly but surely. Not in the clear yet, but I know he'll pull through. The guy's too annoying and stubborn to give up and die anyway."

He smiles and nods. "I remember. He's a good man. I know how hard this must be for you."

I smile faintly. "Got plenty going on to distract me..."

"Well, I hope everyone involved is aware of how this is likely to end?"

He smiles, like a friend would smile when they offer you reassurance about something. My jaw muscles tighten as I think about how *exactly* things will end here.

Very badly. For Pellaggio, anyway.

I flick my gaze over to Chambers, who remains silent. "I think there's a certain level of understanding, yeah."

"Well, as always, Adrian, if there's anything I can do to help, let me know." He turns to speak to Chambers. "I'll head over to your office now and assist Agent Wallis in any way I can." He looks back at me. "Good to see you again, Adrian."

He turns and walks out, leaving Agent Chambers and me staring at each other by Josh's bedside.

She looks at me and smiles, then leans over and gives me a kiss on the cheek.

It catches me off-guard, and I'm not sure how to react. "What was that for?"

"My way of apologizing for the things I said to you. And to thank you for saving my life—more than once."

I feel humbled by receiving thanks and praise for doing what I do. It feels a little uncomfortable being this... this human in front of someone. First time for everything, I guess.

I just shrug. "Forget about it."

"No one is ever going to see past what you do, Adrian. At its core, you kill people for a living. Whatever justification you give, that will always be what you do. But you're a good man. And the things you've done... what you're capable of doing... that's almost superhuman. You have a gift, Adrian—

if you can call it that. I just hope, in time, you'll put it to better use."

We hold each other's gaze for a few more moments. That's probably the nicest thing anyone's said to me in a long time. I feel the moment overwhelming me. I actually feel close to her. I've not thought about a woman this way in what seems like a lifetime. Not since Janine.

I quickly clear my mind and look away. I feel like I'm betraying my wife by even looking at another woman. I'm not ready to put her behind me yet. Maybe I never will be. I don't know.

She takes a step back and adjusts her clothes. "Anyway, I'm going to head off. I want to catch up at the office and see where we're up to with trying to figure out what Pellaggio's next move is."

I nod. "Good idea. I'm going to hang around here for a bit. I want to keep an eye on Josh, just in case Pellaggio decides to lash out. Plus, I want to be here when Manhattan wakes up."

She looks at me with concern.

I roll my eyes and smile. "Don't worry. I'm not gonna kill him. I'll find out what he knows and come straight to you, I promise."

"Okay. Stay out of trouble."

She walks out and closes the door behind her, leaving me alone once more with Josh. I drag a chair from against the far wall and move it so that it's facing the bed. This way, I can see whoever's coming in and out of the room and keep an eye on Josh without leaving myself open to an unseen attack.

I sit back in the chair and cross my arms, lean my head back, and stare up at the ceiling. This is the first time I've rested in two days.

My eyes are heavy...

September 25, 2014 — 07:37 PDT

I snap awake with a grunt. I blink hard and rub my eyes to clear the grit from them. I gaze wide-eyed around the room, trying to focus as my mind comes out of what I suspect was a long and deep sleep. The door's still closed, which I take as a good sign. I look over at the window and see the pale skies of another sunny day peeking through the blinds.

I look over at the bed...

"Fuck me!"

I jump a clear foot off my chair. My heart's hammering into my ribcage with shock.

Josh is sitting bolt upright in bed, eyes wide open. He's staring straight at me and smiling, tilting his head slightly to the left like a goddamn psychopath.

He bursts out laughing, his familiar British accent interlaced with his lovable yet annoying happiness. "Boo!"

"Jesus Christ, Josh! What the hell?"

"Hey, Boss. Miss me?"

"I *was* missing you until you nearly give me a heart attack, asshole!"

He laughs. "I've been staring at you for half an hour... it was totally worth it."

"How are you... why are you awake?"

"The nurse came in a few hours ago, checked my bits and bobs, and gave me a chance to wake up on my own. I did—go me!"

I let out a heavy sigh as I finally calm down and process

the good news. God knows I'm due some. "It's good to have you back, man. How do you feel?"

He shrugs. "Still sore where the bullets got me, obviously. Bit tired, a little hungry, but other than that, I feel good. You?"

I smile. "Well, seeing as you've stopped being such a pussy and finally woken up, I may as well fill you in on what you've missed."

He smiles enthusiastically and sits back, adjusting himself to get comfortable. "Go for it!"

I take a deep breath. This might take a while...

08:02 PDT

Josh frowns. "You really figured out it was Danny Pellaggio from me getting shot?"

I nod.

"Really? Like, all on your own?"

I flip him the middle finger.

He laughs. "So, we still don't know how they blew up the SWAT van, nor how they know our every move?"

"Nope. But the smart money would be on an inside man at the FBI. Question is, who? I've only really spoken with Grace and Wallis, and I'm comfortable vouching for them."

He nods in agreement. "Maybe mention it to Agent Chambers?"

"Yeah, I will next time I see her. Tricky subject to raise, though."

"Yeah, never nice being told your house isn't in order. I can't believe you managed to take out an entire Triad operation at the same time as a black-market weapons dealer. That's pretty crazy, man."

I smile. "Would you have let me do it if you'd been there?"

"From what you've told me, I probably would've suggested it to *you*!"

We laugh again. I realize just how much I miss him when he's not around.

"So, what do we think Pellaggio's plan is?"

I shrug. "I have no idea. I'm hoping to get something from Manhattan when he wakes up."

"He's still got most of the weaponry he bought from Turner, right?"

"We assume so."

"I imagine he'll be looking to use it, then."

I nod. "So, anyway, when are you getting out of here?"

He points at me, laughing. "I *knew* you'd missed working with me!"

I pretend to think about it. "I wouldn't say *missed*, but I definitely seem to get blown up slightly more often on my own than when I have you talking in my ear."

"Well, I feel good, all things considered. Wouldn't mind getting out of here and getting something to eat."

I smile. "Shall I see if they can fix you up a plate of delicious hospital food?"

"Oh, boy, *would* you?"

I raise my eyebrow.

He rolls his eyes. "Sorry, I forget you're still learning the fine art of sarcasm. It's always been more of a British thing, hasn't it?"

"No... *really*?"

He laughs and claps his hands like a child. "You've been practicing!"

I bow gracefully. "Been saving it for a special occasion."

We laugh again. Everything doesn't seem so bad now. I know I'm guilty of forgetting many of the rules I operate by because of everything that's happened recently. But an important rule is: don't think too much. I've been thinking an awful lot lately because my mind hasn't been able to focus. Thinking too much leads to second-guessing, doubt, and hesitation. All of which will get you killed. You need to just do whatever it is, like a reflex or an instinct. You can worry about it afterward. After speaking with Josh, I feel it's finally time to stop thinking and start doing.

My phone rings. I take it out and click it. "Yeah?"

"Adrian? It's Wallis. You all right?"

"Yeah. Josh is awake, so I've just been catching him up."

"He is? That's great news. Pass on my regards."

"I will, thanks. So, what can I do for you?"

"Just thought you might want to know, we've had word from the hospital. Jimmy Manhattan's awake too."

"Really? I'll head up to his room now."

"Oh, and Adrian? Agent Chambers has asked me to remind you that Mr. Manhattan needs to stay alive..."

I smile. "He will. Don't worry."

"But between me and you, feel free to punch the bastard a few times if he doesn't talk."

We both laugh.

"You're all right, Wallis."

"Take care."

He hangs up, and I slide the phone back in my pocket.

"Good news?" asks Josh.

I nod. "Agent Wallis is glad you're not dead. Oh, and Manhattan's awake. Are you up for paying him a visit?"

"Just try and stop me."

He throws the bed cover back and swings his legs over

the side. He slowly puts his weight on them and eases himself to his feet. He pulls the wires off his chest, the clip from his finger, and the IV out of his arm. Everything starts beeping, and within seconds, a team of nurses burst through the door with practiced efficiency.

He's a little unsteady on his feet but seems to be managing well enough. He holds his hands up to try to calm them down as they all shout over each other, trying to order him back into bed.

He chuckles. "Ladies, ladies, don't panic. I'm fine."

They all go quiet and start trying to fuss over him, but he waves them away.

"Can someone please just find me some pants?"

I move over to the door, so I don't get in everyone's way. I catch his eye and smile. "I'll give you a minute."

I walk out of the room and along the hallway, toward the main waiting area. It's a large, open-plan area with two main corridors branching off opposite the one I've just walked down. There is a circular desk area with clerical and nursing staff busying themselves behind it. Across from the nurses' station is a seating area with rows of chairs linked together by the legs, laid out in a small grid, and a TV mounted on the far wall.

I walk over to the desk and signal to one of the nurses to get her attention. She's quite a big woman with dark skin, like coal. She has big brown eyes and long black hair that's tightly dreadlocked and ponytailed. Her uniform struggles to stretch over her frame. But her smile is infectious.

"Hi, could you please tell me where a friend of mine is? He came in a few hours ago with gunshot wounds. His last name's Manhattan."

She beams at me. "Jus' lemme check, sugar." She walks over to the computer on the other side of the desk and taps away at the keyboard. After a few moments, she walks back over. "He's in Room Five, B wing—one floor up."

"That's great. Thanks for your help."

"No problem, sugar." Her tone is a little more flirtatious this time.

I smile politely back and make a hasty retreat to Josh's room. He's just finished getting dressed. He's stretching cautiously. "All right, Boss?"

I nod. "Yeah, just found out Manhattan's room number. You ready?"

"Lead the way."

He walks gingerly at first but soon loosens up. Despite some obvious and understandable discomfort and a slight limp, he seems fine. We walk side by side through the waiting area. As we walk past the desk, the nurse I just spoke to smiles and waves coyly over to me, which Josh picks up on instantly.

He grins. "You been making friends, you sly dog?"

"Screw you, Josh."

"What will Agent Chambers say?"

"Do you wanna be manually put back into a coma?"

He smiles and motions that he's zipping his mouth closed and throwing away the key.

I smile. "Asshole."

We carry on toward the elevator. I press the button and we wait for the doors to open. My mind quickly flashes back to Turner's apartment building, which is the last time I was in an elevator. Well, an elevator shaft, anyway. I hope this won't end as dramatically as that did.

The doors ding open and we step inside. Josh pushes the button for the floor above. Just as the doors are closing, a man rushes over and puts his hand on them to keep them open. He smiles apologetically and steps inside, standing in front of us. He's a nondescript guy in plain, generic clothes. Short hair, no beard. He glances at which button is lit up and waits silently for the doors to close.

It's a short ascent, and the doors open again almost as soon as they close. The man steps out and turns right. We follow him out, looking at the sign on the wall directly in front us to figure out which way we need to go.

Josh points to it. "It says B wing is to the right."

We set off down the corridor. After a short walk, it splits at a T-junction, with another sign mounted on the wall.

I gesture at it with a nod. "Rooms One to Five, left."

We turn and head left. The guy from the elevator is just up ahead. He's walking purposefully. After a moment, he stops at the first door on the right. He looks both ways and sees us, but clearly does not give us a second thought. He enters the room without knocking.

His body language was strange, which made him appear conspicuous...

I won't say anything. I'm probably just being paranoid.

We walk on, looking for Manhattan's room. We pass the first door on the right.

Room Five.

Huh... maybe I'm not being paranoid.

Josh looks at me, clearly thinking the same thing I am. He raises an eyebrow. "Hitman?"

I nod. "Hitman."

20

———

We position ourselves on either side of the doorway and listen intently for any sound or movement from within. I motion to Josh that I'll go in and he should wait outside. He frowns, but I point at him with raised eyebrows, addressing the fact he's in the hospital and therefore not exactly a hundred percent. He rolls his eyes and makes a dismissive gesture with his hand, as if to say *yeah, yeah... fine!*

I count down from three and burst through the door.

Jimmy Manhattan is lying in bed, hooked up to various machines and tubes, with an oxygen mask on his face. The man we just saw enter the room is standing over him on the far side of the bed, facing us. He's preparing to inject something into the drip.

"Oh, no, you don't!"

I dash over to the bed and reach across. I grab the man's wrist and twist it sharply clockwise, causing him to drop the needle. I let go long enough to make my way around the other side and get a better hold of him. He's not really had time to react yet, so he's just kind of standing there.

I hear Josh walk in behind me and shut the door.

I grab the hitman's throat and drag him away into the corner of the room. I pin him to the wall. My arm's fully extended, and I'm standing almost side-on as I hold him, making my body a smaller target and harder for him to hit.

I lean in close, almost snarling with anger. "Who the fuck are you? And why are you trying to kill Jimmy over there?"

The guy's breathing heavily, struggling against my grip. Both his hands are around my wrist, but I can squeeze like a vice when I need to, so he's not moving unless I allow it.

"Answer me!"

"Adrian, you're crushing his windpipe," says Josh behind me. "He *can't* answer you..."

I glance back at him. He's standing at Manhattan's bedside. "Fair point. Smartass..." I turn back to the guy and loosen my grip a little. "There... now answer me."

He grits his teeth, like he's pissed at himself for giving in and talking to me. "Mr. P-Pellaggio sent me."

"Why?"

He moves up on his tiptoes as I re-tighten my grip slightly. My fingertips are applying pressure to the fleshy part of the neck where the pulse is, just behind the bend in the jaw.

"I—I'm following orders. That's it."

I sigh. I don't have time for the formalities of interrogation. I look back at Josh. "Would you mind?"

He nods. "On it." He leans over Manhattan and pulls the oxygen mask off his face, then pats him gently on the cheek. "Jimmy? Jimmy? You awake, mate?"

He looks up at Josh, disoriented and blurry-eyed.

Josh smiles. "There he is! Listen, Jimmy, why would Danny Pellaggio try to kill you?"

Manhattan raises his head slightly, visibly struggling with the concept of speaking. "Because..."

He flops back down heavily, letting out a long, tired sigh.

Josh looks up at me and shrugs. "I'm getting nothing."

I look back at the hitman. I look him right in the eye. I see fear, which is a good thing. It makes this next part a little easier.

"Do you know who I am?"

He nods hurriedly but says nothing. I tighten my grip even more around his throat, making his eyes bulge.

"Good—that saves me some time. Now pay attention. You're going to live, understand? You're gonna go back to that piece of shit who hired you, and you're gonna tell him he's a dead man walking. You tell him if he wants a genetically perfect predator, then he's got one. He walks around calling himself *the Shark*... Well, lemme tell you, I can smell blood, and I'm coming for the kill. Nod if you understand."

He does.

"Excellent."

Without warning, I swing my arm around, leading from the hip, and smash my elbow into his temple, causing his head to snap violently sideways. He loses consciousness instantly. When I release my grip, he drops to the floor with a thud. I look down at him and see the severe bruising around his throat.

I walk over to the bed and stand across from Josh, where the hitman had been. I look down at Jimmy. He looks... old. I mean, I know he's probably quite old anyway, but he's always had an aura about him that exuded power and confidence. Looking at him now, he's merely a shadow of his former self.

He looks at me, but I see nothing in his eyes. Just a frail old man. I smile. "Getting shot and betrayed sucks, doesn't it, Jimmy?"

He doesn't say anything, but he holds my gaze.

"Right, Jimmy, you'd better start talking. Given I just saved your life, arguably for the second time, I figure you owe me. Tell me what Pellaggio is planning."

He takes a long, deep breath and closes his eyes momentarily. He looks first at Josh, then me. "I honestly... don't know the full extent of... what he has planned."

He grimaces from the strain of talking.

"You can't really expect us to believe that?"

He smiles. "Probably... not. But it's... the truth. I helped him... trained him... put him in touch with... with the right people. I funded his whole... fucking operation. But for me, it was always about getting... getting to you. Danny didn't just blame you for what happened... to his father. He blamed that... fucking terrorist, Ketranovich."

"He's already said he wants to make it look like the Russians are to blame for whatever it is he's going to do, but we need you to fill in the blanks, Jimmy."

He clenches his jaw as best he can, out of either anger or frustration, but he remains silent.

I sigh. "Jimmy, this isn't the time for misplaced loyalties. Danny's tried to kill you twice now. He obviously doesn't need you anymore. I don't care if you want me dead, but I *do* care about a potential threat against countless innocent lives. Help me, Jimmy."

He coughs, struggling for breath. He reaches for his oxygen mask and hurriedly places it over his mouth. He takes a few deep breaths, then removes it again to speak. "He has a Russian with him called... Gregovski. He's an extremist who wishes to... sever his own ties with the Motherland for... different reasons. Danny's going to use Gregovski as the... face... and voice of his attack. He'll publicly claim the attack as Russia's. That will be enough to... light the fire. The media and the government will... do the... rest."

I look over at Josh. He shakes his head in disbelief. "Jesus Christ..."

I look back at Manhattan. "You have to tell me what he's planning and when."

"I don't know!" He pauses to cough. "I swear I'd tell you if I knew... but I really don't. I only know he's got something big planned, and... it involves the Russian."

My gut says he's telling the truth.

"One more thing. When you had me tied to a chair, I asked you how you managed to stay ahead of the FBI for so long. You never told me."

Manhattan squirms in his bed, staring at me. He's beaten and he knows it. He owes Pellaggio nothing. Yet he's still reluctant to divulge anything to me. It must be pride.

"C'mon, Jimmy... this is your chance to do something good for once."

He sighs. "We have a man inside... the field office on our... payroll."

"I fucking knew it! Give me his name."

"Agent... Green."

"The piece of shit who arrested me? Sonofabitch!"

I take a deep breath and pace slowly away from the bed, trying to process the information. It's all starting to make sense, which is kind of annoying. The more I find out, the more I think I should've figured it out sooner.

Josh remains close to Manhattan. "Here's a question. If that's all you know—and let's be honest, it's not much more than we already have—why does Pellaggio, Jr. want you dead so badly? Why did he shoot you in the first place? And why send such a pathetic excuse for an assassin to try to finish the job?"

Manhattan's eyes shift back and forth. That's a damn good question.

I look at him. "Jimmy?"

He closes his eyes for a moment. "I... I started asking what his plan was after he... captured you on the bridge and brought you to... the warehouse. He lost control—started saying it wasn't my... business and I... should stop trying to look out for him. That I wasn't his... father."

I frown. "He just snapped?"

My mind kicks into overdrive, running through events again in my head, piecing things together. I remember when we first arrived at the warehouse and everyone surrounded Chambers and me. He flipped like a switch when he grabbed her. And even before that, standing on the bridge— I remember asking him if he suffered from survivor's guilt, purely to get a reaction. But he changed instantly and attacked me.

I should've seen it sooner.

"He *snapped*..." I look at Josh for confirmation of my theory, but he doesn't seem to know what I'm getting at. I look back at Manhattan. "Pellaggio's fucking insane, isn't he? You're still trying to protect him, but he's a couple of cans short of a six-pack."

Manhattan takes another drag on his oxygen mask. "I think he lost his... grip on reality after your attack... if I'm being honest. But the training and... and the planning kept him focused... kept him in check. It's only since he's finally caught up with you that he seems to be... struggling."

"You've been looking after him all this time, and when you found out there was more to this than getting at me, you became curious. Pellaggio took that as some kind of personal attack, and that's why he shot you, isn't it?"

Manhattan nods.

"Sonofabitch..." says Josh. "You basically created a monster and kept him as a pet. You wound him up and he turned on you. Now he's off his leash and rabid on the streets."

I crack my neck, loosening up. "I guess someone should go and put him down, then?"

We leave Manhattan and the unconscious hitman and make our way back down in the elevator to Josh's floor. I'm not bothered if Manhattan gets taken out anymore. We've got everything out of him that we'll be able to use.

Josh walks over to the nurse's station and starts going through the process to discharge himself. I take out my phone and call Agent Wallis. I figure Chambers could do with a break.

He answers. "Wallis? It's me."

"What have you got for me?"

"We just stopped someone from trying to kill Manhattan. Pellaggio sent them to finish him off."

"Oh, shit! Really? What happened?"

"The guy's out cold on the floor. Manhattan's fine. We had a nice little talk."

"And?"

"We don't know what Pellaggio's next move is. Manhattan has no idea."

"And you believe him?"

"I do. I also have a name—Gregovski. Mean anything to you?"

"No. Should it?"

"Dunno. He's a Russian who hates Russia, apparently, and he's going to be the poster boy for Pellaggio's big finale.

Their idea is to frame Russia for whatever it is they intend to do, and hope it causes an international incident."

"Why? What's Pellaggio got against Russia?"

"He blames them for the death of his entire family."

"I thought that was *your* fault?"

"Me too. I did kinda do all the hard work. But he blames the circumstances surrounding my motivation on the Russians, so..."

"Christ. Okay, I'll run the name Gregovski, see what comes back. Good work, Adrian."

"There's one more thing... about Pellaggio."

"What?"

"The guy's insane."

He chuckles. "I could've told you that!"

"No, I mean, genuinely fucking *nuts*."

"Oh, I see. That's... not good."

"No, it's really not. It's all been a nightmare so far, but knowing he's mentally unstable and the worst is yet to come, I think we need to get some contingencies in place."

"I'll pull his medical records from last year, see if there's anything in there."

"Good idea. Josh and I are on our way to you now, so I'll see you soon."

"Okay. Watch your backs."

He hangs up. I pocket the phone as Josh limps over.

"I'm free to go," he announces.

"They okay with that?"

"Not really, but they can't stop me."

"True. You sure you're all right? It's okay if you need to rest up, y'know."

He waves his hand dismissively. "I'm fine. You tell them about Agent Green?"

"No, I'm going to save that little revelation for when we get there."

09:25 PDT

We left the hospital and, realizing we had no transportation, set off walking to the FBI field office. I offered to call a cab, but Josh said he'd prefer the exercise and the fresh air after being in the hospital for the last couple of days. He was moving comfortably enough, considering.

We spent the first twenty minutes or so catching up some more, throwing theories around and generally trying to get back into our rhythm, so we're ready for battle. Whatever's coming from Pellaggio, we know it will likely be pretty big, and we need to be ready for anything.

We passed a restaurant, and Josh pointed out he could *eat a dead horse between two rusty Walmart trucks*—which I assumed was a British euphemism for him being hungry. We walked in, stood in line for ten minutes, and then ordered a breakfast bagel and a coffee each.

We're sitting in a booth across from the entrance. It's pretty busy in here. A mixture of singles, couples, families, and groups chat and laugh and eat like there's nothing wrong with the world. Ignorance really is bliss. I wouldn't wish my current list of stresses on anyone.

A plasma TV is mounted on one wall, showing the news. I look over at it and notice whatever news channel's on is reporting from outside the warehouse on Pier 17 that I got blown out of yesterday. I walk over, turn up the volume, and watch intently, trying to ignore the protests from people sitting nearby. Josh appears next to me. The female news reporter is mid-broadcast.

"...officials are keeping details to themselves, early reports from both police and FBI agents on the scene lead us to believe this could've been a terrorist attack. There's also speculation that this could be related to the recent attacks around the city, but so far, there has been no evidence released to support that.

"We have some video surveillance footage of the blast, being shown now for the first time, exclusively on WKRN. It seems to show three people being caught in the explosion. We'd like to advise viewers that they may find this footage disturbing."

The screen shows a poor-quality, black and white video feed of me, Chambers, and Wallis being blown into the bay in slow motion.

Josh leans close. "Is that you?"

"Sadly, yes."

"Jesus!"

"See what happens when you're not around?"

"Adrian, that happens when I *am* around. You're a magnet for random explosions."

"Yeah... lucky me."

The news reporter comes back on the screen. "The police are urging anyone with information about these people to come forward."

I go to turn and walk back to my seat, but Josh grabs my arm to stop me and points to the screen again. "Wait a sec."

The reporter's still talking. "In other news, preparations are under way for the opening ceremony later today on board the S.S. Jeremiah O'Brien, which you can see docked just behind me, further along the bay. It's being turned into a war museum as part of the continuing seventieth D-Day anniversary celebrations, and a large turnout is expected. Both serving and veteran military and naval personnel are being commemorated as part of the event. The service will begin at around eight o'clock this evening and will finish with an address by U.S. Secretary of Defense Ryan Schultz, followed by a firework display. Security will obviously be high in light of recent events, but it's expected to go ahead as planned. For WKRN, I'm Shelley Prince."

Josh turns to me. "Say, Adrian, doesn't that look like something a terrorist might consider a worthwhile target?"

"It really, really does, Josh…"

We hold each other's gaze, both seeing the other's mind racing, trying to assess every conceivable outcome of a theoretical attack against that ship. No scenario ends well.

Shit!

How did the biggest naval event in years *not* cross people's minds as something Pellaggio might be interested in?

Shit! Shit! Shit!

"I think we have a big problem."

"I think you're right, Boss."

"C'mon. We've got to let people know."

We rush out the door, not bothering to go back to our table.

09:51 PDT

This time, we *did* hail a cab. We pull over outside the field office, clamber out of the taxi, and sprint through the main doors. We ride the elevator up to the eleventh floor. The doors open with a ding, and we head toward the conference room where we've spent much of our time.

We rush into the open office space, and everyone stops and turns to stare at us. I look out at the room, focusing on no one in particular. "Where's Agent Chambers?"

"She's in a meeting," says a female agent who's standing next to a computer terminal.

"Okay. Agent Wallis?"

"He's with her."

"Shit. Where?" They look a little unsure about telling me. "Goddammit, *where*?"

"Across the hall with the ASAC."

"Thank you."

I turn and run down the corridor. I can hear Josh trying to keep up behind me.

"Hey!" I hear them shout after us. "You can't just..."

I ignore them. I'm not going to hang around, so someone can tell me I can't do something when they can't actually stop me from doing it.

We head into the larger office area. It's bustling with activity, and we move unhindered through the maze of desks toward the far end. There's a large room with a window that runs floor to ceiling. The blinds are down but open, and I see both Chambers and Wallis sitting side by side, looking unhappy. I can't see who they're talking to.

I glance at Josh. "C'mon."

"Adrian, maybe we should wait until they're done?"

"Why? Pellaggio fucking won't!"

He sighs. "Fair point."

I shrug. "Look, wait here if you're going to be such a woman about it."

I walk over to the office and open the door without

knocking. I walk in, and they both turn to look at me, their faces both confused and a little embarrassed.

I quickly look around the office. It's nice—lots of dark wood everywhere. The desk in front of them, in particular, looks really expensive. Sitting behind it is a broad man, probably a few years older than me. He has thick, dark hair with flecks of gray above the ears. He's leaning back in a big leather chair, his elbows resting on the arms and his fingers bridged together in front of his face, like he's deliberating. He looks up at me but doesn't look shocked or confused—and certainly not embarrassed. He doesn't make a gesture to stand, and he doesn't look questioningly at either Chambers or Wallis. He simply regards me silently.

I look at each of them in turn. "We have a big fucking problem."

"Adrian!" hisses Chambers. "Now *really* isn't the time!"

"It's all right, Agent Chambers," interjects the man behind the desk. The nameplate at the front of his desk says *Assistant Special Agent-in-Charge Webber*. "It's obviously something Adrian Hell deems to be of great importance, so let's hear him out."

His voice is deep and powerful. I imagine he's used to commanding respect from people. But I pick up on something in his tone that I don't like. I turn to Josh, who's standing just outside the room. "Josh, was he just being sarcastic? I'm not sure."

He steps inside and waves awkwardly at everyone. "Erm... a little bit, yeah."

I turn back to Webber. "Okay, I don't know you, therefore I don't trust you."

I make a point of turning my back on him to face the others.

Chambers looks embarrassed. "Adrian, he's my boss! You can't just—"

"So? He's not *my* boss. Listen, guys. I think I know what Pellaggio is planning."

Wallis sits up straight and tenses. "What?"

I look at them both in turn. "I think he's going to launch an attack on the S.S. Jeremiah O'Brien... tonight."

21

I've never heard so many people say "Shit!" in such a short time.

Pellaggio's target is glaringly obvious. The U.S. Secretary of Defense, along with a who's who of military and naval personnel, are going to be in the same place at the same time—aboard a ship. And because everyone was so concerned with *me* being the main target, no one's thought outside the box and considered the bigger picture.

Chambers and Wallis exchange worried and frustrated glances.

"Shit!" they say again in unison.

They look at their boss, silently asking permission to leave. Webber thinks for a moment into his bridged fingers, then nods.

They both stand, but I hold my hand up to stop them. "There's one more thing..."

Josh steps further inside the room and closes the door behind him.

I look at Chambers. "Grace, do you trust your boss?"

She frowns and looks over at him. "Yes, absolutely."

I trust her judgment. I look over at Josh, who nods. "Okay." I look at everyone in the room in turn. "Before we left Manhattan, I asked him how Pellaggio managed to stay one step ahead of us this whole time. He said Agent Green is working for him."

Everyone looks at each other with a mixture of disbelief and anger. I think the thought had crossed everyone's minds about an inside man, but that doesn't make it any easier to accept when it's proven.

"Do you believe him?" asks Webber.

"Yes, I do."

Webber looks at Chambers questioningly.

"How do you want us to handle this, sir?" she asks him.

"Get his ass in here. Now."

I raise a hand slightly. "Can... I suggest something?"

He shakes his head. "No. This is an FBI matter, and we'll handle it. Your contributions to our investigation have proven useful, and your methods of obtaining information for us are effective—if not questionable at times. But we're capable of handling our own problems."

"Of course, you are. That's why I've been working my ass off to help you all week..."

"Make no mistake, Adrian. I signed off on your involvement on Senior Special Agent Chambers's recommendation, but don't think for one second I approve of it."

"Well, luckily for me, I'm not an FBI agent, and I couldn't give two shits about your approval. You asked for my help, and I gave it. And people around here seem grateful for it. Now I've got to go and stop a terrorist from killing the secretary of defense, but before I do, I'd like to suggest a way of dealing with your... rat problem. End of the day, he's putting my life in danger as well."

We regard each other silently for a moment. I can feel the tension in the room. Everyone else—even Josh—seems awkward and on edge.

Webber sighs thoughtfully. "I've read your file, Adrian. You and I have a lot in common, you know?"

I scoff. "I doubt that..."

"We both served. I did two tours during Desert Storm before hanging up my boots and joining the FBI."

"I joined up not long before Desert Shield started. I missed out on the conflict that made the headlines but made up for it by fighting in countless wars that no one will ever know about."

"Ah, yes—you're referring to the large gap in your career history, I presume? What was it? Black ops? I bet those mission files are interesting to read..."

I smile. "What files?"

I hear Josh chuckle quietly behind me.

Webber's face darkens momentarily, but he glances at Chambers and eventually lightens up a bit. "Agent Wallis, go and get Agent Green. Agent Chambers, round everybody up outside and de-brief them. If Adrian's theory about Pellaggio's target is correct, we need to move quickly."

They both leave the room, leaving Josh and me alone with Webber.

I look at him and raise an eyebrow. "You think my theory might be wrong?"

Webber shrugs. "I'm not saying it doesn't make sense. I just don't want to run with something if there's any doubt about it."

"That's fair enough. Mind if I stay while you speak to Agent Green?"

"Depends on whether you're going to behave yourself."

"Well, *that* depends on the extent of his betrayal."

Webber nods slowly but says nothing. There's a knock on the door and Wallis enters, followed by Agent Green.

He eyes me warily as Wallis shuts the door behind them and stands guarding it. I walk past him and stand with Josh at the back of the room, looking on intently.

"Take a seat, Agent Green," says Webber, gesturing to one of the chairs in front of him.

He sits casually.

If he's guilty, he's good at hiding it.

"You asked for me, sir?"

"Agent Green, I'm going to be frank. We have evidence that suggests you've been leaking critical information about this investigation to Daniel Pellaggio and Jimmy Manhattan. Would you care to comment on this?"

Green shakes his head wildly, looking shocked and appalled. "Sir, that's ridiculous!" He glances back at me. "Who told you that? *Him*? Sir, he's held a grudge against me ever since I brought him. He assaulted me, and I went along with the FBI's decision to overlook that. But I'm not going to sit here and be accused by this—"

Webber holds his hand up to silence him. "Agent Green, will you calm down? To clarify, are you denying these accusations?"

"Of course, I am!"

"What if I were to tell you it wasn't Adrian who brought this to our attention?"

Green looks over his shoulder at me again and frowns before turning back to Webber. "So, who was it?"

Webber glances at me. I shrug and nod. I'm sure they

wouldn't normally divulge this kind of information in this kind of situation, but we're running out of time.

"Jimmy Manhattan. He named *you* specifically."

From behind, I watch Green's body language change. He slumps his shoulders slightly and shifts uncomfortably in his chair. Having just found out he's been sold down the river by the guy topping up his pension fund, Green's realizing he's on his own and likely to both lose his job and face jail time.

If it were me, I know what *I'd* do...

I take a small step forward, anticipating his next move.

In a flash, Green stands, knocking the chair over as he reaches for his sidearm in a blind panic.

Yeah, that's what I'd have done. Except I wouldn't be panicking. And everyone would already be dead.

Before he can draw his gun, I stride toward him and kick the back of his knee, causing him to buckle and lose his balance. He forgets his firearm, opting to use his hands to steady himself instead. I grab his wrist and push down on his shoulder, forcing him to the floor. I hold his arm at an awkward angle, putting pressure on his elbow, ensuring he stays where he is.

"Don't be silly." I look at Webber. "You need to interrogate him formally—find out if there's anything else he knows."

Remaining perfectly calm and seated, Webber nods. "Agreed. Agent Wallis, will you please take Agent Green into custody? Adrian, I believe you've got work to do."

I nod and decide against saying anything else to him. Josh grabs the door and holds it open for Wallis as he escorts Green out of the room. Josh follows them and I walk out last.

Outside, Chambers is standing in the middle of a large

group of agents, explaining the theory about Pellaggio's grand finale and organizing our response. The room falls silent, and everyone watches as Wallis leads Green through the crowd, off to an interrogation room. Josh and I hang back, standing near the exit.

"Okay, show's over, folks," says Chambers. "You know what we're up against and what you need to do. Get to it."

There's a rush of activity as the group disperses and everyone sets about their new tasks. Chambers walks over to join us just as Robert Clark appears from behind us.

"Have I missed the excitement?" he asks.

I smile. "Yeah, sorry, Bob."

Chambers looks at us each in turn before addressing our small group. "Listen up. We need to find out how Pellaggio intends to carry out this attack. I can't see the parade being postponed. At best, they'll increase security, but I fear that won't be enough."

I nod. "Agreed. Pellaggio's going to make a big, loud, bold statement with this attack. He wants the whole world to sit up and take notice, so he can then blame the Russians."

"Will the world's governments buy that Russia did it, though?" asks Josh. "I mean, just because one guy goes on TV and says they did, it doesn't mean we'll all instantly believe him, does it?"

Chambers shrugs. "It's difficult. Worst case scenario, we lose Secretary Schultz tonight. The people are going to want someone to blame. They won't care what makes sense and what doesn't. They'll see someone own up and they'll cry for blood."

"The White House will have to respond quickly with a big, decisive move," adds Clark. "I know how these things work. They'll need to make sure they look strong, so they'll lash out at the person the public is begging them to blame."

I clench my jaw muscles to restrain my anger. "I won't let that happen."

Too many times in the past week, someone has come a-knockin' on my door, asking my Inner Satan to come out and play. And too many times, he was held back or distracted. But as things stand, the path to my door is finally clear. No more games. No more secrets. Directly in front of me is the finish line. The only thing stopping me reaching it is Pellaggio. He has blood on his hands, and he's begging me to come after him.

And I'm going to give him exactly what he wants.

I look at Wallis. "You've got access to satellite imaging here, right?"

He nods. "Yeah. Only what we used to look at Pellaggio's warehouse the other day, though. It's pretty basic."

"Maybe I can help?" offers Clark. "Wallis, if you grant me access to your servers, I can get some of my guys to link up and give you access to *our* satellite network. Josh, I believe you're familiar with the interface?"

Josh smiles with a mischievous glint in his eye. "I've used it before, yeah."

I nod. "Good. I want to see exactly what we're dealing with."

"I'll leave you boys to your toys," says Chambers. "I'll follow up on Gregovski and see what I can find. We'll meet up in an hour in the conference room down the hall, agreed?"

We all nod, and Chambers heads off, leaving the four of us huddled together. Wallis moves over to one of the desks further down the room. It has three monitors and two keyboards set up on it. He pulls the chair out and gestures to Clark. "Do what you need to do."

Clark sits down without a word and takes out his phone. We all step away, leaving him to work his magic, and congregate around another unoccupied desk nearby. Wallis logs onto the computer and starts typing.

Josh looks at me. "So, what are you thinking, Boss?"

"If I were going to mount an attack against an old warship docked in the San Francisco Bay, how would I do it?"

"Do I *wanna* know how you'd do it?" asks Wallis, looking up from the screen.

I shake my head. "I doubt it. I just hope Pellaggio doesn't think the way I do."

Josh laughs. "Well, he's certifiably insane, so if he does, it says more about you than him."

Wallis chuckles. "Yeah, I've got his medical records here from when he got shot." He begins reading from the screen. "After his wounds healed, he showed signs of post-traumatic stress, so they referred him to a psychiatrist following his discharge from hospital. He only went twice, and the notes from those sessions detailed, and I quote, *a rapid decline in mental stability*."

Josh turns to me. "So, you shot him and made him crazy? Nice going there, Chief!"

"Guys, we're hot."

That was Clark. I'm going to have to save my sarcastic retort for another time...

Josh practically runs over to the computer, barely giving Clark chance to stand before sitting in front of the screen and tapping away on the keyboard.

I smile to myself. He looks like a kid at Christmas—leg wound be damned.

I walk over and stand just behind him. "How does it feel?"

He grins. "Ah, man—I've missed being part of the team."

Clark and Wallis stand on either side of me as I lean on the back of his chair. "Well, you can start making up for lost time right now. Get me a live feed of the Jeremiah."

"What are you looking for?" asks Clark.

"Not sure yet. But I'll know it when I see it. Wallis, have you got that shopping list of hardware I took from Turner's laptop?"

He fumbles around with the few papers he has with him, then hands a sheet to me. "Here it is."

I scan down the list. God, I hope he hasn't got one of them on here...

Shit. He has.

I look at Clark. "Okay, the bad news is Pellaggio has one of your FIM-92 Stinger missiles."

He shakes his head. "Christ..."

"What's the range on one of those things? About three miles, isn't it?"

He nods. "That's about right, yeah."

"Okay, Josh—can you give me a three-mile radius from the ship on the screen? If I'm right, Pellaggio is going to fire the Stinger missile at the ship, but he'll have to be within that radius to do it. At least we might be able to narrow down our search, figure out where he's going to be."

"Is that what you'd do?" asks Wallis, sounding genuinely curious.

"Absolutely. A big target needs big firepower to damage it. He won't be able to get close enough to set any charges or anything physically on board, so a ranged assault is the only real option."

"One Stinger wouldn't cause that much structural damage, though," says Clark.

I think for a moment, then shrug. "Maybe he's not after damaging the ship. Maybe he just wants to take out a large portion of the people on it?"

Wallis shakes his head. "Man, I would *hate* to be able to think the way you do..."

I smile and shrug. "It's not my job that makes me think this way. It's my training. I'm no different than any other soldier."

"Here you go," interrupts Josh, pointing to the screen.

We all lean forward and look at the monitors. A blue circle, like a radar screen, is visible over the top of the live feed. He points to the screen. "That's a three-mile radius from the Jeremiah. Not much to go on, as the ship is mostly surrounded by water. Looking at what land there *is*, there aren't many viable options for a strategic ranged assault."

I sigh. "There's one..."

I hate being right. Well, sometimes I do. In situations like this, definitely. But logically, it makes perfect sense. I point to the screen, and everyone groans and sighs as they see what I've just seen.

It's roughly one and a half miles away from the Jeremiah. It's secluded, and it gives Pellaggio the perfect line of sight to launch the Stinger.

I *really* hate being right sometimes.

Danny Pellaggio's on Alcatraz.

22

We're all sitting in silence around the big table in the conference room, waiting for Chambers. I'm at one end, with my back to the TV screen, facing the door. Josh and Clark are sat on one side, with Wallis opposite them.

The room is quiet. There's a palpable tension between us.

I hope Chambers has better news than we do.

Alcatraz is pretty much impossible to approach unseen. I have to assume Pellaggio's already there and preparing his assault. Josh said there's clearly been some recent activity on the island after looking at the satellite feed. All the regular ferry tours are postponed due to the celebrations on the Jeremiah, so it had to have been him...

It's not the first time I've been up against it. As much as I would prefer an easy life, I just hope I'll still be around when all this over, for the good times and the bad.

Chambers walks in and closes the door before sitting down at the opposite end of the table to me. She looks at each of us, spotting the subdued expressions. "I'm guessing you have something?"

"We're almost certain Pellaggio is on Alcatraz," says Wallis. "And we're pretty sure he intends to fire a Stinger missile at the S.S. Jeremiah O'Brien."

Her eyes widen. "Christ!"

"Please tell me you have some good news?" I say to her.

She has a file in her hand, which she puts down on the table and opens. "That depends on how you define *good* news."

Everyone looks on patiently as she sifts through the papers in the file to find what she wants. "I have two pieces of information. The first didn't seem that relevant to begin with, but now you've mentioned Alcatraz, it makes more sense."

I raise an eyebrow. "Go on..."

"Remember those two naval officers we found murdered near Pellaggio's warehouse? Well, we ran their names through the system to see what they were doing in the city on active duty. And you guessed it—they were assigned as security liaisons to the Jeremiah."

I close my eyes momentarily, silent cursing myself for not picking up the link earlier. "And you think Pellaggio's got men on board using their IDs?"

She nods. "I think that would be a justifiable assumption, yes."

I sigh. "Shit. If he's got men on that ship, then there's every chance he's got bombs on there too. You need to get word to the team you've got on the ground there to relay this information to the Secret Service. Use it to convince them to call this whole thing off."

She nods again. "I agree. But it won't be getting postponed, no matter what we do."

The room falls silent for a moment.

"What else did you find out?" asks Wallis.

"Well, this is where your good news come into play." She looks at me. "I ran the name Gregovski through every database we have access to. The man we're looking for is Ivan Gregovski—born 1965 in Nevelsk, Russia. Served eight and a half years in a Siberian prison for war crimes in the eighties. Kept a low profile upon release, married in the early nineties, no children. Became active again in 2001, working alongside mercenary groups under various aliases..."

She falls silent, seemingly hesitant to continue. Everyone looks at each other in confusion.

Wallis frowns. "What's wrong?"

Chambers looks quickly at Josh, then focuses on me. "Adrian, Gregovski's wife had a brother who had two children. Twins."

I shrug and shake my head, failing to see her point.

"Her brother was also a well-known mercenary— Nikolai Salikov."

I sit up straight in my chair. My mind rushes into action like I've trained it to do upon hearing certain keywords.

Salikov.

Images come flooding back to me from Heaven's Valley. The compound. The furnace. Natalia and Gene.

I look over at Josh, who's staring at me with a worried expression. "I killed Gregovski's niece and nephew, didn't I?"

Chambers nods. "This keeps linking back to you and what happened last year in Nevada."

"Bloody hell!" says Josh. Everyone stares at him. "Danny's basically recruited the remnants of Dark Rain to come after you, hasn't he?"

"Looks that way..."

I'm distracted. My mind's still working on the word association. Salikov. Dark Rain. Nevada. Uranium. GlobaTech. Jackson... Clara!

I look over at Josh. I think he's just arrived at the same tenuous conclusion I have. I see it on his face. We think the same way.

He reacts before I have the chance to move—something he's had to become adept at over the years, to ensure I stay calm, free, and alive. He almost jumps out of his seat, rushing and stumbling as best he can to stand between the door and me.

"Adrian, we don't know she's involved, okay? Just take a breath and think this through before you, y'know, go all *Adrian* on us."

Wallis alternates his gaze between the two of us, frowning with confusion. "What's going on? Who are you talking about?"

"Clara Fox," says Clark, breaking his silence. He looks at me. "You think she could be involved?"

I sigh. "No, I don't think she's involved. If she were, we'd have known about it before now. She has a bigger grudge against me than Pellaggio. But I think we were right to rule her out of this one the other day."

Chambers closes the file and stands up. "Well, as nice as it is to stand around and discuss all the people who want you dead, we have work to do."

Her short tone takes everyone by surprise—including me.

I regard her for a moment, then nod. "I know. Your priority needs to be getting to the Jeremiah and alerting whoever you need to in order to stop the parade going ahead."

"And what do you intend to do?"

"I'm gonna go to Alcatraz and stop Pellaggio and Gregovski before they can launch their attack."

"I think you should leave that to the FBI and local authorities, don't you?"

"And what are they gonna do, Grace? You're gonna have Secret Service all over that ship. NCIS will likely be on their way to investigate the murders of their dead sailors—if they're not here already. Local PD will be on standard security duty anyway and will need to know of your involvement. Everyone is gonna be stretched thin and on high alert. You can't even look at Alcatraz without Pellaggio seeing your move coming a mile away."

"Okay, so what will you do that we can't?"

I turn to Clark. "I need a favor."

"Name it," he replies without hesitating.

"I need a gun and a speedboat."

Wallis raises his eyebrows and looks at Chambers, who doesn't look impressed but remains poker-faced and silent. Josh shakes his head and smiles. Clark doesn't look particularly fazed by the request either, although he's had experience with helping me out before. I look at them all one by one.

"Pellaggio's got at least one Stinger missile and God knows how many more RPGs. Any approach by air will end badly, as we've already seen." I look at Chambers, who clenches her jaw and momentarily glazes over. I suspect she's having a flashback to the Golden Gate Bridge yesterday. "Now I can't exactly swim there, but if I can get in a speedboat, I can loop round in a wide arc and hopefully stay out of sight. Even if I'm spotted, I'll be harder to hit than a helicopter, and he won't risk wasting too much ammunition on me. By the time I'm close enough to hit with bullets, it'll be too late for them anyway. Plus, I know there's all kinds of stealth technology nowadays..." I glance at Clark. "I'm sure you can come up with something that might help?"

Chambers and Wallis look at each other. They know I'm right, even if they don't want to admit it.

Clark stands up. "I'll make preparations at once. Globa-Tech will be happy to help in any way they can." He walks purposefully out of the room.

I look at Josh. "I need you to stay here and be my eyes and ears, yeah?"

He nods. "Business as usual, Boss."

"I'll show you where you can work from," Wallis says to him. "I'm gonna sit in on Agent Green's interrogation, so I'll take you on my way there."

He leaves the room and Josh follows, leaving me alone with Chambers.

"Grace—"

She holds her hand up. "Adrian, it doesn't matter. You have nothing to apologize for. I just don't like hearing about what you do for a living and what you've done in the past. It's easy to put it out of your mind when you're actively fighting on our side, but it's still hard to picture you being that person."

I smile and look at her for a moment. "I wasn't going to apologize. I was gonna tell you to get your head in the game because tonight is when all this ends. I can't guarantee the safety of everyone on that ship, so I need you to handle that while I stop Pellaggio."

She's visibly taken aback but smiles at my directness. "Y'know what? I believe you. And I *can* guarantee the safety of that ship and everyone aboard."

I nod and walk toward the door, but she steps in the way,

blocking my exit. We're standing inches apart from each other. She's looking at me, her eyes searching mine for a sign that I want what she does. She moves her face closer to mine and steps up on her tiptoes.

My heart's beating so fast, I'm worried it might actually burst through my ribcage. Not because of nerves or excitement. There are no butterflies, like two young lovers realizing their mutual attraction for the first time. She wants me to kiss her, and part of me wants to oblige. But I can't betray the memory of my wife. I'm not ready to put her to rest. Not just yet.

I take a deep breath and step back—a subtle gesture that I don't wish to meet her advances. She immediately senses my body language and backs off too.

"I'm sorry," we both say simultaneously. We laugh awkwardly.

"I'm sorry," she says. "I just... I shouldn't have tried to..."

I chuckle. "Hey, I'm sorry too. I didn't mean to offend you. I'm just not ready to—"

"It's okay, really. Let's just forget about it, all right?" She smiles, but it looks forced. I think she's either hurt, embarrassed, or both.

I nod, but I feel awful. "Yeah, sure. Come on, we've got work to do."

She turns and leaves the conference room. I stand alone for a moment, taking a slow, deep breath in and exhaling heavily. "Christ..."

16:21 PDT

. . .

The last few hours passed slowly. I spent most of the time pacing aimlessly around the office, feeling useless. Josh and Wallis monitored Alcatraz Island and came up with a bunch of scenarios for me to figure out how to deal with without getting myself killed. Chambers wasn't around much; she was liaising with people on board the Jeremiah, trying to convince them to search the ship for explosive devices. As expected, it was proving harder to do than we'd hoped. I think she was right—there's no way anyone will agree to postponing the celebrations later tonight. The best we can hope for is that the Secret Service realizes we're not trying to interfere and actually listens to us.

I've not said much to anyone. I've eaten a little, but I didn't have much of an appetite. I keep thinking about Agent Chambers... Grace, and our moment in the conference room earlier.

Am I mad?

I mean, she's an attractive woman. And she likes me, despite what I do for a living. I doubt I'll find many women who are so accepting of the fact I'm a professional assassin. Especially ones who are also FBI agents.

But every time I think about her, I get mad at myself because I know I should be thinking about Danny Pellaggio. He's on Alcatraz with Ivan Gregovski and an arsenal of weaponry that includes Stinger missiles—at least one of which he intends to fire at a ship that has the secretary of defense on it.

You'd think I'd be prioritizing a little better...

I'm in the larger of the two office areas, which is deserted now. Many of the agents are already en route to the Jeremiah. Josh and Wallis are at their computer terminals with satellite and drone feeds of Alcatraz displayed on their screens.

I walk over to them. "How's it going, guys?"

Josh is lost in the computers and ignores me.

"We've got thermal imaging up and running," replies Wallis. "We've got eyes on eight bodies."

"Pellaggio, Gregovski, and six for practice."

"We've been over every inch of the island and run every simulation we can think of. Adrian, you're not getting there via speedboat. You'll be seen and shot at."

I let out a tense sigh. "Josh?"

"He's right," he says without looking up from his keyboard. "It ain't happening."

The frustration is getting to me. "There's got to be a way. If I don't get to them before the fireworks start tonight, it's game over."

"Maybe I can help with that," says a voice behind us.

I turn and see Clark walking toward us, carrying two large black duffel bags, one in each hand. He's smiling from ear to ear. He drops the bags at my feet.

I look down at them and grin. "Oh, Bobby, you sure know how to treat a guy!"

He laughs and picks up one of the bags, resting it on a nearby table. He unzips it and holds it open. Wallis and Josh walk over, curious.

"Gentleman, this... is the latest in climbing technology. It's a prototype I've... ah, *borrowed* from our research facility."

He takes out a large grappling gun, maybe four feet long. It looks like a small rocket launcher, with an imposing four-pronged metal claw poking out of one end.

"Now I'll concede it's a little noisy when you fire it, but honestly, I don't think anyone will notice over the sound of the waves. You simply aim and fire—the claw will penetrate almost anything. The cable attached to it is a strengthened nylon polymer and will tie around a special body harness that's also in the bag for you. You shouldn't have any trouble scaling the side of the island with this."

Josh lets out a low whistle. "Jesus..."

"That's brilliant, Bob—really. But these guys are saying a speedboat isn't going to work... I can't climb it if I can't get to it."

He smiles again as he packs the grappling gun away, zips the bag closed, and picks it up. "I've got that covered too. Grab that other bag and follow me."

I frown, slightly confused, but pick up the bag and follow him as he walks off.

"What's in the one Adrian's carrying?" Wallis asks Josh behind me.

Josh laughs. "Oh, you probably don't wanna know that... what with you being a federal agent and all."

"Huh. Right."

I smile to myself as we all follow Clark out of the office, down the corridor, and into the elevator. We take it down to the first floor and step out into the lobby as the doors ding open. He walks outside, and we all look at each other, getting more confused by the second.

We trail after him, stepping out into the late afternoon sun. Clark is standing in the parking lot, the bag on the ground next to him, in front of a sports car. It's nice—a convertible. A Lotus, I think.

He gestures to it. "Here you go."

I shrug. "Nice wheels, Bob, but I think you might've misunderstood what I need. This is a terrorist attack, not a mid-life crisis."

Josh walks over to the vehicle and leans forward, running his hand over the wheel arches and the chassis.

Clark watches him as he stands and makes his way around the car, inspecting it with his educated eye. Wallis is next to me, looking as confused as I am.

After a minute, Josh moves next to Clark and stares at us, one hand over his mouth in genuine shock. He looks at him. "Is this..."

Clark nods and smiles.

He laughs and claps his hands. I swear to God, he would've jumped and clicked his heels if he could.

I frown at him. "Josh, you look like you've just won the state lottery. What's wrong with you?"

"Adrian, my loveable, un-educated friend, *this* is an amphibious sports car."

I raise an eyebrow. "It's a what now?"

He rolls his eyes at my apparent ignorance. "It's an underwater car."

I'm trying to understand how those two words can appear next to each other in a sentence, but I don't have the mental capacity for it.

"An *underwater* car? That's a thing now?"

Clark pats the hood like a proud father. "It runs off an electric motor powered by six batteries. It's capable of seventy-five miles an hour and can submerge to depths of up to three hundred feet."

"So, it's a submarine?"

Clark nods.

"Well, ain't that somethin'..."

"I hope this helps."

He extends his hand, which I shake. "This is incredible, Bob. Thank you."

"Any time, Adrian. And now I'm going to do something I learned to do long ago—stay out of your way while you go kill people." He shakes hands with the others. "Josh. Agent Wallis."

He disappears back inside the office.

Wallis pats my shoulder. "Well, looks like you're all set. I'm going to be on board the Jeremiah with Agent Chambers. Good luck, Adrian."

"Thanks. You too."

He walks off, and as I watch him go, Agent Chambers comes out toward us. They exchange a quick word as they pass, then he carries on inside.

She approaches us. "Nice wheels."

I pat the bonnet, like Clark did moments ago. "It's also a submarine."

She looks confused.

Josh smirks. "I'll leave you two to it." He reaches into his pocket and takes out an earpiece. "Adrian, take this. I'll be with you every step of the way."

I take it from him and smile. "Thanks, man. See you on the other side."

"Bet your ass."

We bump fists, and he walks off, leaving me standing next to the car with Chambers in front of me.

"So, you're all set?" she asks.

I look at the two black bags at my feet and the car behind me. "I reckon so, yeah."

"I'll do everything I can on the Jeremiah. Just stop Pellaggio, okay? Whatever it takes."

"I fully intend to. You be careful. If there are bombs on board, you need to be ready to get people off that ship if things go wrong at my end."

"I will. But you'll stop him. I know it."

I smile and we hold each other's gaze for a moment.

Then I pick up the bags and drop them on the back seat, walk around the hood, and open the driver's door.

"Is this really a submarine?" she asks skeptically.

I shrug. "Apparently..."

"Huh..."

I climb inside and start the engine. I look at her one last time, then drive off toward the pier.

23

My phone rings. It's Josh. I put my earpiece in and answer the call.

"Hey."

"Where you up to, Boss man?"

"I'm a few minutes away from the docks. I've hit some traffic."

"That's to be expected, I guess, what with everything going on over there."

"How are things with you?"

"This place is mental! I think the Secret Service is finally starting to take our concerns seriously, but they aren't being very cooperative in allowing the FBI access to the ship. Agent Chambers is shouting a lot on the phone. I think she's intending to set off for the Jeremiah with Agent Wallis any minute."

"Unbelievable. They'll be cooperative when they get blown to shit and the FBI says *I told you so*."

"If only people would listen to *us*, eh? Anyway, go do your thing, man. I've got your back here."

Instead of hanging up, Josh starts playing music down the line. I smile as the opening guitar riff from *Smoke on the Water* drifts into my ears.

I focus on the road and steadily navigate through the traffic, which is getting heavier the closer I get to the docks. As I hit The Embarcadero, vehicles are almost at a standstill. Cops are standing in the middle of the road, directing cars. I lean out the window and look ahead. The sun's slowly turning orange as it begins its descent, and it's casting a subtle glow on the never-ending line of traffic ahead of me.

Goddamnit!

I check the clock in the car. According to that news report I saw, the service aboard the Jeremiah is due to start at eight p.m. I'm running out of time, and I'm probably ten minutes away from where I need to be.

The music fades away.

"Still with us?" asks Josh.

"Just about. Although, I'm going to start shooting people if this traffic doesn't clear up soon."

He laughs. "Hang on a second. Right, I'm tracking you via the GPS in your phone. You still have a way to go before you reach Pier 33, and the traffic's only going to get worse, but you can turn off early onto Pier 29 and drive along there —it might save you some time."

"Excellent, I can see the turn just ahead. So, here's a question for you... have you ever driven an underwater car before?"

He laughs again. "Can't say I have..."

"But you're familiar with them?"

"Probably more than you are, yeah."

"So, what am I meant to do when I reach the end of the pier, exactly?"

"You drive off it!"

"Josh, I'm being serious here."

"Adrian, so am I! How else do you expect to get underwater?"

"What, I just... drive off? Will I not drown in the car? This sounds like one of those things I really need to get right first time, y'know."

"Have you got a lever at the side of you?"

I take a look. "I've got two."

"Right, well one's the emergency brake. The other, you need to pull as soon as you're airborne but before you hit the water."

"What will it do?"

"It'll make sure the roof and windows are sealed to make them airtight and waterproof. It will also disengage the main electric engine and switch on the secondary supply, which is used to power the water-based part of the vehicle."

"Christ, this is some real-life James Bond shit, isn't it! How do I steer the damn thing?"

"You'll be able to push and pull the wheel as well as turn it—this will control your depth. Forward for down, backward for up."

"Huh. Well, this should be entertaining."

"Assuming you manage it, our comms will be down until you re-surface, so you're on your own until you reach Alcatraz."

I see a gap in the traffic and take it, accelerating quickly and stopping again. The turn for Pier 29 is just ahead.

"Fair enough. Tell Agent Chambers good luck from me."

"I will..."

He falls silent.

"What?"

"Nothing."

"Josh, I can hear you smiling down the phone. What?"

He laughs. "Oh, I'm sorry. Did you think all the awkward, uncomfortable flirting you two have been doing wasn't visible to the rest of us?"

Shit.

"I don't know what you're talking about."

"Uh-huh..."

"Josh?"

"Yeah?"

"I have absolutely no issue with shooting you. You know that, right?"

He laughs again. "Whatever you say, Boss man."

"I'm just about to turn onto the pier. I'll call you once I get to the Rock."

I hang up and take the turn, slowing to a stop at the beginning of the pier. There's a parking lot which is half-full, with spaces along the side of a building. Luckily, there aren't many people around. I set off again, slowly, toward the end of the pier.

I must admit, I'm not confident with driving into the water and pulling a lever so that I don't drown. I get that technology is amazing and useful nowadays, but it doesn't mean I trust it. I just want to make sure I know what I'm doing. No use going to all this trouble if I die before I even make it to Pellaggio.

I stop at an angle as I reach the edge of the pier and get out of the car. I look around and come across the first of what I suspect will be many roadblocks I encounter before all this is over. The pier is fenced off, so I can't drive off the edge.

Great. *Now* what do I do?

I look around. There's no one this far down the pier. I walk over to the barriers. They're interlinked metal gates, maybe three feet high and five feet wide, welded into place. If I drove at them full speed, I'd probably write the car off and injure myself. They're also too high to start trying to build a ramp.

Shit.

Hang on...

I walk quickly back to the car and open the black duffel bag on the back seat that doesn't contain the grappling gun. Inside is a Heckler and Koch MP5 submachine gun—my personal favorite—resting on top of a pile of spare magazines. Lining the bottom of the bag next to it is a selection of grenades. Smoke, flashbangs, white phosphorous, and...

Frags.

I pick one up and look at it in my hand. There's no one around, and this would almost certainly blow at least one section of barrier off, which would leave a space wide enough to drive through.

I turn to walk back to the barrier when something inside the bag catches my eye. I reach inside and retrieve a back holster, identical to the one I used to wear. Resting in it are two brand new, custom Berettas. My eyes widen like a kid on Christmas morning who's just opened a present and found the one thing he wanted more than anything in his life. They're not the A1 model that I'd loved and lost but the more prominent FS variation. I take one out and hold it in the palm of my hand, feeling the weight. I look at it and smile. On the butt, where I'd had the sigil of Baphomet engraved previously, is an intricate image of a smiling devil's face. Every aspect of the gun is jet-black, but the engraving is blood-red.

I tuck it into my waistband at my back. I'll leave the

other one in the bag for now. I walk over to the barrier once more and measure it up, casually tossing the grenade up and catching it as I concentrate.

My earpiece is still in place, so I dial Josh.

"You not drowned yet, then?" he says when he answers.

"Not yet... listen, is Grace still with you?"

"No, she and Wallis are en route to the Jeremiah. Why?"

"Can you get in touch with her?"

"I have her number, yeah. Why, Adrian?"

"Let her know that if she hears any reports in the next few minutes of a small explosion on Pier 29, there's no need to worry—it's just me."

There's a moment of silence on the line.

"Yeah, okay."

"Thanks."

I hang up and pull the pin from the grenade, letting it cook for a second before rolling it along the ground toward the railing. As soon as it leaves my hand, I run back to the car. I reach it just as the explosion sounds out. It's deafening and couples with the noise of screeching metal as the barrier blows out. A small cloud of smoke fills the air, raining down rubble and splintered wood.

I climb in behind the wheel and wait for the dust to settle. As the cloud fades, the gap I've created appears, which is plenty big enough.

Excellent. Now I just need to drive off the pier...

I put the roof up on the sports car and make sure to fully raise the windows. I reach down and grip the lever that isn't my handbrake. I let out a heavy sigh.

I do some really stupid things sometimes...

Without hesitating, I push my foot to the floor and set off screaming down the pier toward the gap. As I approach, I look to my left and see the outline of Alcatraz Island in the distance. At least it's not hard to find.

I fail to suppress a guttural scream of adrenaline as I fight every natural urge I have to slam my brakes on as the end approaches. I feel the car leave the ground, the engine revving loudly. The water of the bay appears in front of me, rushing toward me faster than I could've imagined. I quickly pull the lever, hard enough that I momentarily worry I've snapped it. I hear one loud mechanical noise as a million tiny components all adjust themselves milliseconds before I plunge into the water. Instinctively, I close my eyes and take a deep breath, holding it as I grip the wheel until my knuckles turn white. I count to five and open my eyes. I give it another two before exhaling.

I start laughing.

Holy shit, I'm underwater!

I try the wheel. Sure enough, the steering column now allows me to push the wheel forward or pull it back. To put my mind at ease, I press my hand against the seats, the floor, the roof, the windows, everything. All watertight.

Un-fucking-believable!

Clark's outdone himself this time.

I gently press the gas and pull back on the wheel. I surge forward, leveling out. I drive in a straight line... Am I driving? After a few moments, I realize it's harder to navigate than I thought it would be, so I pull back on the wheel as much as I can and climb. The wavy glare of the sun gets closer and brighter until I break the surface, causing a big splash around me.

I survey the waters, bobbing gently up and down on the waves. I'm facing just to the right of Alcatraz. I give it a little gas and line myself up, glancing at the crowd of people lining the neighboring piers and pointing at me. Luckily, I'm far enough from the streets that the main crowds and patrolling authorities haven't seen me yet—but that's surely only a matter of time because of the explosion.

I take a few deep breaths and gun the engine again, pushing forward on the wheel as I do. I slowly sink beneath the surface once more. The dash is lit up with screens that tell me depth, speed, and a whole bunch of other stuff that makes little sense to me. I focus on going in a straight line.

Maybe a mile and a half ahead of me, Danny Pellaggio, along with Ivan Gregovski and whoever else he has with him, is preparing to commit an act of terrorism that could potentially start a second Cold War. He has no idea I'm coming for him. My Inner Satan has two black bags and plenty of reasons to be pissed.

I smile at the irony of the situation. He's been running around calling himself the Shark, and here I am, a predator far above him in the food chain, approaching with deadly intent below the surface of the San Francisco Bay. I can smell the blood. I can *taste* it. And I'm looking to spill a whole lot more...

Who's the shark now, asshole?

I can't help but hum the theme tune from *Jaws*.

17:19 PDT

I cover the distance in minutes. Seeing the outline of the island ahead, I steer left, looping around in a wide circle to approach from the far side of the island. When we first looked at Alcatraz, we all agreed that Pellaggio would fire the missile either from the right-hand side, on the roof of the main prison, or near the Quartermaster's building, where he'd have line of sight and a better angle to fire from.

I drop my speed and slowly climb to the surface again. I wish I'd put a fin on the roof—that would've been brilliant!

I come to a stop and immediately dial Josh.

"How am I looking?" I ask when he answers.

"I've just picked you back up on the GPS. You're looking good. How was it?"

"Being underwater? Fucking weird!"

He laughs. "I bet! At least you didn't kill yourself."

"Yeah, always a bonus. So where am I, exactly?"

"Pretty much bang on where you need to be. The north-west corner of the island is just ahead. You should come up on West Road at the back of the lighthouse, which will provide you with enough time to get yourself prepared. Thermal imaging from the GlobaTech drone we've got over the area is showing minimal movement on that side of the island. There's one guy patrolling, and he's heading over to the lighthouse as we speak. Take him out and you should have a clear run toward Pellaggio. Steer another couple hundred yards, and you should see a small inlet in the rock formation that's level enough for you to climb onto. It's the best place to begin your ascent."

I raise my eyebrows, not surprised but impressed by how much detail he had waiting for me. I expect nothing less from him, but it's just further evidence of how talented Josh really is.

I laugh. "See, *this* is why I don't shoot you."

"Any reason's a good reason!"

It's good to hear his trademark enthusiasm when there's little to look forward to. When I'm not on a job, it can irritate the shit out of me—which he knows damn well. But when I'm working or facing a particularly awful situation, it relaxes me knowing someone can still be so happy.

"Oh, Clark got me some new guns. Berettas again, but the 92FS model, not the 92A1's. They're beautiful."

Josh chuckles. "Aww, ain't he a sweetheart?"

"He's somethin' all right. What's the latest from Grace? Any news from the Jeremiah?"

"Secretary Schultz is due to arrive in the next twenty minutes. Like she said, they're going ahead with the parade no matter what. Secret Service has tightened up their security, but they're still denying the FBI full access."

I press the button on the dash that I assume opens the roof. This is a convertible sports car, after all, and the button has a small image of a car, side-on, with the roof partially raised.

Educated guess.

I'm right. It folds slowly back, revealing the cold sea breeze and the setting sun. I reach behind me and open the black bag with the grappling gun in it. I take out the harness Clark had mentioned and start putting it on.

I shake my head to myself. "That makes no sense. Surely, they'd want as much help as they could get?"

"My guess would be because they already have military and naval security on board, plus the Secret Service, they don't want to draw attention to themselves by suddenly having the FBI on there as well. There's no reason for them to be there normally, so people might start asking questions if they saw them working security. Plus, I think it's probably a pride thing. They wanna handle it all themselves."

I take a deep breath as I slowly stand and tighten the fastenings around my waist. "Well, that pride is gonna get people killed. We got anything we can use from Agent Green yet?"

"Nothing we don't already know. Jimmy Manhattan set the whole thing up, as far as getting to you is concerned. Everything else was planned by Pellaggio behind Manhattan's back."

"Any word on *his* condition?"

"Manhattan? Still breathing as far as I know. Do we care?"

With the harness firmly in place, I reach down and take out the grappling gun. I heave it up in my arms and taking aim.

"Not particularly."

It goes quiet on the line, and I use the time to line up my shot. I've never used one of these things before, and I'm only going to get one chance at planting this grappling hook in the top of the cliff ledge.

"Oh, shit!" shouts Josh in my ear.

I let out a tense sigh. "More good news?"

"Adrian, that guy patrolling the perimeter is closing in on your position."

"Where is he?"

"Approaching the helipad now, just a couple hundred yards east of the lighthouse. You're gonna come up on the Agave Trail. That path winds up to the top of the island. He's gonna be directly above you as you're climbing."

"Wonderful. Is he going to hear me fire this grappling gun?"

"Possibly."

"Great..."

I line up my shot again and steady myself. I lean into the weapon slightly so that any recoil doesn't knock me backward and overboard.

"Keep an eye on him," I whisper.

I close one eye and adjust my grip, taking a deep breath

and holding it. I steady myself and breathe out, squeezing the trigger as I do. The gas-propelled grappling line roars out of the gun, making a noise like a firework. The *thunk* as the hook penetrates the cliff side overhead sounds loud, even over the noise of the bay.

Clark wasn't kidding about it being noisy. Jesus!

"Christ!" yells Josh. "How loud?"

"Tell me about it." I tense my jaw muscles. "Has the sentry heard me?"

"It doesn't look like it, no. He must be deaf."

"Pardon?"

"I said he must be... oh, piss off!"

I chuckle. "Got you."

"Whatever. I hope he shoots you."

"If he does, I'm gonna come back and haunt you."

"Adrian, you always say that, but we both know when your time's up, you'll be trapped way down in the pits of Hell with no hope of escape..."

I smile at the visual. "Fair point."

I detach the rope from the gun and tie it to the harness. It's like a sleeveless jacket but thick, like a Kevlar vest. It has compartments on every side for weapons and grenades. Two straps run down each shoulder, and another wraps around the waist with a small device clipped to it. The rope feeds through the straps and into the device, which will then wind up the rope, helping speed up and control the climb. At the top, I'll simply disconnect the device and walk away.

I put the strap of the Heckler and Koch MP5 over my shoulder, securing it at my back. I load up the side pockets with grenades and attach my back holster with both Berettas in it. There's a pair of fingerless gloves in the bag as well. They have tough leather sewn onto the palm and a thin layer of padding over the knuckles. I put them on and carefully step out of the car and onto the shallow bank at the foot of Alcatraz.

"Right, Josh, I'm beginning the ascent now. How's it looking up top?"

"The guy's still wandering around near the helipad. You're gonna need to be quick and quiet."

"Roger that."

I look up at the imposing cliff face and take a deep breath. I hate heights and being exposed. I loop my right arm once around the rope and get a firm grip with my hand. I pull hard to test if it'll take my weight. I'm happy it will. I grab it with my left hand and place my left foot on the cliff in front of me. Slowly, I begin to climb. The device at my back whirs away automatically, and it makes things much easier, taking a lot of pressure off my arms. Within minutes, I'm almost halfway up.

This is like walking—like in the old *Batman* TV show from the sixties with Adam West. They'd scale a building, but if you tilted your head, you could tell they were just walking, and the camera was on its side.

Whoa! Shit!

My foot just slipped on the cliff face, and I crashed forward into the rock, banging my left shoulder and knee.

"Ah, shit…"

"Adrian, you all right?" asks Josh.

"Yeah, I slipped."

"Jesus. Be careful, will you?"

"Josh, I'm hanging off the side of a fucking cliff. It's not exactly the safest thing I could be doing."

I push off gently and find my footing again, take a deep breath to compose myself, and continue with the climb.

A few more minutes pass without incident. I'm soon at the top, level with the grappling hook. The steel prongs are lethal and fully penetrated the rock. I slowly place one hand on the flat surface directly above me. After a couple more steps up the side, I bring my other hand up and heave myself onto the ledge. I swing one knee over, then the other. I rest on all fours and catch my breath before unclipping the device from my back and regarding it in my hand. It's a great piece of tech, but my arms are still burning from the effort. I stand and a pain shoots through my shoulder, making me wince. I look down to see blood soaking through my top and the harness.

Oh, yeah, I got stabbed... forgot to get that looked at.

I look around me. The lighthouse is to my left, standing ominously against the skyline. The path beneath me is muddy and leads off to my right on a steady incline.

"Josh, I'm up. Where's the guy?"

"He's stopped level with the helipad. His heat signature's spiked a bit, so I'm guessing he's just lit a cigarette or something."

I take one of the Berettas from my back and attach the suppressor to it, which I'd shoved hurriedly into my pocket before I started the climb. I grip the gun tightly in my right hand. I take a last look over the edge of the cliff. The amphibious sports car is bobbing gently on the waves below me. I must be over a hundred feet up.

Man, I hate heights...

I crouch slightly and move quickly along the path and around the bend. The Agave Trail runs uphill on a slight gradient to the helipad before leveling out on top of the island. I keep to the right, moving along the outside of the path as it curves up and round to the left, to keep out of the guy's line of sight for as long as I can.

"He's about thirty feet in front of you," whispers Josh. "Just as the path veers right up ahead."

I don't respond to minimize the risk of giving my position away. I change my stance, standing straight and holding my gun in both hands—right arm locked, ready for any recoil; left arm bent but firm, to steady my aim.

I need to be fast. A one-man patrol this far away from anyone else will definitely have a radio, and I don't want to announce my presence here any sooner than necessary.

I edge forward, peering around as much as I can. I see a small plume of smoke fly out and evaporate a few feet in front of me from around the bend. The wind isn't blowing in that direction, so the guy must be just around the corner, facing me.

I take a slow, deep breath to compose myself. I quickly step out, drop to one knee, and raise my gun up, taking aim at the guy. He doesn't even have time to register surprise or shock. He just looks at me impassively for a brief second before I squeeze the trigger twice. A double-tap—one in the chest, one in the head, in quick succession. He crumples to the ground, lifeless. The dirt around him turns dark as blood flows from his wounds. I walk over to him, twisting my foot on his cigarette as I pass.

I shake my head disapprovingly. "Those things'll kill you, asshole. One down, Josh."

"Seven to go," he replies.

24

I quickly search the body. He's got a radio, which I slide into an empty compartment in my harness. He also has plenty of spare magazines for his gun, but I don't need his weapon, so won't need his bullets either.

"Right, Josh, where am I going?"

He clears his throat. "Okay... Head straight along the West Road. When you get to the main prison building, you're gonna need to head inside and cut through, which will bring you out on the East Road. You'll see the water tower on your left as you do. The Quartermaster's building is just beyond that. I can see three heat signatures in there. My money's on one of them being Pellaggio."

"Any other movement I should worry about? Where are the other three?"

"Nothing of any consequence. You should have a clear run into the prison at least. The rest of them are milling around near the East Road at the moment. Looks like a loose patrol."

I set off along the West Road at a slow jog. I look to my left and see the outline of Angel Island State Park illuminated by the pale orange glow of the sun as it begins its descent for the night. It's a beautiful evening—a little breezy, but that's understandable, considering I'm surrounded completely by water. It should be a nice evening, which will likely see fireworks on board the S.S. Jeremiah O'Brien.

Hopefully not the bad kind.

I make good time and come up on the main prison within ten minutes. The building is old, and the brickwork has fallen away in places over the years. Steel railings block the entrance—presumably for the purposes of the tours they operate on the island. There's one door on the side wall, which looks like a service entrance. It's rusted metal, dark gray, with thick bolts studding along the edges.

I stop and crouch. "Okay, Josh—I'm here. Is this the only way in?"

"Seems to be... I'm checking the schematics now. That door should bring you into a small corridor that leads into the main prison holding area."

"Okay. Anyone nearby?"

"No sign of life beyond. Everyone is still where they were a few minutes ago."

"Great. I'm moving in."

With my Beretta in hand, I try the handle slowly. The door is unlocked, which I half-expected—I figured this was the way the guy I just killed had come. I open the door an inch and look up and down the gap, checking for wires, just in case it's been booby-trapped. Ahead, I see a short, narrow, open-ended maintenance corridor that seems to lead into the main prison area, just like Josh said. Mold stains cover the walls, and the old cement covering the ground is mottled with damp patches.

I lower my voice. "Looks clear. I'm heading inside."

"Copy that. Still looks good here."

I push the door open and take a step inside.

Click.

I close my eyes. Oh, fuck...

I spin around and see a small, black, circular device attached to the wall behind the door, which I immediately recognize as a trip mine. A small laser fires out from the top of it. If that beam is broken, it triggers the explosive on a slight delay.

The door just broke it...

I probably have about three seconds before it explodes. I lunge forward, urging my legs to sprint as fast as they can into the main prison. Unfortunately, my body is moving faster than my legs seem to want to, and all I end up doing is lunging forward through the corridor and out into the prison.

In mid-air, I hear the explosion go off behind me. The roar of the flames is deafening, and the heat is intense. As I land, I cover my head with my arms, looking underneath me as best I can.

Oh, shit!

The blast has ripped the metal door from its hinges. It's flying toward me, propelled by the explosion.

I scramble to my feet and try to dive away to the right, but I'm too slow. The door lands on me, smashing against my back and the back of my head. The force of the impact sends me flying forward and skidding across the floor.

I roll over on my back and lie still for a moment, assessing the damage. I feel like an eighteen-wheeler has just ran over me. I have a pulsating ache across my back, and my ears are ringing. My headache is beyond words, but other than that, it seems like I'm in one piece—which is a goddamn miracle.

I prop myself up on my elbows and look around. My vision's a little hazy, but there's not much to make out anyway. I roll over and push myself up on all fours. My hands are resting in shallow puddles, and the floor is uneven and muddy around me. The area I'm in looks small—maybe thirty feet square, max. There are large double doors on both sides, with holding cells lining the wall in front of me, facing the corridor I just got blown out of. I try to stand, moving my leg forward to take my weight.

Woah... nope!

I barely got my knees off the floor before I toppled over. I landed awkwardly on my shoulder.

I groan and blink hard, trying to focus. I'm in so much pain that anything new doesn't even register anymore. I tap the earpiece absently with my hand.

"Josh? Josh... you there?"

I get no response. When I tap it again, I get feedback in my ear. Great. I guess I'm on my own. I take it out and throw it across the floor. I struggle to get on all fours again. I'm facing the corridor and look across the room at the doors.

They're open.

Wonderful... what now?

I sense I'm not alone. I squint to focus, dealing with the onset of a concussion and the dim interior lighting, which aren't helping clear the haze. Three men rush toward me, armed, approaching in a loose, wide arc. All three of them are dressed in nondescript black denim, combat boots, and black T-shirts. They look military, so I'm guessing they're Pellaggio's own men, as opposed to leftovers from Manhattan's leftovers reign in charge. They've got me covered from every angle.

I push myself up further, so I'm kneeling back, resting against my heels. I'm breathing heavily, grimacing from the pain that's shooting around my body with each breath.

I hold my hands out to the sides, exhausted. "I don't suppose... you boys wanna surrender now... do you? Save us all... some time and effort... later?"

The guy on my right steps toward me while the others hang back and raises—

Ah!

Shit!

He didn't say a word. He just slammed the butt of his rifle into the side of my head—hard enough to make me dizzy, restrained enough to keep me conscious. My concussion doubled in severity almost instantly, and I fell forward to the floor again, fighting the urge to vomit.

I push myself back up on all fours and shake my head, trying to clear the cobwebs and stay conscious. I spit out a little blood to the side and look up at each of them in turn.

"Huh... guess not."

The one in the middle steps forward now. "Mr. Pellaggio has been expecting you."

I struggle to one knee. "Well, I hope he's got a cold beer waiting for me... I'm parched."

"Get up!" yells the guy on the right.

I ignore him and spit a little more blood out on the floor next to me. I feel inside my mouth with my finger for a cut. I can't find anything, which I'm assuming means I've got some internal bleeding. I can breathe okay, so I've not got a punctured lung.

"Hey! Get your ass up!"

I sigh. "I'm doing my best... asshole. How about you get

yourself blown up, then hit in the face—see how quickly *you* can move after?"

He steps forward and raises the butt of his rifle once again, but the guy in the middle stops him. "Jones, enough. Pellaggio wants him in one piece. It's not our job to beat the shit out of him, remember?"

I look up at him and smile weakly. "Thanks."

He smiles back smugly and shrugs. "I wouldn't thank me if I were you. You've not met the guy who *will* be beating the shit outta you!"

I look back down at the floor, grimacing through another deep breath. "Great..."

The guy on the left and the one in the middle move over to me. They let their rifles hang loose as they each grab me under an arm and heave me up, holding me steady so that Jones can frisk me. He takes my phone out of my pocket, tosses it to the floor, and drives the heel of his boot down hard on it, smashing it beyond repair. He then unfastens the harness, along with my back holster and the strap of the MP5, letting them all drop to the floor at my feet.

Jones looks to the guy on the left. "Pritchard, pick his shit up." Then he looks at me. "You, move."

I sigh and let them lead me over to the open door, breathing slowly and painfully. High above, the hanging beams of light crackle away, doing nothing for the earth-shattering headache I have. There's no natural light inside here, and I imagine there's little outside by now, either. I think about the Jeremiah and realize I'm running out of time to stop Pellaggio.

I frown. "What time is it?"

"Time for you to shut the fuck up," replies Jones.

I shrug. "Wow... helpful. Thanks."

Josh would be so proud at how well I'm doing with my sarcasm.

They push me again, making me stumble forward and almost fall over. I'm definitely not firing on all cylinders. It's too risky to attempt to take them all out now, although not impossible. I need to bide my time, mess with their heads as much as possible, and get them good and pissed for when it *is* time to kill them. The more wound up they get, the better the chances of them making a mistake. Right now, I need all the help I can get.

We walk through the doors and into a long corridor with old, empty offices either side. We walk to the end, where it becomes a crossroads. I stop, looking both ways. To the right I see the corridor to the prison cells. Left looks to be the old dining hall. The guy behind nudges me in the back with the barrel of his rifle, which I take as a sign to go straight. After a short walk, the corridor opens up into a reception area, with two large doors ahead.

I wish Josh were still in my ear, telling me where I'm going and what's coming. I hate flying blind, especially when I'm outnumbered and barely conscious.

Pritchard moves ahead and opens the doors. He steps through and holds them open for the rest of us. He's carrying the harness, my holster, and the MP5 by its strap, all in his left hand. We emerge outside of the main prison block, on a pathway that seems to wind down the front of the island, all the way to the main docks.

We make our way down it, along the outside of the prison and dining hall. Pritchard is ahead of us, with Jones and the remaining guy either side. The sun is low on the horizon. Its orange glow is silhouetted against the shadowed skyline of the San Francisco Bay as dusk settles in. I can just about make out the shape of the Jeremiah in the distance.

The secretary of defense will be on board by now, I suspect. It has to be close to seven p.m. by now, so they'll be making their final preparations before the service begins. My money's on Pellaggio waiting until the end, so he can be sure Schultz will be on the stage giving his speech. He'll want to make certain he kills *him* if nothing else.

Tick-tock, Adrian.

I sigh, clenching my jaw muscles. I silently fight the headache and the pain in my neck and back that's beginning to throb more prominently now.

After a few minutes, the path turns sharply to the right and works its way down a slope as we gradually head toward the East Road. It starts out with relatively new, well-maintained cement underfoot, but the farther we walk, the worse the path gets. It slowly becomes gravel with patches of old, stained cement dotted around.

I try to walk a little faster—no use to me going downhill. Essentially, they're above me, giving them any physical advantage there is over me. Once we get back on level ground, I need to take these monkeys out before we get too close to Pellaggio. The guy before made it sound like I'm in for some serious punishment when I get to where we're going—I imagine from either Pellaggio himself or Gregovski.

I can hardly wait...

The path turns, going back on itself yet again. Looking down, I can see the main East Road not far below. Farther away to my right is the main dock. I can just about see one boat and what looks like the back of another that's partly blocked from view. Must be what Pellaggio and his crew came over in.

A few minutes later, we come out on the East Road at a junction just before the old Officer's Club building, which is away to the right. The road doglegs slightly to the left, which is the way we're going, apparently. The guy with my stuff takes point, and the rest of us follow him, with the other two still on either side of me. A few hundred yards along, up ahead, I see the Quartermaster building.

I'm running out of time.

I turn to look at Jones. "So, what's Pellaggio planning on doing once he's fired his Stinger missile at the S.S. Jeremiah?"

He frowns and looks nervously at his colleagues.

I chuckle. "Oh, sorry—was that meant to be a secret?"

"Quit talkin', asshole," says Pritchard.

"I'm just curious. I figured, if you guys told me now, it'd save him doing it later. He could use the time more effectively, like for torturing me. I'm just thinking of him, really."

"You really don't know when to keep your mouth shut, do you?"

I shake my head. "Not usually."

Jones takes two quick steps forward and stops in front of me, gun raised and aimed at my chest. The guy on the right takes a step back and looks on. I glance over my shoulder at him, then at Pritchard, who's stepped to his right. They've got me covered, forming a loose triangle around me.

"I reckon we can have a *little* fun with this prick..." says Jones to no one in particular.

"We could say he tried to get away, and we had to stop him?" adds Pritchard.

He sets my equipment down beside him and casually aims his rifle at me.

Perfect!

I look at each of them in turn. "Hey, c'mon, guys. There are three of you and one of me. I'm concussed and can barely walk. Surely, you don't need the guns? How about you all put them down, and we settle this the old-fashioned way? Give me a sporting chance, huh?"

Come on... take the bait, assholes. Take the bait...

They all exchange glances and smile at each other, their grins filled with bad intentions. One by one, they rest their guns on the ground.

Bingo!

I know I have to be careful. I'm still a bit unsteady on my feet and have limited maneuverability after the blast. I can't afford for any confrontation to get dragged out.

I take a step back, turning the loose triangle surrounding me into a square, with me in the bottom left corner. Pritchard is in the opposite corner to me. I figure he'll make the first move because the other two seem to be running things by him, so he might be more senior.

I'm right. Pritchard edges forward, one step at a time, his hands up in an amateurish boxing guard. I stand loose, turning slightly side on, with my arms by my sides. Even on my worst day, I'm twice as fast as any of these idiots. And today is definitely not one of my better days.

He's approaching with all his weight on his back foot. He's in an orthodox stance, meaning his weaker, left hand is out in front. He's going to get close and immediately swing a big, lazy right haymaker in an attempt to knock my head off my shoulders. It's so obvious, I almost feel sorry for the guy.

I let him get two paces closer before reacting to the punch he's about to throw. I move forward as fast as I can, bringing my arm up across my chest. As his haymaker comes up and round from his hip, my hand snaps to meet it and pushes it away, sending him off-balance. I got to it before his momentum could get going, which made deflecting it easier.

As he's leaning away from me, I take a step forward, raise

my foot, and kick his front leg at the knee. I step through, pushing my foot through his kneecap and instantly breaking his leg. The snap is sickening and sounds loud on the near-deserted island, but it's quickly drowned out by his agonizing screams.

I bring my leg back, waiting for him to fall toward me. As he inevitably does, I bring my knee up to meet him, catching him flush on the nose. I feel the thin bone and cartilage give way under the impact, sounding like a wet explosion as blood splatters across his face.

He crumples to the ground, unconscious and broken. I take a couple of hurried steps back, narrowing my angle to the other two guys, who are standing in shock, yet to react to what's happened.

I try to ignore the pain I'm feeling from all this moving around. I look at each one in turn. "Who's next?"

They look at each other. Panic and confusion spreads across their faces. The confidence they had is suddenly—

BANG!

Huh? That gunshot came from farther up the East Road.

I look over and see a figure walking toward us. Both men do the same and then turn back to me, smiling but also looking a little uneasy. The man walks over and stops between the other two.

"Enough. What's going on?"

His voice is loud and angry and Russian.

Hello, Gregovski.

Fuck me—the guy's huge! I'm no slouch. I'm a little over six feet tall and probably around two hundred pounds. I'm a pretty powerful guy when I need to be. But Gregovski has five inches on me, easily. And probably a good fifty pounds. And it's all muscle. He looks younger than he is. He could comfortably pass for early forties, despite his FBI file confirming he's approaching fifty. He's got a shaved head and dark eyes.

I relax my stance. I think my little rebellion is over... for now, anyway.

Jones takes a step back, seeming to physically shrink, clearly intimidated. "We, ah... He tried to escape, so we surrounded him, tried to teach him a lesson."

Gregovski looks over at me. I simply shrug. He then looks at Pritchard, unconscious on the ground with a busted nose and broken leg. He looks back at Jones. "You didn't teach him well, it would seem..."

He moves over to Pritchard and nudges him with his boot. No reaction. He aims his gun and fires once, putting a bullet in the back of his head. He then turns and puts another bullet in Jones, right between the eyes. No emotion, no hesitation.

I like his style.

He turns the remaining guy, who's shitting himself to my left. His eyes are wide, and his body language is tense. "Get his bag."

The guy obeys without hesitation.

Finally, Gregovski turns to me. "So, you're Adrian Hell?"

I shrug. "Last I checked, yeah..."

He raises his gun and—

BANG!

25

??:??

I cough as a heavy boot buries itself into my stomach, waking me up. Not the nicest alarm call I've ever had. I slowly open my eyes. I try to lift my head and look around. My vision's blurry and my body feels like it's on fire.

I'm sitting on the floor with my back to a wall. I'm inside a large, dilapidated building that resembles a warehouse. The Quartermaster building—it has to be. It's long and narrow with pools of water on the floor. It's mostly hollowed out inside, except for two rickety wooden staircases climbing up the far side of the building opposite me. The wooden gantries above look equally decayed from this angle.

I hear some faint movement coming from above, but I can't see anything. Looking around, I seem to be sitting at one end of the building. On either side of me are three rows of windows stretching up. Out of the left side, I see the dusk fading into night and the skyline of the San Francisco Bay lighting up as daylight fades.

I must've been out well over an hour... shit! I can't afford to keep losing time. I have to stop Pellaggio before he fires on the Jeremiah. I quickly run through a self-assessment. My right arm is throbbing and burning. I slowly put my hand on my shoulder, feeling the wet, blood-soaked material of my shirt and jacket. I look down, blinking rapidly to clear my vision and focus. The bullet Gregovski put in me went through the fleshy part of my arm, on the outside, below the shoulder. It hurts like hell, but it hasn't caused any permanent or troubling damage.

Oh.

Gregovski is standing a few feet away to my right, glaring down at me with a mixture of anger and disgust. My God, the guy's a monster! There's no sign of anyone else with us. I guess they're either upstairs or outside.

It's just him and me.

He takes a step forward and kicks me again in the stomach, just below the ribcage. I crease over and fall to my right, coughing up more blood.

I hold up a hand. "Okay, okay! I'm awake already!"

"Your pain has only just begun, Adrian Hell."

His voice is slow, deliberate, and full of hatred.

I manage to push myself back into a sitting position and hug my knees to my chest as I look up at the menacing beast looming over me. This situation is going to get worse before it gets better. That's assuming it actually *does* get better...

"Wonderful. Is this because you're pissed at me for killing your niece and nephew last year?"

Without a word, he leans down at full speed and punches me across the face, sending me down again.

Christ... that one's going to leave a mark! Good job I can

take a hit. But this guy is going to kill me if I let things carry on as they are. I need to do something to take this guy out, and I need to do it soon. I'm honestly not sure how much more of this I can take.

I sit back up again and stare at him. His eyes are wide, and he's snarling through gritted teeth like a wild animal. He looks barely in control, and I've not even started trying to piss him off. I can see why Pellaggio wants this guy as the poster child for his attack on the Jeremiah. He's a convincing terrorist-slash-psychopath.

I smile weakly. "So, is this anger all about me? Or is there any truth to the rumor that you hate Russia, America, and everyone else as well?"

He doesn't answer me. He still looks incensed with rage. His eyes are burning with hatred. He reaches down, grabs my throat with both hands, and—

Whoa!

—heaves me off the floor to my feet.

My eyes go wide. I balance on my tiptoes, trying to keep the ground beneath me as he lifts and squeezes, restricting my ability to breathe. I grab his wrists with both hands, frantically trying to loosen his grip.

That doesn't work.

I start hammering down on his elbows, trying to force his arms to bend and take some of the pressure out of his vise-like grip.

That works a little, but he's not letting up that easily.

My lungs start to burn as I gasp for oxygen, not getting anywhere near the amount I need to stay awake. My arms are throbbing in agony from the wounds inflicted on both my shoulders now, so I can't get as much power behind the blows as I need.

When in doubt, go low.

I position myself as best I can and launch my foot into his balls, like I'm kicking a fifty-yard field goal in the Superbowl.

That loosens his grip.

He yells as he lets go and staggers back, clutching his groin. I take a few paces back myself, to put some distance between us while I recover. My throat's sore and feels like it's starting to bruise already from where he gripped me. I look around the expanse of the old Quartermaster building, trying to find my equipment. Where the hell are my guns?

Oh, *there* they are... in the middle of the room, next to a couple of upturned crates on the floor. Behind Gregovski.

Fucking brilliant.

I guess I'll have to fight this sonofabitch, won't I?

He looks up, shaking the effects of my kick away. He runs at me with a speed not befitting a man his size, arms wide and high, ready to slam down on me. He looks like a Neanderthal on steroids—a big, thick brow and long arms the size of my legs. He's definitely strong. But he's still slow, hindered by his size and weight. I haven't been a hundred percent for a few hours, and I'm certainly nowhere near that right now, but I figure I'm still quicker than he is. And that's my only advantage. That's how I'm going to beat him. I'm faster than he is. And I can guarantee I'm better trained and more violent than he is too.

As he comes at me, I quickly play out every possible defensive technique in my head. What if I move left? What if I duck and feint right? I consider what could work and what definitely won't.

Ah, when in doubt...

I let him get maybe five feet away from me, then jump forward. I snap my forehead toward him in an arc, as if it were a dead weight. I time it perfectly with the jump and connect with the bridge of his nose, where it angles out in between the eyes. It's like he ran into a wall. The impact takes away all his momentum instantly. He stops dead, stunned by shock and pain in equal measure.

His arms are by his sides, so his face was unprotected. I stare at him for a moment, frowning to ignore the throbbing pain in my head, seeing what he's going to try next. He's just standing there, eyes still wide, but confusion replaces the anger. I'm going to launch a right elbow at his head, just in front of his ear. That should—

"What the fuck is going on?"

Huh?

I look up. It's Pellaggio. He's on the top floor, looking down over the railing. We lock eyes for a moment, then he disappears out of sight.

"Shoot him!" he shouts.

I hear footsteps along the gantry as the last of his men set off running for the stairwell at the far end.

I should probably get my guns...

I take a step toward the MP5, but Gregovski cuts me off, blocking my path. He seems to have made good use of the small reprieve and has recovered well.

He looks at me and smile with bad intentions. "I'm looking forward to killing you, Adrian Hell!"

I grin. "Yeah, you wouldn't believe how many Russians have said that to me. And every one of them is dead from trying."

"Not all of them," he replies cryptically.

What does *that* mean?

He swings his arm around slowly, aiming at my head. I duck under his right hand but catch his follow-up left on my ribs. I see him go for my throat again and block it. I duck down and deliver a left hook to his liver. It knocks him back a little, so I roll under and do the same on the other side—a straight right to the gut, central, aimed once more at the liver. Again, it sends him back and looks like it hurt him a bit more this time. Regardless, he remains stubbornly upright in front of me, his large arms held high in a loose fighting guard.

The magical thing about a blow to the liver is that it has a devastating effect on the body, causing pain, nausea, and loss of balance. But it has a delayed reaction. It takes your body roughly ten seconds to process the impact and react accordingly. He just took two nasty punches to his, so he's about to have a bad day...

We stand looking at each other as the seconds pass. He bares his teeth again, like a caged beast taunting its prey. I simply stand and smile.

Three... Two... One...

Gregovski's eyes go wide. He keels over and drops on all fours, vomiting profusely. Then he falls over into a fetal position; his body is going into shock as his brain finally registers the shots to his liver.

Goodnight, sweetheart!

That's him down for the count. I make my way over to my guns and crouch to take a Beretta from the holster. As I draw it, I hear the familiar sound of a gun being cocked behind me.

No... *two* guns.

Oh, no... three guns!

I look up and see three guys standing over me—Jones with someone on either side of him. They must've made it down the stairs quicker than I thought they would. They've both got me bang to rights, and I doubt they're going to hesitate.

Shit!

Jones smiles, and I see his finger tense on the trigger. "So long, asshole!"

I can't believe I let them get the drop on me like that. I didn't give them anywhere near as much as credit as I should've. I was too busy focusing on Gregovski.

Shit, shit, shit!

I close my eyes and take a long, deep, painful breath as I wait for the inevitable.

Three gunshots sound out, and I flinch with surprise.

What the...

I open one eye and look around. Then I open the other, just to be sure. Then I pat myself down as a final check.

Nope—definitely not dead.

I look at the three guys who were about to shoot me. Jones and his friends are lying on the ground with blood pouring from bullet holes in their chests.

Seriously, what the fuck just happened?

I look all around the building, quickly resting my gaze on the main door. It's open, and Senior Special Agent Grace Chambers is standing in the doorway, gun in hand.

She's smiling at me. "Hey."

I frown. "Hey. What are you doing here?"

"Saving your ass, by the looks of it."

"Yeah, thanks for that. But seriously, why aren't you on the Jeremiah?"

She walks over to me. "Agent Wallis has it covered. He's working with the Secret Service. Obviously, they remained steadfast that nothing will change, so I figured I was more use to you. I took a speedboat over here, then spoke to Josh to find out where you were."

"I've not spoken to him. I lost comms when I got blown up earlier."

"When you got—Jesus Christ! What happened? Are you all right?"

The fact she's concerned about me is a nice a feeling. And the fact she has my back is even better. I can feel myself beginning to trust her.

I see her gaze flick above us, looking at something behind me. "Adrian, look out!"

A hail of bullets streams down, narrowly missing us both. I look up and see Pellaggio screaming from the top floor, leaning over the balcony and firing down at us.

No rest for the wicked.

"Grace, find cover!"

I pick up my back holster containing both Berettas and sprint as fast as my broken and beaten body will allow over to the far wall underneath Pellaggio, to limit his visibility.

I have to find a way up those stairs, so I can stop him.

I look over at Chambers. She's picked up my MP5 and moved behind the doorway outside. She leans in and fires off a couple of bursts at Pellaggio, forcing him to duck away.

"I'll cover you!" she shouts.

I take my Beretta out of the holster, tuck one in my waistband at my back, and keep hold of the other. I take a couple of deep breaths and look over to the door to make sure she's okay. She breaks cover and unleashes another burst of fire at Pellaggio.

Yeah, she'll be fine.

I set off running for the stairwell on the back wall, which immediately draws more fire from above. I glance behind me and see Chambers move back behind cover. I keep my head down and make it to the stairs. I duck down at the side of it. It offers precious little cover but allows me to squeeze off a couple of rounds in Pellaggio's direction, which buys me some more valuable seconds.

I hold out until Pellaggio pauses to reload, then set off up the stairs as fast as I can, taking two, sometimes three at a time. Every inch of my body still aches from the explosion earlier. Both my arms are throbbing as blood continues to stream out of the wounds caused by Manhattan's blade and Gregovski's bullet. But the pain can wait. I have to stop Pellaggio, that's all that matters.

Another hail of bullets shreds and splinters the wooden staircase as I come up on the second floor and race around to begin my ascent to the top. I hear Chambers fire a few more short bursts, which buys me more time. I hold my gun out in front of me, ready to fire as I dash up the final flight of stairs. I come out on the makeshift walkway at the top.

I aim my gun at Pellaggio, who's leaning over the balcony, firing at Chambers below. "Danny! It's over. Drop your gun and step away from the edge."

He stops firing but doesn't move, keeping his gun trained on Chambers. I look down and see she has her gun pointed at him too. The scene is frozen in a deadly stalemate.

He glances at me. "Throw your gun over the side, Adrian, or I'll cut her in half!"

"You won't get the chance, and we both know it. Just give it up. You've lost."

In the blink of an eye, he snaps around and levels his rifle at me, flashing a wicked smile. "No, I've not."

I hear a muffled cry below, and I glance back down over the balcony. Gregovski is back on his feet, standing behind Chambers with one hand over her mouth. His other hand is holding her right arm out to the side. Her gun is on the floor a few feet away from them.

Shit!

Pellaggio glares at me. "Now throw your fucking gun over the side, or he's gonna snap her pretty little neck!"

I sigh and begrudgingly throw it over the side.

"Adrian, don't!" yells Chambers, who has apparently struggled free from Gregovski's grip.

Pellaggio smiles. "Touching. Now how's this for real power, Adrian? I'm not even gonna keep my gun on you. You stay right there, or your little FBI bitch will die. Understand?"

Arrogant bastard. But I have little choice if I want to keep her alive. I nod reluctantly.

He puts his weapon down, turns, and walks a little farther down the walkway. There's a sniper rifle leaning against the wall. As he gets level with it, he pauses. His gaze alternates between the rifle and back over his shoulder at me.

He picks it up, holding it in his arms like a new father would hold his baby for the first time. "Well, this brings back some fond memories. This... this is what I used to shoot your friend. How's he doing, by the way?"

The anger erupts inside me, coursing through my veins and consuming me. But as pissed as I am, I'm smart enough to see the opportunity I need to stall him.

I take a few valuable seconds to calm myself. "Oh, yeah. You won't have heard, will you? Since we found your inside man at the FBI, you won't be in the loop anymore. Josh is fine. In fact, he's watching all this unfold via a satellite feed at the FBI field office right now."

Pellaggio's face drops, but he quickly recovers. "No matter. There's nothing anyone can do to stop this happening. And then we will watch as a brave new world blossoms in the aftermath."

I shake my head in genuine disbelief. "You're a fucking

idiot. Do you know that? Why do you think I'm here? We figured out most of what you were doing on our own, and your old pal Jimmy Manhattan filled in the blanks. As we speak, the FBI and Secret Service are clearing that boat, so all you're gonna do is play a really expensive game of Battleship on your own."

I know that's not strictly true, but he doesn't. He looks quickly in every direction, like he's trying to follow a fly. His eyes are wide. He seems to be teetering on the edge of control, about to lose it completely and snap. I can handle whatever he comes at me with, as long as he isn't focusing on firing at the Jeremiah.

But he doesn't snap. He doesn't come at me. He struggles, but he exercises restraint and simply smiles back at me. An evil, twisted, intelligent smile. "Nice try, Adrian. I don't care if anything you just said is true or not. I've been planning this for a year, and nothing's gonna stop me from succeeding."

He drops the sniper rifle, continues along the walkway, and stops beside a large black box that looks like a huge briefcase. He crouches beside it and flicks the lock open. He lifts the lid, rests it against the wall, and reaches inside. He takes out an FIM-92 Stinger missile launcher.

I quickly look at Chambers. She isn't afraid, but she's panicking. She can see how close we are to failing. Gregovski is staring up at me with menace in his eyes, his hand holding her steady by the side of her neck. He dwarfs her, towering a good foot over her. She struggles against his grip, but it's more of a futile gesture than a serious attempt at escape.

I look back at Pellaggio, who's hefted the launcher up on his shoulder. It's a tube about five feet long—just a bit longer than the missile itself. His left hand is supporting the end, in the way you would a regular assault rifle. The butt and trigger are close to the shoulder, and his right arm bends as he grips it, finger on the trigger guard. On top of the tube, coming out at roughly a forty-five-degree angle, is a thin piece of metal similar in size to a computer keyboard. Along the top edge of it is the sight, which he's looking through now, out the window and across the bay, lining up his target.

The way the targeting system works is, you look through the scope and see a computerized telescopic sight. Once you get the target in your sights, you hold it steady while the on-board computer locks onto its position using a combination of GPS and laser-guidance. Once the screen confirms the target's locked, you fire.

The missile is propelled out of the launch tube by a powerful stream of argon gas, which is kept cool by a battery pack fitted into the butt of the launcher. It travels at around nine hundred miles per hour and will penetrate its target before exploding like a powerful fragmentation grenade, causing an insane amount of damage.

I'm screwed if he fires that missile, but if I move for him, Chambers is dead.

I clench my jaw muscles, running through every outcome in my head. There are no perfect endings.

Except one. Maybe.

I move my hand slowly to my side, thinking about the Beretta I still have at my back. It's risky, but it's the only option that stands even a remote chance of working. Pellaggio is about to fire his missile. If he does, everything we've done would've been for nothing.

I take a deep breath.

Fuck it.

26

I'm fortunate to have natural ability when it comes to what I do for a living. I received a lot of training during my time in the military, but—and I say this with no ego at all—to get to the level I operate on, you have to have some natural talent to begin with. It has to be in your blood.

I have two main strengths when it comes to shooting: speed and accuracy. If we lived in the Old West, I'd have been a quick-draw champion—no doubt about that. Hand-eye coordination has always come naturally to me, which obviously has a positive effect on my level of accuracy.

You can train people to shoot the wings off a fly at a thousand yards, and that's great. But I can take one look at my target, instantly shoot from the hip, and hit it—every single time. I don't aim with my head. I aim with my eye. My brain then tells my hand to point at what my eye's looking at and it does, like an instinct... a reflex. There's no thought involved. I just point and fire. And I never miss.

It's quite a handy skill to have when you kill people for a living.

I look down one last time at Chambers. We lock eyes and time slows down around me. All noise disappears, leaving nothing except the two of us, staring at each other for what feels like a lifetime. I can see the panic in hers. She'll be able to see the killer in mine.

I wink at her and take one last breath...

My hand disappears behind my back, re-appearing a second later holding my Beretta. I whip it around to aim at Pellaggio. I arc the swing of my arm out over the balcony as I do, and fire once. The bullet hits Gregovski in the center of his forehead, narrowly missing Chambers by a few inches. She screams as Gregovski shudders and falls heavily to the floor. A spray of blood catches her down her left side.

As confident as I was with that shot, it's harder when there's someone you care about in the way.

I save the sigh of relief for later. I know Chambers is okay, and there's no time for celebrating.

I continue the swing, bringing my gun level with Pellaggio. But I hesitate. I can see his finger tensing on the trigger. If I shoot him, it will likely cause him to twitch and get the shot off anyway. In a split-second, I change my mind and drop my gun, racing toward Pellaggio as time resumes its normal speed. I can hear the launcher start to beep as it acquires its target.

Goddammit! Come on, Adrian—faster!

With gritted teeth, I approach him at full speed. I jump and aiming my elbow at his head. I smash into him, catching him flush on his temple at the exact moment he squeezes the trigger. He collapses to the floor, falling with me on top of him.

But I'm too late...

The loud whoosh of the missile firing fills the building.

I punch the floor in frustration. "Fuck! Fuck!"

Chambers appears at the top of the stairs. We look at each other. Her eyes go wide and she runs along the gantry toward me. "No!"

I scramble to my feet and shake my head. "No, this isn't over!"

I'm Adrian Hell. I don't fail, and I certainly don't miss.

I lunge for the Remington sniper rifle that Pellaggio taunted me with earlier. The same rifle that put two bullets in my best friend. I slide to a stop on one knee, grab it, and jab the barrel into the glass of the window in front of me, smashing it. I quickly chamber a .300 round and place the scope to my eye, lining up my shot.

My brain is running at a thousand miles per hour, calculating everything with practiced efficiency.

The Stinger missile is moving at around nine hundred miles per hour in a straight line. The bullet I'm about to fire will move at over twice that speed. The downside is that the range of my bullet is over half that of the Stinger, so the timeframe I have to work with is measured in split-seconds at best.

I track the missile through the scope. It's a small target already, but I'm pretty sure that if I can just hit it, that'll be enough to knock it off course—or, ideally, detonate it early.

I hear Chambers approach me.

"Adrian, you could've shot me back there! I can't believe you would..." She stops, mid-sentence. I've not acknowledged her, but her silence tells me everything I need to know. "Adrian, you can't be serious?"

I don't respond. This is probably the biggest shot I've ever had to take—not wishing to add more pressure to myself or anything.

My whole body aches, and my arms are screaming as I try to hold the rifle steady. But this is it. I look through the scope at the missile. If I miss and it reaches the Jeremiah, the consequences will send shockwaves felt the world over.

I take a deep breath and hold it. Everything around me fades away. I breathe out slowly, squeezing the trigger as the air leaves my lungs. The sound of the shot echoes around the hollow interior of the building. I immediately throw the rifle down and look through the window. I feel Chambers's hand on my shoulder. I reach up and grip it.

One... Two...

The missile explodes, and a small cloud of fire erupts briefly in the sky over the bay. Seconds later, fireworks start flying, signaling the end of the service aboard the Jeremiah.

"Oh my God!" Chambers shouts, sounding both surprised and excited. "You did it!"

I stand up slowly and look at her. A pulsating ache resonates around every inch of my body. My legs feel weak, and I can barely support my own body weight. She steps in close to me and throws her arms around my neck, hugging me tightly. It hurts like hell, but it's totally worth it.

I let out a heavy sigh. I've done it. After everything we've all been through over the past few days, in the space of a few seconds, it's finally over. I step back from Chambers and turn to look at Pellaggio. He's—

—running full-speed toward me. Shit!

I'm too slow to react, but I manage to push Chambers away. He drops his head and spear-tackles me, sending us both crashing into her and to the floor.

His eyes are wild with rage. "You sonofabitch! You've ruined everything! I'll kill you!"

He gets into a full mount position on top of me, resting on his knees as he straddles my chest. He starts raining blow after blow down on me, connecting with my face and chest. I struggle to bring both arms up to protect myself, writhing to evade the punches and look for an opportunity to escape. As I turn away from a big right hand, I steal a glance at Chambers to see if she's okay. She's lying on her side a little away from us, not moving.

Uh!

A punch just caught me on my cheekbone—punishment for getting distracted. I feel myself almost lose consciousness, but another punch to my right cheek knocks the cobwebs away again. I look into his eyes, seeing the unbridled fury burning behind them. He's not going to stop. I know I can't take many more shots like these.

I move my upper body to my left as much as I can, narrowly avoiding another powerful right hand. I catch his arm at the wrist and buck with my hips, using every ounce of strength I have left. It's just enough to dislodge him. Using his arm for leverage, I manage to roll him off me.

I seize the opportunity and struggle to my feet, standing at roughly the same time he does. He comes at me again, but toe-to-toe in a straight-up fistfight, he's got no chance against me, even in my current condition. Plus, he's so far gone with his anger, he's not thinking at all. He's operating on pure hatred, and he's going to be easy pickings for me.

He's holding his hand behind him as he moves toward me. I can see the swing coming a mile away. Don't get me wrong—if it connects, it'll do some serious damage. But it's so easy to telegraph, there's more chance of Elvis hitting me than Pellaggio.

I dodge backward as the punch comes and watch as he hits thin air. His momentum carries him nearly all the way around. As he spins, I smash my elbow into his temple. He drops like a stone and skids toward the edge of the walkway.

I bend over, resting my hands on my knees while I catch my breath. I look over at Chambers and see her making her way slowly to her feet. "You... okay?"

She's holding her head but seems unscathed. "I'm fine. You?"

I stand up straight and stretch my back, making the *okay* gesture with my hand.

She looks at Pellaggio, then at me. She takes a deep breath and walks back along the gantry to where I dropped my Beretta. She picks it up by the barrel and walks back over to me, holding it out to me. "It's unfortunate I wasn't able to make an arrest, what with Danny Pellaggio catching a stray bullet during a shoot-out..."

She raises an eyebrow but never quite manages the smile that should've gone with it. I take the gun from her and nod.

Pellaggio's making his way to his feet, holding onto the railing as he drags himself up. "Okay, you got me." He lets out a desperate laugh. "Well done, you! I'll come quietly. Due process and so on."

Leaning back on the railing, he holds his hands out to Chambers, his wrists together in a gesture of restraint.

She finally manages a smile before turning her back on him.

He frowns, then his eyes grow wide. "Wh-what are you doing? I'm surrendering!"

I take a step forward and raise my gun, so he's looking directly down the barrel. "You're past the stage where you get to just come along quietly and sit in a jail cell. The FBI *know* you died on Alcatraz."

The panic in his eyes gives way to fear. "B-but I'm still alive! I'm giving myself up! I'm surrendering!"

"To whom?"

I pull the trigger and put a bullet through his left eye. The force of the impact pushes him through the old, wooden railing, and he plummets two stories, landing with a sickening thud on the floor below. I glance over the edge and see his crumpled body staring back at me. A large, dark red splatter has formed where his head impacted the concrete.

I should've done that twelve months ago. It would've saved me so much trouble.

I look back at Chambers, who's walking toward the edge. "I wouldn't if I were you. You don't need to see that."

She looks at me, her jaw clenched and her eyes looking the darkest I've ever seen them. "Yes, I do."

I nod and walk along the gantry toward the staircase, leaving her to have her moment of closure. I make my way slowly down the stairs and retrieve my other Beretta. I take a quick look around the old Quartermaster building. For a brief moment, my gaze rests on Gregovski's body. I stare at it but soon realize I feel absolutely nothing. I walk across the floor and stand in the doorway. I look out at the prison complex, farther down the East Road. The dark sky periodically lights up with a flash from the fireworks on the Jeremiah.

Chambers appears next to me. I turn to her. "What now?"

"I need to call Wallis. I left him in charge on the Jeremiah."

I nod.

She puts her hand on my arm. "What about you?"

I shrug. "That depends. Am I still a person of interest to every agency in America?"

She smiles. "After this? I wouldn't think so. Not to the FBI anyway—I'll see to that."

"Thank you."

"Any idea if you're going to stick around? Maybe help us with the aftermath of all this?"

"Probably not. I think the best thing for me to do is put some distance between myself and this city for a while."

She shrugs and smiles. "I guess you've earned a *little* holiday..."

I look over my shoulder at the bodies of Pellaggio and Gregovski one last time, then set off walking. I stop after a few paces. I glance back at Chambers and gesture with my left arm, silently asking her to link it. "You coming?"

Without a word, she strolls over to me, takes my arm, and we set off together down the East Road. This time, I'll take the easy route back to the harbor.

27

After Chambers and I made it back to the mainland, we linked up with Wallis on the Jeremiah. He told us they had managed to track down Pellaggio's men and get them to confirm where they had planted the other bombs on board. I was then taken away in an ambulance, courtesy of the FBI, and driven to the hospital, where I got patched up. Chambers rode with me, holding my hand the whole time.

We both got some much-needed and long-overdue sleep while we were there. In the early hours of the next day, we returned to the field office and de-briefed Josh on what had happened. He said he'd seen some of it on the satellite feed but got worried when he'd lost contact with me.

Chambers was escorted away to give the official de-brief to Assistant Special Agent-in-Charge Webber, so Josh and I took that as a sign to leave quietly. We made a quick call to Robert Clark, thanking him for his support and offering our services in return, should he ever need them. He was grateful and we left it at that.

We ate, drank, and rested for the next day, keeping a low profile as we watched the various news channels around the city report on what had happened. Or, at least, what the authorities had told them had happened. I suspect some of the official statements omitted a few of the grittier details.

Then I got a call from Chambers to say the FBI had arranged a funeral service for Special Agent Johnson, and we'd be welcome if we wanted to pay our respects. I watched that man get gunned down in the line of duty right before my eyes because of a situation I still hold myself accountable for. So, despite our initial differences, I absolutely had nothing but respect to give him.

It's early afternoon now, and the sun's beaming down as I stand in the National Cemetery on Lincoln Boulevard. Close friends and family are sitting in two rows of chairs directly in front of the open grave. FBI agents are standing solemnly just behind them. I see Chambers stood beside Wallis. She's wearing a black trouser suit. Even in mourning, she looks as great as always.

The coffin's in front of the grave with the American flag laid over it.

I'm standing under the shade of a large tree with Josh beside me. We figured it would be best to keep a respectful distance. I've cleaned myself up and I'm on the mend. I'm wearing my jeans and boots, a black shirt, and my leather jacket. Josh is wearing his usual T-shirt and jeans with sneakers and a zip-up hoodie. We don't really have the wardrobe for this type of thing. We usually just focus on putting the body in the ground, not pausing to pay our respects afterward as well.

I bury my hands in my pockets and stare at the grass,

lost in thought. I feel Josh staring at me. I don't look up. "What?"

"Nothing..."

I sigh. "Come on, out with it."

"Well, there's something bothering you. I can tell, so don't waste your time denying it. If you don't wanna tell me, I'm cool with that. But I'm worried about you. This has been a really shitty week, Boss, even by your usual standards. Are you sure you're all right?"

He knows me too well for me to hide anything from him.

"Something Gregovski said back on Alcatraz."

"What was it?"

"We were fighting, and I said every Russian who has tried to kill me died in the process."

He shrugs. "True..."

"Gregovski said, and I quote, 'Not all of them.'"

"You think he means—"

"Clara? Yeah, I do."

"Look, you know we ain't letting her go. If she's alive, we'll find her when the time's right and play hide the bullet with her head. But don't let it eat at you, man. Stay focused on the future."

I finally turn to him. My jaw clenches as I struggle to find the right words to say. It's something I've been meaning to say for over eight years, and now the time's finally come for me to say it, I want to make sure I do it right.

"But things do eat at me, don't they? I'm not sure I *can* look to the future without first addressing my past."

Josh frowns. "What are you saying, Boss?"

"I'm saying, I think it's time."

"Really?" His voice is a mixture of excitement and concern.

I shrug. "You said yourself, me and Agent Chambers—

we clearly feel things for each other, but I can't allow myself to move on like that. Not with the death of my family still hanging over my head. I need to go back to the beginning, to Pittsburgh. Put things right and deal with Wilson Trent once and for all. Put the memory of Janine and Maria to rest, along with my guilt. After everything I've been through over the last few days, I realize now that the life we lead might not afford me many more opportunities to do it. And I need to move on. It's time, Josh."

I let out a sigh. That wasn't easy for me to say.

He puts his hands over his face for a moment, then runs them up and through his hair. "Man, you don't know how long I've waiting to hear you say that, Adrian. Watching you sweep those demons of yours under the carpet time and time again, carry the guilt on your shoulders the way you do— none of it was your fault. It was Wilson Trent who murdered your family, not you. And until now, you've never been ready to aim those Berettas of yours back at him to avenge your wife and daughter. I've got your back, Boss, as always."

Before I can say anything else, Josh nudges my arm and nods at Chambers and Wallis, who are walking toward us.

Wallis shakes both Josh's hand and mine in turn. "Hey."

"I'm glad you could make it," says Chambers, smiling.

"I'm sorry about Agent Johnson," says Josh. "I know how hard it is when you lose a colleague. He was a fine agent."

She nods. "Thank you." She looks at me. "Adrian, there's someone who wants to talk to you."

I raise a curious eyebrow and look at Josh. He simply shrugs. She turns and walks off, so I follow her without another word.

Up ahead, across the cemetery, over by the far gates is a black limousine. It's surrounded by four men wearing suits, earpieces, and black sunglasses. As we approach, the door opens and a man steps out. He's shorter than me, maybe five-nine or five-ten. He's got silver-gray hair, but he isn't that old, maybe early fifties. His weathered face indicates a hard life, but he's managed to retain a certain youthfulness about him.

Chambers stops in front of him and turns to me. "Adrian, this is—"

"Ryan Schultz, Secretary of Defense for the United States. And you are Adrian *Hell*."

His strong, Texan accent sounds just like it did on the phone the last time I spoke to him.

I nod. "That's me."

He strokes his chin, takes a deep breath, and rests his hands on his hips. "I have a dilemma, Adrian. See, this is the second time you've done our great country a service now, son."

I shrug humbly and nod, briefly recalling the last time, down in Heaven's Valley last year.

"But this time, you saved my damn life, so I hear."

I shrug again. "You're welcome."

"You're welcome... what?"

I shake my head. "Don't push your luck, Ryan."

The Secret Service agents around his car all flex their shoulders back and shift uneasily on the spot. Sensing it, Schultz half-turns and gestures with his hand for them to relax. He looks back at me, holding my gaze. "All right, fair enough, son. You've done your job, and on behalf of the United States, I'd like to extend our appreciation."

"Does this get me off the government's hypothetical shit list?"

Schultz frowns and glares at me for a moment in silence.

Then he waves his hand dismissively and turns back to his car. "Doesn't mean I like you, son."

He climbs in the back, and one of the Secret Service agents slams the door shut behind him. A moment later, the limousine drives off.

I turn to Chambers. "Nice guy."

She smiles, and we both set off walking back toward Josh and Wallis. "So, what now, Adrian? Do you still intend to leave?"

"I do."

She nods but fails to hide the disappointment from her face. "Where are you going? Do you know?"

I take a deep breath, pausing for a moment. "I'm heading to Pittsburgh."

Saying it out loud makes it seem more real. This is going to be one of the hardest things I'm ever likely to do in my life.

She frowns. "What's in Pittsburgh?"

I lean forward, kiss her on the cheek, then take a step back, away from her. I look deep into her steel-gray eyes and set my jaw. "Closure."

THE END

Dear Reader,

Thank you for purchasing my book. I hope you enjoyed reading it as much as I enjoyed writing it!

If you did, it would mean a lot to me if you could spare thirty seconds to leave an honest review on your preferred online store. For independent authors like me, one review makes a world of difference.

If you want to get in touch, please visit my website, where you can contact me directly, either via e-mail or social media.

Until next time...

James P. Sumner

CLAIM YOUR FREE GIFT!

By subscribing to James P. Sumner's mailing list, you can get your hands on a free and exclusive reading companion, not available anywhere else.

It contains an extended preview of Book 1 in each thriller series from the author, as well as character bios, and official reading orders that will enhance your overall experience.

If you wish to claim your free gift, just visit the website below:

linktr.ee/jamespsumner

*You will receive infrequent, spam-free emails from the author, containing exclusive news about his books. You can unsubscribe at any time.

Made in the USA
Columbia, SC
08 August 2023

21420360R00190